# BACK OF BEYOND

## By Lisa J Comstock

2018

2012, by Lisa J Comstock

This is a work of fiction: all names, characters, businesses, places, events and incidents are either products of the author's imagination or used in a fictitious manner. Any resemblance to actual persons, either living or dead, or actual events is purely coincidental.

Enclave Productions, LLC has allowed this work to remain exactly as the author intended, verbatim, without editorial input.

Softcover ISBN: 978-0578412559
PUBLISHED BY ENCLAVE PRODUCTIONS, LLC
USA

Printed in the United States of America

# LOOK FOR THESE OTHER BOOKS BY
# LISA J COMSTOCK

**Back of Beyond is dedicated to my husband: Stephen Comstock**
**Thank you for letting me dream!**

I have so many wonderful people in my life
that have helped make my dreams come true.

I want to thank everyone that has helped inspire,
encourage and assist me along my path of being
an author.

I have a few special people I want to give
extra thanks to:

Steve Comstock, my husband

Jane Witham, my mother

Nina Liv Witham, my sister and fellow author

And my dad, Royce Witham –
looking down on me from heaven but always
in my heart!

I would not be where I am today without
all of you!

# 1

# They Come From the Dark

Callie Summers was moving her index finger over the smooth surface of a crystal ball that was on a golden stand shaped like a bird's talon set in the center of a table before her. The tip of the digit was making what appeared to be smoke inside it spin. The fingers of her other hand were unconsciously fiddling with the velvet tassels hanging off the purple, blue and green paisley print scarf that was being used as a tablecloth.

She was staring up at the phosphorescent yellow planet and star mobile that was spiraling above her head, wishing she were somewhere else. She was beginning to question all her beliefs and convictions.

As early as her pre-teens, Callie had always felt she had a special connection to the cosmos, *to the beyond* – as she called it. She didn't consider what she was doing as giving fortunes, which were basically only repeating a person's wants and desires back to them, what she did were true fore-tellings. She would relay to them actual events that she could see coming about. Now all was blank. Something had changed a few weeks ago. It was like the connection to the beyond had been severed.

She could fake it well enough; she was good at reading people, with a few well-asked questions she could give the impression she had learned it all by reading a person's mind, but if she kept doing this she would be what many thought she was – a fake.

She didn't know how to get the connection back. She had dried meditation, fasting and even several drugs, but got nothing but a clear head, sick from being hungry or high from them. There was a day she would have reveled in the idea of not being able to see into people's minds but it had become so much a part of her that she now missed it like she would miss a severed hand.

Callie jumped as the brass bell over her door rattled shrilly telling her someone had just entered her shop, *Summer Sage*. She hoped they were only interested in a love potion or wanted a poultice to get rid of headaches. She started to stand up to find out when the face of an older woman with tight curled purplish hair peered through the black velvet curtains she had set up inside the booth to make the people feel they were getting the full treatment. It was a bit clichéd but people had certain expectations when they went to have their palms read.

"Hello, ma'am," said Callie. She tried hard to get an image of the woman's name or why she was there but was seeing only a dull blankness... There was a day all of a person's most intimate details would flood into her mind as soon as she saw them. She had learned how to block out those details and focus only on the ones she needed. It was useless; she was getting nothing but a fuzzy picture of a patchwork quilt with lots of pinks and purples.

The woman stepped fully into the room and said, "I... I am..." She was wringing her hands and kept wiping tears from her red and swollen eyes. "I need..."

Callie was about to ask if she was looking for a lost dog; praying that was what she was there for. She didn't think she could take another person calling her a complete fraud to her face. She got very lightheaded all of a sudden and fell back in her seat.

\*\*\*\*\*\*\*\*\*\*\*\*\*\*\*\*\*\*\*\*

The elderly woman had been frightened to enter the shop but she was unsure where else to turn. Something was drawing her to this shop; something was telling her she would get help here. She started to the room hidden by the curtain, knowing it was there she wanted to go. As she stepped into room they were shielding another feeling came over her, one that said she was wrong. What she heard next made her sure she was going mad.

\*\*\*\*\*\*\*\*\*\*\*\*\*\*\*\*\*\*\*\*

Callie got a clear and distinct phrase in her mind as she looked into the woman's eyes; she spoke it aloud, "They come from the dark."

"Wha... what?" the older woman said as she was backing away. She was certain she didn't want to be here now, what she saw next confirmed this.

The younger woman's eyes went all cloudy and she began to speak in an odd voice, one that couldn't possibly come from her throat on its own. It was about two octaves deeper than most men's voices would be. "You cannot get away from us. You will help to complete our proviso." The thing possessing Callie's body made her rise to a standing position then it brought her arms up and her hands, which were twisted and curved like three fingered claws, moved toward the older woman's throat.

That woman was frozen in place, her eyelids and the tears running down her cheeks the only parts of her that seemed able to move. A strange feeling came over her then and she heard an equally deep voice say, "You must stop this now," just as the younger woman's twisted hands met her throat. It had come from the old woman's lips. Her own eyes were now solid black and glossy.

Callie fell back then, screaming and clawing at her own throat.

The older woman's eyes cleared and, in her own shaky voice, she said, "No... no... not again." She turned and ran from the small booth and out the door of the shop, slamming it hard against the brick wall beside it.

The bottom panel of glass cracked from the hard impact but the toughening of the pane, which was a security measure, kept it from breaking completely. The transparent film that lined the inside of the double pane was holding all the tiny cuboid pieces in place making hundreds of tiny prisms form in the light of the streetlamp reflecting off it.

The crashing of that door woke Callie with a sudden jolt. A wave of dizziness washed over her and she began to shake violently. She jumped and fell back again as she got a flood of images. Her hands went to the sides of her head, trying to keep it from splitting open from the onslaught.

She saw the woman who had just been in her shop running frantically up the dark alley her shop was at the end of. She was looking over her shoulder as if she was being chased. It was a strange viewpoint, like she was having an out of body experience. Her soul was flying above the woman. She was sucked inside the older body when the woman opened her mouth to scream then she was seeing through the other woman's eyes – seeing what it was she was running away from.

She had never seen anything so frightening in her life; three gray humanoid forms with no real features and only short stubby arms held tight to their bodies were gaining on her, on them, very fast. They weren't really running, more floating a few inches off the road, and they didn't cast shadows, only odd blackish holes showed beneath them. She watched the devoid silhouette of one of these things move over a puddle of water in the alley and gasped as the surface rippled erratically like it was getting ready to boil then she saw its reflection – it looked like it was only smoke coalescing tightly.

Callie wished she could make the old woman run faster but she couldn't move her body, she also couldn't get herself out of the woman's body. She felt sure her heart was going to stop when the three forms reached them, and that it had when she felt the deathly cold grip of their three fingered hands close over the other woman's arms.

The cold spread out from those tight grips and engulfed the older woman's body. Callie's mind, inside the woman's mind, screamed then suddenly she was thrust out of the woman's body with a jolt.

It took the young woman a second to realize where she was because she didn't recognize the room. She saw a queen size bed beneath her. A hand woven quilt in a patchwork, like she had gotten an image of when she first saw the woman, was covering two bodies in that bed. One looked like it had once been an elderly man by the wispy gray hair on his head. His body looked like it was dry and shriveled up like a mummy without its wrapping. The other was the woman that had been in her shop.

*How could she be here in her bed and in my shop at the same time*? Ran through Callie's mind, she was beyond confused now.

She was about to call out to the woman when she saw three blackish gray forms like what had been chasing them step from the deep shadows of the corner – out of the very shadow itself.

Callie watched in horror as the things floated to the woman's side of the bed, raised their stunted arms over her and began to chant in an eerie sounding language she didn't understand. It was raspy and harsh and made the hairs all over her body prickle. The woman's back arched violently then her body came off the bed and she twisted up, first this way then that, as if huge invisible hands were wringing out a washcloth.

Callie held her breath as she heard the last breath leave the woman's body then she watched her soul leave it. She had seen death many times, been witness to many a soul depart living flesh. It didn't frighten her but it still made all the hairs on the back of her neck rise and goose pimples form all over her body.

This woman's soul didn't float up to the light as she had watched other people's do; this one seemed to struggle. One of the beings by her side brought out what looked like an urn. It took the cover off this vessel then the woman's soul was sucked inside it.

Callie panicked as she felt her own soul getting pulled down, then even more when she saw the beings turn and raise their faces, or where their faces should be, to look at her. They didn't have eyes or mouths, only two small holes like nostrils and a hole on either side of their heads, like ears.

She opened her ethereal mouth to scream and shook herself awake.

\*\*\*\*\*\*\*\*\*\*\*\*\*\*\*\*\*\*\*\*

Callie opened her eyes but she couldn't see anything, there was only pitch-blackness around her. She thought for a moment she had been struck blind. Her breath was coming in painful hitches, her throat was raw and dry, as if she had been screaming and she was covered with a cold sweat. She began to panic as she realized something was on top of her. She kicked out hard with her legs and felt whatever it was move off her quickly.

Her eyes had begun to adjust to the sparse light around her now. She breathed a sigh of relief when she realized she was in her own bedroom and bed, and it was only the thick comforter, which she had doubled over because it was especially cold when she went to bed, that she had felt the weight of.

The woman's drafty loft apartment was hard to keep warm on a typical night but this one was one of the coldest of the year. In fact it was the coldest on record for Indigo City, whose nights on average didn't fall below thirty degrees – even in the dead of winter. It was early spring by the calendar but the temperature outside this night was only fifteen degrees. Inside her bedroom, which was on the north side of her apartment, it might have been forty degrees.

She was wearing only a thin tank top and pajama shorts but she actually didn't mind the cold air that was rushing in to replace the warm blanket at that moment. Except that it was drying the sweat fast and making her shiver with a frenzy. Some of this was due to the adrenaline rushing through her veins just then as well though.

She tried to tell herself she had only had a bad nightmare but she knew better. It had been months since she'd had a premonition and she had never had one like this before – it had seemed so real. She wouldn't mind if it was many more before she had another, if ever again.

Callie took a deep breath and pushed the sweat dampened golden hair from her young, angular face. She used the edge of the blanket to wipe her forehead, neck and the exposed part of her chest then she lay back down and fought to make her heart rate slow. The cold was beginning to only feel cold now so she pulled the blankets back over her. She lay staring at the ripple effect of the moon reflecting off the river that ran beside her loft on her ceiling. Most nights it had a calming effect on her, this one it only made her more anxious.

Finally, she allowed her heavy eyes to close again. An image of a male lion with a thick mane, a long tufted tail and the head, wings and talons of an eagle formed in Callie's mind just as she was falling asleep again. She couldn't say why this helped calm her; she had always thought a Griffin was a horrid looking creature.

# 2

# **The Griffin**

A blondish brown haired six foot three man stood in the center of a large picture window. He was gazing down at a symbol that had haunted him all his life and had been one of great comfort to him. It was of a mythical creature with the body, tail and thick mane of a lion and the head, talons and wings of an eagle – commonly known in mythology as a Griffin.

He had often used a symbol like it on his written correspondence growing up, sometimes doodling it on the corner of his school papers in place of his name since it was the same only spelled different.

The symbol Gryphon Blake was staring down at this day was a profile of the creature in a proud seated stance on a backlit sign that was spinning on an axis in the center of a flowerbed full of red, yellow, purple and pink tulips in full bloom in the courtyard in front of his business, Griffin Concepts, Inc. Another like this sign graced the side of his building. The window of his office was set in its head and stone versions of the creature were set on each side of the drive up to the building.

GCI was a scientific think tank that held contracts with many major scientific, medical, environmental, pharmaceutical, technological and aeronautical companies, government agencies, a few military and private facilities and many colleges. His company was involved in everything from developing the norm: medicines, vaccines, weapons of war, space rocketry, communication satellites and multi-functional robots, to the unthinkable: a failed attempt to create a time travel device and a machine that was supposed to detect ghosts.

He knew a lot of the agencies his company dealt with, as well as much of the scientific and academic world, thought he and his employees were jokes but it didn't stop many of them from offering financing when they needed it for their unconventional concepts – more than willing to take some of the credit if the concept proved true.

Gryphon was preparing for a seminar he was giving at Northern Biscayne University, his Alma Mata, tomorrow on his phase shift device; another of his company's, and his own personal, inventions that was thought to be a complete joke.

He sniffed with indignation.

He couldn't care less if he ever received public recognition as an asset to the scientific community but he hoped someday his company, and the brilliant people employed here, would be.

Gryphon jumped as a soft tapping came from the door behind him. He said, "Come in," over his shoulder in a voice far calmer than he expected it to be. He had no idea how much longer he might have stayed at that window if not for the interruption.

The door opened slowly to the face of a woman of about twenty. She had big green eyes and bright red hair, which was pinned up in a loose bun on top of her head; a number two lead pencil was stuck through the center of it like an old schoolmarm.

"Excuse me, Dr. Blake," said this woman.

"What is it, Sandra?" asked the man. He turned from the window and walked to his large mahogany desk, which was set cattycornered and off center in the center of the room. He lifted the cup of coffee he had poured himself before going to the window for a moment of reflection. It was still steaming. He blew across the top of it then took a sip.

"The car has arrived for you," said the woman as she stepped inside, his dark brown leather and suede briefcase in her hand.

Gryphon had only a blank stare on his face.

Sandra was dressed in a gray tweed jacket over a light pink cashmere sweater that was tight enough to show every lacey detail of the bra beneath it and a pink and purple plaid skirt that was so short she couldn't bend over without the bottom of her underpants, which were just as lacy if Gryphon didn't miss his guess, would be showing. She was wearing black stiletto heels with no nylons so her well-tanned, muscular legs, which went all the way up, were clear as well – hoping to catch his eye he guessed. He knew she had a crush on him; she had let it be known in little ways since the day he had first seen her in his office, interviewing for the position of his secretary and assistant. His business partner and best friend, DJ, had asked him jokingly if he hired her in hopes of an easy lay – or at least he hoped it was a joke. The man could be very crass at times.

He wondered himself why he had hired her. She wasn't the brightest of the candidates for the job, nor the most qualified, but there was something about her that felt comfortable. He was certain it wasn't thoughts of bedding her.

He hadn't been with a woman in close to six months, which by coincident had been just about the time Sandra had come in for her interview. He hadn't sworn off women, he did hope someday to date again and maybe, one day, to get married, but his last relationship had ended rather hard. He had fallen deeply in love with that woman, deeper than he had admitted even to himself until it was too late. He had been hurt bad when it ended abruptly.

It hadn't been over another man or another woman it had been over his work.

She had said, through shouts at the top of her lungs, the last time Gryphon saw her, that he cared more about his stupid science projects than he did her. He would later admit to himself that he had spent far too much time at the office at the end of their relationship. He could never make her understand that brainstorms came when they came, sometimes even in the middle of a romantic dinner or making love. He had never found anyone that understood that except for DJ, who'd never been able to keep a relationship going for long either.

He supposed there was a reality in this thought process he should look deeper at but he wasn't in the mood just then.

"Tell Jacob to leave my car out front, I'm not quite ready to go yet," said Gryphon in a monotone voice. The woman stayed in the doorway, as if she had something else she wanted to say. He thought seriously about waving her away but instead he said, "Was there something else, Sandra?"

"I wanted to tell you I hope your seminar tomorrow goes well," said Sandra.

His eyes left her as he lifted the cup to his lips again. "You and me both, Sandra, you and me both," said the man.

"I… I also wanted to let you know that I believe in your work, Dr. Blake. I really think someday you will be recognized as you should be."

"Thanks, Sandra," said Gryphon. He had started for the panel between two floor-to-ceiling bookcases that his the door to his executive washroom as he said this. He realized the woman was still standing in the doorway as he reached it. "Something else?" he said over his shoulder.

"Um… I noticed you never left for lunch today and didn't order anything in… You really need to keep up your strength… I am sure I don't need to remind you of how long it took you to get over the flu last month."

He had truly been sick for a few days but he hadn't been as bad as he had told her he was. He could have made it in the fourth or fifth days of his absence, he just hadn't felt like working. He knew someone would insist he come in to see their latest ideas if he had and he wasn't in the mood to try to be encouraging let alone act interested. The last two days of his days out he was actually trying to get himself back right mentally. The third day of his absence would've been his fourth anniversary with Adrienne.

"I appreciate the worry, Sandra, but I'm feeling fine. Honestly. I had a bag of dehydrated fruit and nuts in my drawer and a bottle of Gatorade from the fridge."

"Oh…"

The fact that she still hadn't left told him she wasn't going to let him off so easy. "You know how little I like people beating around the bush, Sandra, just come out and say what you want to say."

"Did you… Would it be inappropriate for me to ask… Would you be interested in going to dinner with me?"

"I appreciate the invitation, Sandra, but I wouldn't be much for company tonight. I need to practice my talk and go over my notes… which will take me most of the evening," said the man, taking another step.

"You could practice your lecture on me," said the woman's hope filled voice.

"Again, I appreciate the offer, but I am still going to say no. I left a list of things I would like you to see about before the end of the day. I hope you have a good weekend," said the man as he continued into the washroom and closed the door.

Sandra saw a piece of paper on the center of her boss's desk, beside his cup of coffee. She walked over to it, set his briefcase down on the desk and placed her hand on top of it for a moment, just feeling the soft suede and leather material. Her eyes shifted to the paper her boss had been referring to. It was a piece of the man's personal stationary, a mottled gray parchment paper with a symbol of a Griffin imprinted in the top right corner. It was a list of tasks, as he had said it would be, handwritten in his scrolling penmanship. She took the list and looked at the neat writing, wishing it was a personal note to her. She looked at the door the man was behind and wished again he would consider her as more than just an employee.

# 3

# Modesty

Gryphon buttoned up his fly, hit the flush button on the wall over the commode and turned to the black and green marble sink. He waved his hand under the tap of the faucet to turn it on. It shut off as soon as his hands left it. He grabbed a black towel monogrammed with a gold Griffin and his initials G.A.B. from the rod beside him, dried his hands then tossed it onto the corner of the vanity. He was looking at his reflection as he was doing this. He wasn't sure if he liked what he was seeing or not.

He was considered quite handsome. He had, in fact, been voted one of the county's top ten most eligible bachelors – this year he was number one. His business partner, DJ, had immensely enjoyed teasing him for this. He had made an announcement regarding this fact over the paging system of the building just the day before. He had given several of his coworkers a copy of the issue and had paid them to stop their boss and ask him for an autograph. The man had also left a copy on his desk, opened to the middle of the photo spread.

It showed pictures of him taken while he was out walking on the boardwalk a few weeks before. He wasn't dressed in the usual business attire that he preferred to be in when promotional photos were taken but at least he had not looked like a vagrant – the photos showed him in a red cotton polo shirt, knee length khaki shorts and dark sunglasses.

The only reason he had read the article was so he could have any incorrect or inaccurate information corrected in the next issue. He didn't especially care if they got anything wrong about him but he wanted his company shown in the best possible light. As the old adage goes – no publicity is bad publicity.

He sniggered as he remembered reading over his stats, which listed his best attributes as his eyes, his smile and his ass. Those were three things he always thought could use improving.

Gryphon didn't think he was bad looking but he knew there were many that were better looking. He had been told by enough women over the years that he was attractive to believe he was to them but unlike a lot of men who are told this enough times it had never sunk in. He had just turned forty-three a few months before, which had always seemed like such an ancient age until he reached forty.

He ran his large hand through his tousled hair that was in need of a cut; it was beginning to curl wildly along the edges. It was still pretty much the same color it had been all his life – a mottled blondish brown. He didn't have many grays yet but there was more than he would like to see. He was thankful he still had most of it. His business partner, and he guessed he would call his best friend, David Jacob Wright, affectionately referred to as DJ by people that knew him well, was only thirty-three and already had thinning hair and a widow's peak started.

His hair, like his eyes, which were a blue-gray, tended to look a different color depending on what he was wearing and what lighting he was in. The fluorescent lights over his head in this room made his hair actually look a touch on the reddish side and his eyes more gray than blue. The latter also looked very tired and a touch bloodshot. He reached into the medicine cabinet over the sink and took out a bottle of eye drops. He put two drops into each eye then looked back at his reflection.

He was tall, had broad shoulders and was well built; naturally so by luck, since he wasn't one for exercise. He used to jog when he was younger and had even managed to go to the gym for about three months about three years ago but when he realized he hadn't returned in six weeks he decided to let his membership lapse.

He was wearing a slate blue fitted button up shirt, which wasn't tucked in and was unbuttoned down the front more than usual, and an old pair of blue stonewashed jeans. The edges of the pockets and along the bottom of the legs were fraying, and the color was faded more along the tops of the thighs than any other part of his legs. He supposed he should throw them away but they were comfortable. He remembered Adrienne saying he looked sexy this way. He had never really considered himself to be that. He typically wore silk dress shirts, linen slacks and a tie to work and had a sports jacket with him for meetings but he wasn't supposed to be working today. He had only come in to get his notes for his talk tomorrow and had only ended up there all afternoon.

Gryphon practiced his smile in the mirror. He was trying to make it look genuine, not forced. It still looked more like a grimace to him. He finally gave up and splashed water in his face.

He didn't know why he kept putting himself through this kind of torture. He hated public speaking with a passion. Not because he wasn't good at it, he was actually very good at it and he had a voice that was made for it – it was deep, melodic and carried well, without a microphone. He didn't like being judged. He always felt at least half the crowd was there only to see him fail and fall on his face.

He cleared his throat and began to recite his usual opening in his deep speaking voice, "Good afternoon, students, faculty and visitors of the university. I know that you have all come here with certain expectations of what you will see, hear and learn, I promise to do my best to make sure you also understand when you leave. First I want to explain what phase shifting is and what it does." He sniggered a little then and said to himself in his usual voice, which was only a little less deep, "Half of them still won't understand, do you suppose even a quarter of them will care?"

He turned from his reflection, opened the door, stepped back into his office and nearly jumped a foot.

"Who are you kidding, you'd be happy if even a tenth of them do," said the man that was standing at Gryphon's bar pouring himself a scotch on the rocks from his bottle of Glen Livet.

"You do know it is rude to listen in on a person's personal conversations," said Gryphon as he shut the light off in the room behind him and closed the door panel.

"You were speaking loud enough I could have heard you from my office," said the man whose office was about a hundred feet away, on the other side of the building. He held the bottle of single malt up, in offer to pour the other a drink. He set it down when the other man shook his head. He held the glass of amber liquor in his hand up in a mock toast then took a sip.

"And," continued Gryphon, "walking into someone's office uninvited?"

"Like you haven't done it to me in mine a million or more times."

"This is my company, so your office, in essence, is my office as well," said Gryphon. He held a cork coaster with the company logo on it up then tossed it to the other man so he wouldn't set the sweating glass down on his fine wood furniture.

"Touché." The man sniggered and pointed at the door as he said, "I saw the dreamy look in your secretary's eyes as I came in, did you finally tag her?"

"Very crass, DJ," said Gryphon pointedly.

"Like you don't know she would lie down and spread them willingly with even a hint from you."

34

Gryphon grunted in disgust. He put his fisted hands on his hips and said, "Have you come for a reason, other than to eavesdrop, harass me, steal my liquor and make rude remarks about my secretary?"

"Actually, I did. I just got the test results on the rats we injected with the synthetic growth hormone."

Gryphon waited. He knew his friend was pausing because he wanted to be dramatic; he wasn't disappointed.

"As we suspected their muscle mass is larger than usual but their bones aren't keeping up. Their brains aren't developing like they should. They can't even make it halfway through the maze before they freeze up, and they are still developing cancer cells at the same rate," said the man walking around the perimeter of the room.

"So, back to the drawing board on that one?"

"We are getting closer, but yeah, afraid so," said DJ as he sat down on the arm of the coach. He finished the drink then sucked an ice cube into his mouth and chewed on it. "You still freaking out about tomorrow?"

"I *do not* freak out!" said Gryphon.

"The growth hormone had another effect that surprised us," said the man as he went to pour himself another drink.

"Which was?"

"Euphoria."

"And?"

"If you were to take a small dose you wouldn't be worried about tomorrow anymore," said DJ.

"No, but important things might start falling off me... Gee, I think I will pass," said Gryphon. He gave his friend a look that said he wondered why he might think he would want to.

"I am only trying to make you lighten up some, Gryph. We both know you will do just fine. You always do. The women will all be drooling over your hot eyes," said the man, batting his eyes quickly, "and the men will scoff at you because the women are all drooling."

Gryphon held a middle finger up to his friend.

DJ sniggered and said, "Are you here much longer?"

"No. Heading out in a matter of minutes."

"Can I catch a ride with you?"

"What happened to your car?"

"It's in the shop, getting a new paint job."

"Didn't you just get it painted as you put it *the hottest color on the market right now* teal green last month?" asked Gryphon as he opened the briefcase his secretary left him and put his note cards and the slides he had prepared into it.

"Yeah, but we just developed a new paint in the chem lab that changes colors depending on the angle you look at the car... red to purple to blue and back... Think of all the things I could get away with if no one can get the color of my car right."

"I've told you before, David Jacob Wright, you cannot use our technology for crime," said Gryphon. He knew DJ was only teasing but he also knew the man wouldn't be satisfied or stop until he had said something similar to show his outrage. This was like a game between them – for DJ to see how annoyed he could make Gryphon and for Gryphon to see how long DJ thought he could get away with it.

"You wouldn't have to kiss so many asses if I robbed a few banks though," sniggered the younger man.

"You can kiss *my* ass," said Gryphon, as he took the man's empty glass from him and set it in the sink on the bar. He turned back to him and added, "My car is out front. Go on down, I will be right along."

"Yes, massa," said the younger man, bowing to his boss as he backed out the door.

Gryphon couldn't help but smile at the idiot's antics. He took one last look out the window, at the odd pinkish purple clouds of the sunset, then he walked to the door himself. He locked it behind him, walked past the desk of his secretary without even responding to her, walked up to the elevator and pushed the down button.

# 4

# Hide and Seek

Gryphon hated elevators; he wondered almost every day, why he had decided to have his office on the top floor of the building. He drew in a deep breath and held it as he stepped inside the compartment and watched the doors close. He could feel his lungs constricting with them.

This one was much larger than most, or else he would never have been able to let the doors close him in. All the walls were mirrored to make it seem bigger still but it still felt like they were closing in on him. He could see how pale he was getting in those surfaces, hear the wheezing in his breath, and feel the pain building in his chest as he fumbled in his pocket for the medicine he never went far without.

Gryphon suffered daily from three ailments; each exacerbated by the others.

The first was Asthma.

He was having an attack of it now as floor six changed to floor five.

He shook the tube and mouthpiece that made up the inhaler a few times then closed his lips over the mouthpiece and squeezed off a hit of the breathing medication inside of it. He held his breath for a few painful moments as the vapors entered his lungs then breathed out. He took one more hit then leaned against the far wall. He gripped the bar on the wall tight, closed his eyes and counted the seconds until the doors opened and he could breathe again.

His second was fear of confined spaces.

He was claustrophobic and had been since he was ten years old. His therapist said he had to confront his fears if he wanted to overcome them so he made sure to ride this horrid thing at least once a day.

The summer of this tenth year, he and his younger brother, Sammy, had gone to stay with their grandparents for two weeks while their parents went on a second honeymoon to Bermuda. They never minded going over there because Papa and Nana always let them stay up as late as they wanted, let them have ice cream, cookies and soda, even right before they went to bed, and let them watch whatever they wanted on the TV, which they had one of their own in the room they shared.

They had an old Victorian house on a quiet cul-de-sac with lots of great hiding places; hide and seek was Sammy's favorite game. The two usually swapped off which games they played, each choosing one until it was done then the winner of that game would choose the next, and so on.

It had been his brother's turn to pick the game that morning.

Gryphon hadn't really wanted to play hide and seek but he had because he loved his little brother and knew the boy would break down in tears if he didn't. He had started out hiding in all the usual places, all of which his brother found him in quickly, then he hid in a place he knew Sam would never find him, meaning he would win.

Gryphon's plan had backfired on him.

Neither of them liked going into the open expanse at the top of the house – the attic. The different heights and pitches of the roof made many odd peaks and valleys in the ceiling of the room, the exposed rafters looked like the exposed rib bones of some massive beast. Boxes, old suitcases, boiler trunks and ratty and dusty furniture covered with dry-rotted white spreads made it look like someone had once lived in it but had never cleaned it.

Neither boy would have been surprised to find the body of that person still there, having simply sat down and died. There wasn't just bits of dust every here and there, there was whole sheets of it, almost woven together, tons of cobwebs and spider webs, with huge spiders on them, and lots of corners with deep, dark shadows – obscurities he knew hid things waiting to take children away.

He knew Sam wouldn't want to look for him up there so he would win, which meant they would get to play the game he wanted next, which was Mousetrap. He liked the Rube Goldberg type game, watching the contraptions get built as the mice tried to evade capture had fueled his desire to go into physics and science.

He had gotten into the closet willingly, no one had forced him into it, but the door closed on its own, of that he was certain, locking him inside it.

Later, when he was brave enough to go into the attic again, his grandfather had shown him it was only the way the floor sloped in that part of the house, that made the door appear to swing shut on its own.

He had been in that tiny three foot by three foot room for almost five hours. He had cried the first three of them and had sat in a tight ball rocking himself for the next two. Between those hours he had shouted for anyone to get him out and had fought not to fall asleep.

It was just after this that he was first diagnosed with asthma. At first the doctors thought it was just that he had inhaled too much dust and his lungs were only reacting to it but over the years it had gotten progressively worse.

This incident had also fueled his third ailment, which was fear of the dark.

He had felt and heard things in the darkness of that tiny closet he had only ever told one person of, not even his therapist knew – afraid they would think he was crazy. He had confided the story in his former lover and had immediately been sorry for it because in his mind it gave it validity. His scientific mind had tried to explain away this fear but it could not. He truly believed he had heard voices, speaking in rhyme, trying to make him fall asleep – for what purpose he didn't know nor did he care to find out. He knew they belonged to the things that hid in the shadows. He was afraid if he let on that he knew about them they would take him away.

His grandparents and parents, who had come home early when they were called to say he was missing, had been beside themselves when they found him; they had lavished him with gifts of toys, chocolate and ice cream for the next three days, hoping to make it up to him.

As most children do, the whole episode was soon put to the back of his mind, becoming more like only something he had seen in a movie or TV show. Thoughts of school starting and seeing his friends took their place and he became the happy-go-lucky kid he had been.

He had never really thought it was all that traumatic, sure he had an occasional nightmare of the closet and the voices, but he'd had nightmares of other things too, like monsters from movies and TV shows, until the first time he had stepped into an elevator.

This pivotal moment had occurred when he, his brother, his parents and his grandmother were going to visit Papa about a year later. He was at Biscayne General Hospital, in the cardiac intensive care unit on the fourth floor, after having had a mild heart attack. Gryphon had been fine up until the doors of the mechanical lift had closed and the lights over their head dimmed for a second. In that brief interlude of darkness he had heard the voices again and this time heard his name called out.

He was thinking of all this as he wondered again why he had chosen to take the elevator instead of the stairs.

\*\*\*\*\*\*\*\*\*\*\*\*\*\*\*\*\*\*\*\*

"You took the elevator again, didn't you?" DJ asked when he saw how pale the other man was as he stepped from the automatic glass doors at the front of the building.

Gryphon didn't answer, not feeling he really needed to.

"Why do you put yourself through that, Man?"

"My therapist says the only way to get over your fears is to force yourself to confront them."

"I would be afraid of the therapist then," sniggered the man.

"Whom I force myself to see as well," said Gryphon.

"You want me to drive?" asked DJ. He knew it would be a few minutes before his friend was calm enough to be able to. He also knew the man didn't like to be treated as if handicapped so he said it as calmly as he could and waited for his reaction.

"Sure, just obey the traffic laws this time."

"Yes, Daddy," said the younger man, in a voice of a young child.

"Have a good evening, Dr. Blake and Dr. Wright," said Jacob. He was holding a folded up newspaper, which he handed to his boss, then he stepped forward and opened the passenger door for him.

"Thank You. You too, Jacob," said Gryphon as he climbed into the custom vanilla Dodge Magnum he had picked up only a week before and set his briefcase onto the backseat.

"This is such a cool car... for an adult I mean," said DJ as he pushed the button to open the electric sunroof all the way, turned the tuner on the stereo to his favorite hard rock station, turned the volume up then put the shift into drive and revved the engine.

"You're thirty-three years old, DJ, which makes you an adult as well, last I checked," said Gryphon as he turned the stereo down a little.

"Nah!"

DJ owned three sport cars, what had been a teal green Dodge Viper, a candy apple red 1969 Ford Mustang Mach I and a 1973 Red Ferrari Daytona. The third car only came out on special occasions, the second one, part of an inheritance from his grandfather, was getting the interior reupholstered, back to original red and white vinyl, and the first one was at GCI, in the workshop, being painted – for the third time.

He paid DJ quite well, better than the bio-chemist thought he should, but he never complained when he got a raise. Most of that money was sitting in a high yield savings account at the local credit union. His cars were his biggest investments; he hadn't bought a house yet. He considered that something someone that wanted to settle down would do. Because he was far from being ready for all a home meant to him, he was currently living in a two bedroom condo that he leased from his parents on the north side of town. It was the ultimate bachelor's pad: lots of electronic toys and a ten person Jacuzzi on the back deck.

Gryphon had the Dodge Magnum they were in now, a 1947 Plymouth Executive Coupe he was rebuilding in his spare time, since he had none of that it was only about half completed, and three Harley motorcycles himself. He lived in a Tudor mansion on the east side of town, the *ritzy side of town*, as DJ called it. He also had a three bedroom mission style bungalow cottage on Tybee Island off the coast of Savannah, GA, which was where he kept his cabin boat.

His biggest investment was his company. He had used part of an inheritance he had gotten from an uncle when he was a teenager to pay his way through eight years of college, the rest was used to start CGI, which had grown from an office and one laboratory on the NBU campus, leased from the college, to the custom built three thousand square foot facility that had six floors and several dozen laboratories, they now operated out of.

DJ had been a freshman at the university when Gryphon first set up shop on campus. He had come to work for him as a lab assistant in the work study program to earn credits toward his degree in Chemistry. He was one of dozens that eagerly volunteered each year but his unusual ideas quickly brought him to the boss's attention.

DJ had come to work for Gryphon full time only a week after graduating valedictorian with a PhD in Biochemistry. He had taken over as his head of

Chemistry and had made them good profit with medicines he had helped to discover and enhance, and the chemicals he had synthesized for everything from household cleaners to fertilizers – all of which was part of why Gryphon didn't mind paying him so well. For all he was a bit of a noodge, at times, he did know his stuff and he didn't want to lose him to any of the competition.

Other than their love of science, the two men were polar opposites, which was probably why they had gotten along with each other so well, balancing each other out. Gryphon had never really let his hair down and DJ's was always down.

# 5

# Newsworthy

Gryphon opened the paper the valet always had waiting for him when he left the building. He was trying not to pay any attention to how DJ was driving his new car. He knew it would only make his blood pressure rise, give him another asthma attack and an even bigger headache than he already had building.

He quickly scanned the headlines, which were mostly political and financial whinings. He wasn't much for politics and he had people to follow his investments in the market so he had no desire to know what his stock portfolio had closed at for the day. He passed over the big sports stories of the day as well, not much on sports either, except when their home team was in the big game. They had a tendency to trade away a player as soon as they started to shine – not wanting to have to pay them what they were worth – so it wasn't very often. He began to scan the local headlines. His eyes moved over the page first, as usual, looking for any names he recognized. He didn't find any so he went back to the first headline that caught his eye.

*"Mummy Couple Found In West Side Home."*

He sniggered and wondered when the usually newsworthy establishment, The Biscayne Gazette, had decided to run tabloid grade articles. The hairs on the back of his neck prickled and he got goose pimples as he read the story.

'It was like something out of a horror movie,' said one of the first EMT's to respond to the scene; and so it was. They are being called the *Biscayne Mummies* because they were found in a state that can only, and best, be described as mummified – dried up and perfectly preserved.

'The police are baffled as they say all the doors and windows were locked from the inside and there was no sign of forced entry or of anything missing from the home. They also say they found no sign of anyone else having been in the house and they have no clues to what killed the couple: Anne (66) and George (69) Stubbs, in their home. The couple's daughter said she had seen the two only the day before for dinner and both were perfectly healthy.

'They were found dead in their bed by the housekeeper yesterday morning. The woman, who wished to remain unnamed, stated that Mr. Stubbs had recently had a cold but that he had been improving and was in good spirits and that Mrs. Stubbs was a very active woman, both in the community and her garden. She went on to say that both had requested she get and install nightlights in every room. She said: at the time she had thought this was only because of their failing eyesight. Until her employer confided in her – saying she had heard voices in the dark and had felt things clawing at her. She says Mrs. Stubbs said, 'The voices told her they were coming for her, coming from the dark', and 'that she was needed to fill their proviso'.

'We consulted with a literary expert who states a proviso can be a type of qualification or provision. Whether this is how Mrs. Stubbs meant it or why the woman would have chosen this unusual term has yet to be determined.

'Police state the cause of death has yet to be determined but they have not ruled out foul play. The bodies of both were sent to Clarence Medical Center at Fort Hopkins for an autopsy. The date of which has not been released nor has there been any word whether its findings will be revealed to the public – as part of an ongoing investigation.

'The police request anyone with information that will assist in the investigation contact Biscayne Precinct sixteen.'

"Gryphon... Gryphon?"

"Wha... what?" asked the man, suddenly feeling very lightheaded and cold.

"You okay?"

"Yeah, why?"

"I have been calling your name for the last ten minutes."

Gryphon guffawed and said, "I asked you not to speed, DJ," He looked in the rearview mirror expecting to see the blue lights of a police car behind them. They were stopped beside the road but he saw no one behind them, only a row of buildings with manicured lawns that looked very much like the condos his business partner lived in.

"We are in front of my house," said DJ, pointing at the clock on the dash, which read 6:25. They had left the office at 6:00; it took less than fifteen minutes to reach his home going exactly the speed limit.

Gryphon was having a hard time believing he had been that out of it.

"You look about ready to be sick, Man, you need another hit of medicine?" asked DJ, all joking aside.

"No," said the older man, he wasn't having that kind of trouble.

"The flu not done with you yet?"

"Yeah, that's probably it."

"You sure you feel up to doing the talk at the university tomorrow? I know the basics well enough and can stumble through your notes if you want," said DJ, concern for his best friend in his voice.

"I'll take an Alka-Seltzer Plus before I go to bed," said Gryphon. He could see DJ was still concerned and ready to argue. "I promise. I will be fine in the morning."

"I'm more concerned about you getting home all right tonight."

"It's not that far." It was about twenty minutes, across town.

"I can drive you there and borrow one of the bikes to get me back here," said DJ, the excitement building in his voice and the silly schoolboy grin coming to his lips again.

"I don't think so," said Gryphon pointedly.

"You sure?"

"Yeah." Gryphon saw this hadn't convinced his friend. He added adamantly, "Yes. Get out."

DJ wasn't convinced but he knew if he kept pushing the man would get upset. "Call me tomorrow night and let me know how it went?"

"I will give you a call if you promise to be to work on time Monday morning."

"Oh, come on…"

"Get out already," said Gryphon as he climbed out and started around the front of the car, the newspaper still held tightly in his hand.

He watched the younger man jog up the walk beside them, punch his security code into the panel beside the door and enter his condo then shook his head and climbed into the driver's seat. He adjusted the seat, steering wheel and rearview mirrors, pushed the button to close the sunroof and punched the third pre-set station button on the stereo. Soft classical music came from the eight speaker sound system around him moments later.

He really didn't care for the glorified elevator music but it would help to calm his fevered mind.

He put the Magnum into gear, started it away from the curb slowly. His eyes moved from the windshield to the passenger seat where he had dropped the newspaper. It had come open to the page with the article he had been so engrossed in moments before. He wondered what it was about it that had ensnared him so much.

He sniffed indignantly, lifted the paper and tossed it onto the back seat so he wouldn't be distracted by it again as he pulled his car into the intersection and headed towards his home.

# 6

# Memories

Gryphon turned onto Helsing Avenue and drove along the multi colored stone wall with Gothic arch shaped niches built into it, each with a spiral cut conifer in it and red tulips before it, that surrounded his lot. He pushed the button on the dash that opened the iron gates to his property and pulled onto the red and black brick lined driveway.

He pulled his car up beside the front stairs. It wasn't supposed to rain that evening so he wasn't worried about leaving it out but he left it under the portico in case the weatherman was wrong. He knew his butler would put it away in the morning when he arrived. He had given his staff the evening off, wanting the peace and quiet of an empty house with no disturbances and distractions to be able to practice his talk, so he knew there was no one there to open the door for him either.

He grabbed his briefcase and the newspaper from the backseat, climbed the stairs and entered his house. The foyer before him was large and open, the windows on the front of the house and the vaulted ceiling above his head went up three stories; skylights at the top of the tower let the last bits of daylight into the expanse. This helped calm his still overwrought nerves from the elevator ride.

Only a round console table with an original Ming Dynasty vase broke the expanse of tan and rose-colored travertine tiles of the floor before him and only a few pieces of artwork hung on the burgundy walls around him. An oak tread staircase started at the back of the entry hall, went up to the second floor then split into two staircases going up the sides of the landing to the third floor. Hand hewn oak newel posts, styles and rails went up the sides of the stairs and continued along the second and third floor galleys.

His eyes scanned these features then went to the stack of mail sitting on the edge of the console table. He took it in his left hand and set his car keys down in its place then continued to his study.

He passed the parlor, for greeting guest, the arboretum, with its green foliage and year round flowering plants, the formal dining room, with a 1920's oak mission style L&JG Stickley dining table, with eight chairs, china cabinet, sideboard and teacart, and the sitting room with big screen TV and more comfortable furniture for lounging around, and entered the library at the back of the house. It was lined with walnut floor to ceiling bookcases, each filled with books on dozens of subjects. A large two board oak trestle table was in the center of the room with an 1877 hand-colored atlas of Biscayne County setting on a bookstand open to their city, Indigo City. Several side chairs were setting around the room but he walked past them all.

He pushed open the door worked into the panels that opened to his study.

This was the smallest and darkest room in the house but somehow he never felt stifled or confined in it. It had wood panels halfway up the walls and a tan and burnt orange sponged faux finish on the upper walls. He flipped the switch on the wall just inside the door and four mission-style rust colored slag glass paneled wall sconces lit up, which added a warm glow to the room. A dark brown suede sofa was set against the back wall, centered between two windows, both covered with black curtains. A well-stocked bar was on the left wall. A red and black Persian carpet was covering the wide plank wood floor and a large mission style oak desk was set off center in the right corner of the room. A burgundy velvet bloater had some of his brainstorming sessions, scribbled on the backs of napkins, post-it notes and envelopes, stuck under one corner, a hand-carved humidor filled with cigars and a phone on the right side were the only things on top of the desk and a light brown leather executive chair was setting up to it.

He set the mail, his briefcase and the newspaper on the top of the desk and walked into the bathroom off this room. He went to the medicine cabinet, making sure not to look at himself in the mirror, and pulled out a packet of Alka-Seltzer Plus tabs. He took a glass setting beside the faucet and filled it about half full then ripped open the packet and let the two quarter sized tablets fall into the water. He carried the fizzing glass back into the study with him to wait for it to finish dissolving.

While he waited he began to sort through the mail. Most of it was from various charities he had given money to, all asking for more, the rest was junk mail. The latter went into the rubbish bin beside the desk, the others he set back on the desk to review later. The cold medicine had dissolved now so he set his head back and began to gulp it down. He grunted and made a sour face as he set the glass that now had a powdery white residue along the bottom down then sank into the chair, letting it lean back a little.

Gryphon's eyes drifted around the room and came to rest on his leather briefcase. Inside it were his note cards for his talk that he was trying so hard not to obsess about. He had planned to run through them at least once before going up to bed but he really didn't want to. Like DJ said, he knew deep down it would go well, it always did, he just had a tendency to over think things. Adrienne had said that more than once to him as well.

He felt a tightness form in his chest as he remembered the woman who had recently left him. This time it was emotional not physical. He opened the drawer before him and took out an antique gold frame with a picture of her beside a riverbank. Water was falling over large rocks behind her, lush green leaves were hanging from the trees around her and she had a sweet smile on her face that made him smile every time he looked at it – even now. She had soft flowing light brown hair that could be curly if she allowed it to but she usually straightened it, and eyes the color of the water behind her. Even in the two dimensional image the sparkle in them was breathtaking.

She had a tight body with just enough curves, she was only about a B cup and had small hips but she fit him well. This day she had been dressed in a pair of tight blue jeans decorated with gems and sequins in the shape of butterflies down her left leg and on the pockets in the back and a white tank top with the word LOVE in a heart shape on the front that didn't come quite to the top of the jeans, leaving about half an inch of skin exposed all the way around.

When she saw the photos, about two weeks after this, once he finally found the time to pick them up from the drugstore, she had said she looked too much like a teenager in that outfit and had never worn it again. He had liked her in it; it showed the playful side she rarely let show.

The photo had been taken only a few weeks into their relationship. They had gone on a drive up the coast on his Harley. They had stopped beside the brook to eat the picnic lunch they had brought with them. It had been a perfect day, not too warm or cool, and the sound of the water, birds and the wind through the trees had been better than any music they could have brought.

They had talked for hours about every subject under the sun, and laughed at each other's jokes, at a bird playing in a small pool in a niche in a rock the crashing water had created, and at a bent leaf that looked like a tiny gondola that was being pulled into rapids the canals of Venice would never have. As the morning turned to afternoon they had laid back in the soft moss of the bank and watched the clouds lazily go by, pointing out the shapes in them.

They had made love for the first time that day. His smile grew larger as he remembered they had for the second time that day as well. The first time had been on the riverbank, in that soft moss, under those lazily floating clouds. The second time was after swimming in the small cove before them, against a rock with the water rushing around them.

The endearing smile faded and a lump began to form in his throat as he ran a finger down her two-dimensional face and said, "Why didn't we go for more drives?"

Gryphon's heart ached at the thought of never seeing the woman again. He set the frame on the top of the desk, leaned further back in the chair and wondered what she was doing now. His ever-cynical mind said she was probably out on a date with a hot young resident doctor she had spent the day ordering around that was hoping to get to order her around for a bit.

He jumped when the grandfather clock in the library began to chime. Eight times. He knew this wasn't doing him any good so he left the room.

Gryphon walked to the kitchen to see if there was anything good to munch on. He found two slices of the pepperoni pizza DJ had brought over with him the night before on the middle shelf of the refrigerator that would do him well enough. He slid them out of the plastic storage bag onto a plate, put the plate into the microwave oven and set it on one minute. He went back to the fridge, took out a bottle of Guinness, popped it open on the edge of the counter and took a long slug of it. He took the plate from the microwave, grabbed another bottle of the stout beer and started for the stairs.

He climbed them, taking another drink from the open bottle as he did, and went into his bedroom.

His bedroom was in about the back of the house, on the second floor. There were two other bedrooms, each with its own bathroom, on this floor and three more that shared a bath on the third. The house had a total of fifteen rooms and six baths and was setting on three acres of land that included a tennis court, a pool with a Jacuzzi and cabana, a large formal garden with a shed and a six bay garage.

Gryphon's parents, his brother Sam, DJ and Adrienne had all thought he was crazy when he showed them the huge house, which he purchased with cash only about a year ago, but it had spoken to him. His therapist said it was because of his fear of confined spaces.

Either way, it was his.

He pulled the curtains open to let the dying sunlight into the room then opened the French doors so the cool breeze would come in as well. He stepped onto the slate tiled balcony the doors opened to and leaned on the cast iron railing, looking out across his tiny piece of the world. He watched a leaf caught in the swirling of the waterfall in his pool for a moment then shifted his eyes to the garden, and followed along the meandering stone pathway. He took a deep breath and smiled as the scent of the roses, magnolias and wisteria filled his nostrils.

The crickets were just starting to tune up for their night of singing and the sky was just starting to tinge purplish on the edges. This was Gryphon's favorite time of day, not daytime any longer but not night either. Dusk, it was called – he always thought it was such a dark sounding word for it. Twilight – he liked better.

He took a piece of pizza from the plate he was still holding, folded it in half lengthwise and bit into it. He ate the second piece on the balcony as well then went back into his room and emptied the first bottle of beer; the second he left untouched and unopened.

He kicked off his sneakers, pulled off his socks, didn't bother to unbutton his shirt, only pulled it over his head and undid and dropped his jeans. He left the clothes in a pile at the bottom of his bed. He grabbed the remote to the fifty-two inch plasma TV from the bottom of the bed, pushed the power button then the numbers two and one, for the local news channel then tossed it back onto the bottom of the bed and walked through the large closet to the huge master bathroom.

A granite slab in several shades of brown with black and gold specks made up the counter around the black porcelain sink, nickel-plated faucets, cabinet hardware and towel rods made for a striking contrast to this as did the suede-like slate blue walls. Twelve inch mottled blue, gray and green porcelain tiles covered the floor, the whirlpool tub surround and walls of the shower stall. A dark blue towel and a washcloth, both with his initials embroidered into them, hung from nickel-plated rings beside each of these.

The scientist debated taking a bath or a shower; he decided on the shower, not trusting that he wouldn't fall asleep in the tub. He stepped into the five by five stall, turned on the overhead showerhead and the body jets that ran along the sides and closed the frosted glass door behind him.

He was thoroughly pruned and fully relaxed by the time he left the stall. He grabbed the blue towel and rubbed his hair for a bit then wrapped it around his waist and hit the lights as he left the room and walked back through his closet to the bedroom.

It was only eight thirty five Gryphon's usual bedtime wasn't much before ten pm, but he tossed the damp towel onto the top of the pile of his discarded clothes and climbed into bed anyway. He wasn't planning to go to sleep right off in any case.

He turned the volume up on the TV and started to reach for his second pillow to prop himself up. He jumped a touch when the loud sound announcing a special report came from the speaker beside him. He finished adjusting the pillows then leaned back and waited for whatever the breaking news was.

"Pardon the interruption, viewers, but we just got this in. It seems there has been a rash of unexplained illnesses across the region. Reports are coming in from several counties around us, twenty and counting, of strange deaths. Each is described in like terms, the bodies being found in a mummy-like condition. Local authorities and medical personnel are baffled.

"We go now to our field reporter, Les Dugan, who is in the conference room of Clarence Medical Center on Fort Hopkins Army Base where the bodies of all the victims have been sent. We are being been told the chief of medicine is preparing to make a statement. Les?"

"Hello, Katy. As you said, I'm in the conference room of Clarence Medical Center where a colonel, John Graham, has just informed us the press conference is about to begin," said the man who looked as if he had been under the knife recently, his face was too perfect to be real, every hair on his head was in exactly the place it was meant to be and his teeth were so straight and perfect that they looked like they had never come into contact with food.

The camera panned away from the man and moved across the sea of other reporters and camera crews to a podium holding about ten microphones taped together with the seal of the United States government on the front of it, marking this as an official Army hospital.

The camera then moved to the right where four men dressed in army green fatigues and Kevlar vests, one with the medals of a colonel on the breast and triceps, and three people dressed in doctors' smocks, two men and one woman, were entering the room.

Gryphon's heart skipped at least five beats when he saw whom it was that stepped up to that podium.

# 7

# **Betrayal**

The reporters in the room immediately began to shout out questions, talking over each other. The woman at the podium held her hand up and said, clearly and strongly, into the mass of microphones, "Please reserve your questions for the end of the press conference."

The chatter in the room quieted down then.

"Thank you. I am Dr. Adrienne Ivekio, chief physician and head of the bio lab here at CMC," said the woman who had a bright red silk shirt on under the white smock. Her brown tresses were up, in a tight bun on top of her head, she was wearing retro style red thin-framed glasses and had a lot more makeup on than usual. "I know you are all here wanting answers; at this time all we really have are questions."

"What is causing this?" asked an older woman reporter near the front.

"Is it an epidemic?" called a man in the center.

"Is it contagious?" shouted another.

Adrienne only looked around the room – it was a look Gryphon knew all too well – the one that said she could be very patient and would hold her tongue until she was ready to speak. Once the room had quieted down, she said, "As was reported in the papers and on TV, we are currently investigating several unusual deaths in the area. We don't know yet if they are connected although the similarities in the deaths would suggest this. We don't believe it was foul play or natural causes. We are attempting to isolate the cause, which could have been something they ingested or be an environmental hazard they all came into contact with. All this being said, as I said, at this time we have more questions than answers. One thing we do know is this *virus* does not appear to be transmitted by means of contact or air, meaning, to the best of our knowledge, it is not contagious."

"What is the cause?" shouted the same older woman from the front of the room again.

"We do not know at this time. As I said, it could have been contaminated food or some sort of bio-hazard. Not having anyone alive to question or test our theories against, we cannot say for certain."

"What are the symptoms?"

"Who can get it?

"Is any age immune?"

"I repeat, we have only just found out there is a situation. As I stated already, we have no one living with the virus to speak to so we can only speculate on the symptoms, the ways of contracting it or any susceptible ages or races. Not wanting to cause any sort of mass hysteria, we will refrain from speculating on any of what these may be."

"Can you tell us anything?" asked Les.

"Only that we will keep the public informed in the event of or when it becomes an issue that requires it. Thank you all for coming. Have a nice day," said Dr. Ivekio.

The reporters were all shouting at her again but she, the other two doctors and three of the military men quickly went back out the door they had come in. The fourth man, the one earlier identified as Colonel John Graham, stepped up then.

In a deep gravelly voice that mirrored the gruff exterior, he said, "As Dr. Ivekio stated, that is all the information we have for you at this time. Please proceed now to the exit and return your press passes to the sergeant at the desk as you leave the facility."

The camera turned back to the face of Les then. He was smirking. The only emotions he had let show to prove he was indeed an actual human being and not just an anatomically correct android. "As you just heard, Katy, and as Dr. Adrienne Ivekio and Colonel John Graham just said, we have more questions than answers right now. We will bring you more of this breaking story as we receive it. For now, this is Les Dugan for ICTV, back to you Katy."

"Les, who is this Dr. Adrienne Ivekio, what are her credentials?" asked Katy in the TV studio, a picture of the young doctor appearing beside her.

It looked like an I.D. photo. It was from her shoulders up and she was standing slightly in profile. Her hair was down but pulled back from her face, probably in the French braids she liked to wear it in, she had a dangling pearl earring in the lobe of the ear showing and a pearl necklace around her long neck. She was wearing a black square neck blouse that was showing just the tops of her breasts. Gryphon knew this meant she was wearing a pushup bra since she didn't have that much natural cleavage. The slight smile on her face was one that said she was comfortable with who and where she was, which was one thing he had never doubted about her.

"We have been told that she came highly recommended to the position about six months ago. She comes from a microbiological background and has many years of experience in the field of bacterial virus research."

"And that is what they suspect this is being caused by?"

Gryphon muted the TV then, not needing to hear any more of the story right then.

*Six months*? He thought. That was about the time they had ended. She had not said anything about ever having interviewed for it a position at the Army base. It likely would have taken several months of one on one interviews, background checks and security screenings before they would have offered her a position in a government facility. Meaning she had likely been vying for the position for three or four months before that. How could she not have told him? Unless she didn't want him to know just how long she had been planning to leave him…

He tossed the TV remote across the room, got out of the huge bed, grabbed the unopened beer, twisted the cap off it, tossed it into the bin beside the bed and walked out onto the balcony. He stared into the now deep blue night sky for several minutes, drinking gulps of the beer and swallowing gulps of tears with it.

Once the bottle was empty he sank into a lounge chair behind him, closed his eyes and proceeded to fall asleep.

# 8

# In the Light of Day

Callie turned the knob on the front of the gas stove to the left and smirked at it. She didn't know why it never lit right. Only the first couple holes after the gas tube were lit; she gently blew on them and the rest of the burner lit up. She turned it back to barely a glow, set the fry pan on the tiny flames then added a pat of butter to it. Once it had melted and was just starting to sizzle she added two slices of beaten egg, vanilla extract and milk coated bread and cooked them until they were golden brown on both sides.

She put more butter on top of the French toast then poured some of the Vermont maple syrup a friend going to school in the state had sent her for Christmas over the top of it. She used her finger to catch the drip on the edge of the rim before she closed it then stuck that finger into her mouth. She poured herself about half a glass of orange juice from the jug beside her then cut the bread into bite-sized pieces and sat down on a stool beside the cabinet.

She stuck a bite into her mouth as she opened the morning paper. She started to take another bite as she scanned the front page of it. She wasn't interested in politics or sports so she skipped these pages. She mostly only looked at the entertainment page and the one with the comics and horoscopes. She knew it was foolish to read the horoscopes since she was a psychic and could do her own but she liked to see what others had come up with – compare notes, she supposed. She was just about to that page when her eyes stopped on a picture that made her drop the fork she was bringing to her mouth.

It hit the edge of the plate, spilling syrup all over the top of the counter.

"Sugar," she said as she quickly went to get a cloth to catch the sticky, fast spreading, stuff before it reached the floor.

Once she had the mess cleaned up she went back to the paper, hoping what she thought she saw was only a flashback to her nightmare of the night before.

It wasn't.

In the middle of the page was a picture of an older man and woman. The woman was the same one she had dreamed had come into her shop the night before, the one she had followed back to her home and watched the soul getting sucked out of. Chills ran up and down her spine, all the hairs on her body stood as goose pimples swept them up, and her stomach twisted as she continued reading.

The article said the bodies of an older couple had been found in their home in mummified condition. As in her dream, they were found lying beside each other in their bed. The couple's house-keeper said the woman had uttered the same phrases she had heard. It was more than a dream then. It wasn't a premonition; she had those before – not during – the event.

Her mind must have physically manifested into the woman's mind, somehow. She had astral projected before, but never in her sleep. She wiped the sweat that had beaded up on her forehead and neck away with the towel then finished reading the article.

It said the bodies were to be taken to the Army base hospital. Why would they take them there unless they suspected it was something more than natural causes? She knew a couple of nurses that worked at the hospital – it specialized in biological hazards and disasters. Perhaps that was what had killed the elderly couple? Some sort of biological illness, maybe? That was easier to swallow than what she had seen.

What *had* she seen? Had her mind created the ugly beings as a representation of the illness that was ravaging them? It had to be that. They had seemed so real though, she had felt them gripping the woman's arm. How could they be real, though? There was no such thing as monsters and she knew of no animal species like them? Could they be aliens? No, that *was* crazy. Maybe *she* was going crazy as more than a few had accused her of being?

She shook all this off, knowing if she kept at it she would only make herself crazy. She had been having troubles with her abilities for months, as she had in her dream. Chances were she had felt residuals on the lines between here and beyond stretching after receiving the two souls and had only imagined the rest of it.

She flipped the page, what she saw next gave her chills, goose flesh and twisted her stomach up all over again.

What had caused the repeat reaction was an advertisement that filled half the page. It was for a seminar being given at Northern Biscayne University that afternoon on something called phase shifting. She had no idea what phase shifting was or who the man that was giving the seminar was but the image under the man's picture was the same thing she had seen in her mind when she first awakened that morning after the nightmare – a Griffin.

The advertisement said the man worked for a company called Griffin Concepts, Inc. – thus the use of a Griffin in the company logo. The picture of the man giving the talk, G. A. Blake, was a partial profile shot from his waist up. It was in black and white and looked posed. He looked to be fairly young and was quite handsome. The lab coat he was wearing told her he was either a doctor or a scientist, or, at his age, a lab assistant. She didn't see any ring on the ring finger of his left hand, which was setting on his waist on the bottom of the picture and no sign that one had ever been there, telling her he was single and either had been for a while or had never been married. The smirk on his face gave him a look of arrogance or self-assurance; she wasn't sure which. His eyes looked bright and kind but she could also see a pain behind them, one probably only she could. She couldn't tell anything else about him from the picture; if her recent history continued she wouldn't be able to in person either.

She couldn't explain why but she had a feeling she should go to this talk. It was listed to be from two to five o'clock and was open to the general public. She made a mental note that if she had nothing else to do she might just check it out. She set the paper down and stood up. She was pulling her tank top off as she started for her bathroom to get washed up for the day.

# 9

# Surprise

Gryphon jolted awake as he heard a sound he didn't recognize. He looked around, uncertain where he was at first. He realized, as he went to try to sit up and felt all the muscles of his body scream out in protest, that he was still on the lounge chair on his balcony. The noise he had heard, what had awakened him so rudely, was the filter pump of the pool priming and kicking on. It did this every morning at this time but he wasn't usually out on the deck to hear it.

He slung his legs over the side of the chair and sat up. His eyes took in the clear blue sky that seemed far too beautiful for his mood just then. He ran his hands through the hair on his head that was disheveled from being wet when he laid down the night before and the night wind blowing it dry then over the hair on his chest, which was prickling from the cool breeze blowing across them. Another blew across his skin then, reminding him he was still naked. He thought to himself that he would have been better off getting drunk and having a hangover than what he felt right then, at least then his muscles would have been relaxed enough not to cramp up with the position he had slept in.

He stood up and stretched out his shoulder and back muscles. He had kinks in places he didn't know he had. He started back into his room and jumped when he heard someone humming a song in his bathroom. He noticed his pile of clothing was gone as was the towel from his shower of the night before and that the bed was made up. He guessed the humming was coming from his maid, who was only but two weeks into his employ. The sound was getting louder, telling him she was on her way back into the main room. He could imagine how she would react to him standing there naked.

Gryphon sniggered as he moved to the bed. He was just about under the covers on the corner as she stepped from the closet opening. The shocked look on her face almost made him want to laugh.

*********************

The woman, Jayne Abbott, had actually been in Gryphon's employ for about three weeks now, of which she had only seen him once in person; most of the time he was zipping out the front door to go to work just as she was arriving. She knew what he looked like mostly from the photographs she dusted in the parlor and his study – she especially liked the one of him kayaking a river rapid with his best friend. He was a very handsome man, one she wouldn't mind seeing more of – it didn't matter to her that he was old enough to be… a much older brother.

Jayne was thinking this as she was cleaning around the sink of his bathroom. She had an image of him stepping from the shower beside her or waiting for her to enter it with him in her mind. She giggled to herself then went back to humming the song she couldn't get out of her head whenever she thought about the man. She was singing the only line she really knew of it aloud, "You're one of those things I love, but your bad for me…" as she stepped back into the man's bedroom, holding his discarded clothes and the towel close to her front.

She opened her eyes, dropped those clothes and shouted "Oh, my God!" as she saw the man himself standing before her. She couldn't miss that he was completely naked as her eyes watched him walk across the room and dive for the covers of his bed.

\*\*\*\*\*\*\*\*\*\*\*\*\*\*\*\*\*\*\*\*\*\*

"Sorry, Ah… it's Jayne, yes?" asked Gryphon as he sat on the edge of the bed and pulled the covers over his waist.

"Ah… um… yes… yes, sir… it is," Jayne's tongue stumbling through her mouth. Her heart skipped a beat when he said her name, making her blush.

The maid had thought her boss looked quite fine in the photos in his den; all of which she had guessed were from a few years ago. He looked just as fine today. He was quite muscled and was tanner than she had imagined him to be. That image would be forever burned into her mind, which Jayne really didn't mind.

"I am sorry, Sir. I knocked on the door. When I didn't get any answer I thought you were already out for the day."

"It's alright, Jayne. I was on the balcony and didn't hear you. I was going over… over my thoughts for the lecture I am giving today and kind of lost track of time," said the man.

Jayne was almost half his age, which meant he had no interest in her as anything other than an employee, but she was attractive. She had bouncy shoulder length blond curls and a very womanly body. DJ had told him a few things he would like to do to her when he saw her for the first time a few days ago. Things he found himself thinking of now. He had to admit she did look like she would perform them well.

The young woman bent down and picked up the clothes she had dropped in her surprise. She forced herself not to look over at his naked chest, the side of his hip that showed around the blanket or his bare legs, though she wanted to. "I'll go get these to the laundry room… Do you want me to have Aggie fix you anything for breakfast, Sir? She is in the pantry inventorying for a grocery pick-up."

"Um, yeah, some eggs and toast, I guess," he said, scratching his head and yawning.

The movement of this made the covers slip further off him, exposing almost all of his left side and the line of darker colored hair that ran from under his bellybutton to his privates to the woman now.

Jayne couldn't look away from him then. She was frightened and excited at the thought that he was trying to intentionally entice her. "How… how do you want the eggs done?" she asked breathlessly. She was mesmerized as she watched him stretch out his neck and shoulder muscles and at the way his pectoral and stomach muscles were dancing as he did this.

"Over easy is fine, Jayne," Gryphon said through a smile, acting oblivious to her unrest.

"Yes, Sir," she said, forcing her eyes off him.

He didn't even wait for her to close the door before he stood and started for the bathroom.

She looked back as she was closing the door and whistled to herself as she watched his naked body walk out the room.

Gryphon shook his head at the girl's reaction to him naked. He knew he should not have teased her but he supposed he needed the boost to his confidence right then after having learned his previous lover, a woman he had thought he had known pretty well, one had trusted, had lied to him. He again turned on the shower, this time only the overhead showerhead though, climbed inside it and closed the door.

# 10

# Playing Fair

The breakfast Jayne had said she would tell his Aggie, he wanted was waiting for Gryphon in the breakfast nook off the kitchen when he got to the room. He sat down, took up the cloth napkin, spread it over his left leg and began to eat. The chef stepped into the room just as he was finishing the last sip of the coffee she also had waiting for him.

"Gryphon Blake," said the woman in a pointed tone, her hands on her hips and her feet set firm.

"Yeah, Abigail," he asked in his best hadn't-done-a-thing-wrong voice, the sneaky smile that came to his lips moments later told another story though.

Abigail Hendricks was in her late sixties and reminded him a little of his mother, except she still had all of her amber hair; he truly doubted that she colored it. She had worked for him for about ten years now; she was the first person he had hired to work for him at home, while he still lived in the condo just down the street from DJ because he was never home and didn't like to clean up after himself.

"You realize you frightened poor Jayne half out of her wits?" Abigail asked as she started to the table to remove his empty plate.

"I am sorry but she frightened me more than a little out of mine as well."

"Were you so frightened out of yours that you forgot that you were completely naked?" asked the woman, putting her fisted hands on her hips again.

Gryphon only smiled. It was a wicked devilish smile few ever saw because he rarely let himself go enough for them to.

The woman shook her head and said, "Did you have to parade yourself in front of her that way though? It took me three weeks to find her. Now we will be lucky if she comes back in the morning. She likely thinks this is a nudist's home and that she will be expected to go naked as well."

The tiniest curve to the left side of the chef's lips told Gryphon how hard she was trying to control the urge to laugh. "And this would be a bad thing how? Think how much time, money and water we would save if I didn't have any laundry. Not to mention electricity… It could be the start of a global change. No need for animal hides or cotton… or polyester. Heck, we could end so many problems then… Though, the colder climates would be using more fuel, wood and coal to keep warm. Unless we all grew hair like the Neanderthals…" He gave her his best silly look then scratched his head as he said, "Would we still be considered naked then?"

The woman sniffed at this and said, just under her breath, "I think you are a Neanderthal, Gryphon Blake."

"She had my clothing from last night in her hands, and was between me and the closet so I couldn't get more. The only thing I had to cover up with was my hands, which aren't large enough to cover my entire body," he said, holding his quite large hands up. "I swear I went for the covers of the bed as quick as I could." He was enjoying the jesting.

"I am flabbergasted, sir. Why have you never done this before me?" she asked; putting her hands on her hips again, a wild twinkle in her eyes.

"Ah, jealousy is it then?" he asked. "Am I going to find her strung up to the clotheslines and you waiting for me in my bed when I get home this evening?"

"You know my husband would never approve of my having an affair with you, Sir, but that doesn't mean I have to enjoy you flirting with a younger woman," said Aggie as she took the plate from before him and motioned to find out if he wanted a refill on the coffee.

He smiled and stood up then he loosened his tie and pulled it over his head, pulled the bottom of his shirt out of his pants and started to unbutton it. "I must make sure you all get equal treatment. I wouldn't want to be accused of playing favorites. I'm not going to do this for Jerome though; I think he would be offended to see a man naked... Do you wish to volunteer to disrobe for him or should I ask Jayne to do it. Then of course, Jerome will have to do it for the both of you... And I will feel left out and will expect a show of my own... Lord knows where it will end... "

"Are you trying to irk me?" asked the woman, shaking her head and a crooked finger at him in warning.

"No, I just want to be sure you are happy here by doing anything I must, my dear," said Gryphon as he took her slightly wrinkled hand in his and kissed the top of it. "Would you prefer we do this in the bedroom... Will you be able to keep your hands off me after?"

The woman pulled her hand from his, walked over to the sink and set the dishes in it to be washed later, huffing and puffing loudly in feigned irritation. She was enjoying the mood of her employer; she had seen it more often than most but it was not as often as she liked.

Gryphon shook his head, stood up, walked up beside the chef and kissed her gently on the cheek. "Oscar is a lucky man, Aggie," then left the room.

"Damn straight he is," said the woman as she watched her employer leave the room. He was fully clothed but she enjoyed how his slacks clung to him and how his hips moved when he walked. She wasn't surprised so many people had a crush on him. "Mm, mm, mm! If I wasn't married and about ten years younger I would show that man a trick or two." She went back to the pantry then; to finish the inventory she had begun that morning.

\*\*\*\*\*\*\*\*\*\*\*\*\*\*\*\*\*\*\*\*\*

Gryphon was still smiling as he walked into his study to get his briefcase and notes for the talk he was giving in a little more than four hours. He grabbed his gray tweed sports jacket, pulled it on over the crisp white shirt, adjusted the collar and the silk pink and gray striped tie he had chosen to wear and started back out of the room. He jumped when the phone on the corner of the desk rang.

He knew Abigail was busy in the kitchen and Jayne should still be in the laundry room, which was in the basement, so there was no one free to answer it. He set the case down in the hall, walked back to the desk and picked up the receiver.

"Hello?"

"Hi… ah, is Gryph… Is… Is Dr. Blake available?"

It took Gryphon a moment to catch his breath; he recognized the voice in an instant. "He is," he said, a little surprised and hurt she didn't recognize his.

"Gryphon?" the woman asked.

"Yes, Adrienne," he answered.

"Why are you answering your own phone?"

Gryphon thought of a hundred witty retorts but instead he said, with more than a little bit of sarcasm, "Don't you have people to make phone calls for you?"

"Did you… I am guessing you caught the press conference then?"

He said nothing, knowing now she had only called because she was feeling guilty that he had learned of her betrayal in that manner.

"I was hoping… wondering if maybe we could get together and talk over a cup of coffee or… have a drink?"

"Talk over what, Adrienne?"

"Please, Gryphon," said the woman.

He could hear the pain in her voice. He hoped it was at the thought of having hurt him. He wished he didn't still care that she was hurting. "I'm giving a seminar at the university today, Adrienne. I have no idea how long the questions after will take so... I really don't think I can get together with you today."

"I... would you mind if I came to the talk?"

Gryphon almost dropped the phone. In the three plus years they were together she had never once wanted to go to one of his talks. She was a medical doctor; for all there was a lot of science to it she thought his science wasn't the same. "It is open to the public so I cannot stop you being there, Adrienne," he said flatly.

"What time does it start?"

"Two o'clock."

"Should I... is it alright if I hang around after and if you have time..."

"I need to get going to make sure everything is in place so..." he left the rest of the statement unsaid.

"Yeah, poster boards and slides and such... Okay, I look forward to seeing you again."

Gryphon only grunted into the phone then slowly lowered it to the cradle. He tried to put her being there at the back of his mind, guessing she had only made the call as a consolation; the chances that she would actually show up was slim to none.

\*\*\*\*\*\*\*\*\*\*\*\*\*\*\*\*\*\*\*\*

The owner of the house walked down the stairs to find his butler, Jerome, washing his sporty station wagon, as much soap and water on himself as on the car.

"Good morning, Dr. Blake," said Jerome, standing up straight. "Did you want the Magnum?"

"No, Jerome, I thought I would take out the Blockhead today."

"Very good, Sir. That will give me a chance to wax this."

"You bucking for a raise, Jerome?"

"No, sir, you pay just fine, Sir," said the man.

"Can you get the gate for me?"

"Most definitely."

Jerome Chamberlain had been the butler for a wealthy family in town for twenty years but they had restructured their household and his position had been removed. He was actually more than just a butler for Gryphon, he was also his attendant and steward but being an old fashion Englishman, he preferred butler as his title.

He knew the man was serious that he didn't want any more money, like with DJ, and all of his other employees, Gryphon Blake was a very generous man. Jerome had an annual review coming up though, which meant he could give him a small *cost of living increase* without telling him.

Felling a little more like himself again, Gryphon walked to his garage entered through the open bay door and smiled at his three Harley Davidson motorcycles. He had a black 2002 Softail Heritage Classic, a red 2005 Dyna Super Glide Custom and his favorite, a black 1985 Evolution "Blockhead" with the old style kick start, bright red, yellow and orange flames airbrushed on the gas tank and lots of shiny chrome accessories. He liked riding all three but he was in the mood today to take out the old-timer.

He put his briefcase into the saddlebag on the right side and walked to the wall to get his riding gear. He changed his tweed jacket for a black leather one and put on black fingerless riding gloves. He had a choice of helmets on the stand before him. He chose the solid black one. He neatly folded the sport coat and put it into the left saddle bag then put on the helmet, climbed onto the bike. He turned the key, jumped on the rod to kick start it then cracked the accelerator on the right hand grip several times. He just listened to the distinct sound of the engine growl for a bit. He pulled out of the garage, brought the bike up to rolling speed and started down the driveway.

The gate opened just as he reached it so he never even had to slow down.

He had a half hour ride to get him to the campus of the university, going the back way, which would take him through the foothills that surrounded their town. He liked this drive on a bike because the rolling hills and valleys gave the cycle a good workout, which made it feel good between his legs.

More than a few had equated riding a Harley Davidson motorcycle to riding a woman – in some ways one was better than the other and in some ways the other was better than one.

Right now he only had the bike so he would enjoy it as if it was a woman.

# 11

# **False Sentiment**

Saturdays on the campus of Northern Biscayne University were usually fairly busy, there were a few classes but it was mostly a day for the students to catch up on their studies, hang with their classmates and party.

This being a fairly warm day for a change there were a lot of students getting ready to do the latter with fifty gallon drums filled with gas doused wood set around the quad to be lit as soon as the sun started going down. Other half drums were set up with metal grates and charcoal briquettes or smoked wood inside to barbeque steak, pork, chicken, burgers, hotdogs, sausages and miscellaneous vegetables. Several others were set around to put ice in to chill the kegs that would also be showing up at sundown.

He had been to more than his fair share of these when he was on campus as a student and he'd had to collect DJ from more than a few to show him the results of whatever experiment they were running while he was here. He smiled at the students playing with a frisbee and tossing balls and had to admit he missed those days.

He brought his bike up to the curb beside a fiery red convertible Mercedes Benz, took the key from the ignition and stepped off it. He heard more than a few whistles from the students that had watched him pull up on the classic bike, the guys envious of his owning it and the girls wishing they were it. He had to admit it made him feel manly to be seen with the bike. After his night last night and the phone call this morning, he needed this boost to his ego as well.

He swapped the leather jacket for the more business-like tweed one and put the former and his gloves into the saddlebag. He twisted the lock on the clasp then stepped to the other side and took out the briefcase with his notes. He was smiling to himself, listening to the whispers of the students watching him, as he turned toward the campus. That smile faded when he saw Dean Williams walking toward him.

Gryphon started up the cobblestone walkway surrounding the quad, intent on meeting the man in the middle, so he wouldn't think he had the upper hand through intimidation. He wondered if the man was there to greet him or insult him.

Robert Williams had been the dean of students while both he and DJ were students here and hadn't cared for either of them. He had told them both, on more than one occasion, to their faces, alone and together; that he thought their brand of science was a step below that of the Ghostbusters of 1980's movie fame. DJ's comment to this was always, "The man is so stuck in the eighties I doubt he'd know modern science if it was to smack him on the ass and ask *Where's the beef?*" using his best old lady impersonation as he said the famous line.

"Dean Williams," Gryphon said as cordially as he could manage, forcing a smile to form on his face. He stuck the helmet he was carrying under his left arm then extended his hand to the man.

The man ignored the hand, his own clasped tight behind his back. "The faculty and staff would like me to... graciously extend our gratitude for your recent contributions," said the man, very pompously and like it was hurting him physically to do so.

Gryphon said just as pompously, "I have more than a few of this fine establishment's former students in my employ, sir, so I thought it only right to show my gratitude that you allow your students to spread their scientific wings and stretch the perception of modern science in hopes that this tradition will continue."

The dean sniffed loudly, then said, "The material for your seminar arrived yesterday and has been set up in room B."

"Thank you, kind sir. May I inquire as to how many have signed up to attend my talk?" asked the physicist.

"I believe the last roster listed fifty," said the man, sounding as if he couldn't believe even one would.

This was forty-eight more than Gryphon had thought he might get so he smiled. "Was there anything else, sir?"

"We have another seminar, on the cause and effect of one legged frogs in the rain forests of Brazil, beginning at six this evening so please be prompt in clearing out when you are done."

Gryphon wanted to say that should be a short seminar since both was the effects of global warming on the environment but he left it alone, each man's science to his own. He nodded to the man, stepped around him and continued to the Science building.

As the man said, Gryphon found two wooden crates waiting for him when he arrived. One was about the size of a normal shipping box, which was filled with literature on his company as well as information on the device and the science behind it. The other was on its side and was as tall as him and five feet wide – the device itself. There also were two six foot folding tables, a podium with microphone, an overhead projector and a drop down screen as he had requested.

He stood the screen up in front of the chalkboard and opened it, set up the tables beside each other in the center of the floor a few feet in front of the screen, so he could move around them with ease, moved the podium to the far right of the tables, so he wouldn't block anyone's view of the screen and chalkboards, set the overhead projector on the corner of the first table beside the podium, and turned it on to make sure it was in focus, that the image was large enough and that it was aimed at the center of the screen then grabbed the crowbar from the top of the smaller crate and pried the top off.

He took out the envelope of GCI brochures, promotional items and color pamphlets on the project he had asked Sandra to get together for him and opened it. He slid the material out along with a folded piece of paper. He opened it to find it was a note from his secretary that read, *Good luck, Dr. Blake, Sandra*, with a smiley face beside her name. He shook his head at it then folded it back up and put it in his pocket for disposal later.

He placed all the material into neat piles on the table, along with a stack of his business cards. It didn't happen often but he had made some contacts and found some customers at these seminars.

He went to the larger crate, which was still strapped to the four-wheeled dolly cart it had been shipped on. He pushed it to the far left side of the room, opened it and brought out the unit. It wasn't heavy but it was awkward. He set it on the table in the center of the floor and put a black cover over top of it.

He looked at his set up and nodded then looked at his watch. He had about thirty minutes left before the talk would begin so he walked to the chalkboard, grabbed a piece of white chalk and wrote his name and the words, phase shifting, below it in large letters.

At ten minutes to two o'clock, Gryphon grabbed a pile of the literature and moved to the door to greet the people as they arrived. This was marketing 101.

He was surprised and pleased when he opened it, intending to prop it open, to find a line waiting. He recognized some as his former student assistants and, as DJ had said, a majority of them were women. He did see a few teachers and a couple newspaper reporters he recognized as well. It was an eclectic mix of people, most he doubted had any idea what he would be talking about, likely taking the seminar only to get out of class for the day or to get extra credit with a report on the subject. At least he wouldn't be talking to himself.

He handed a packet of information to each as they entered and said, "Good afternoon, sit wherever you like," or its equivalent to each as they stepped past him.

# 12

# Phase Shifting 101

"Good afternoon, students, faculty and visitors of the university. Thank you all for taking time out of your busy lives to see me. I am Dr. Gryphon Blake. I have a PhD in Applied Physics from this university and am CEO of Griffin Concepts Incorporated. I am here to tell you about one of our recent projects. A phase shifting device."

He waited for the expected initial comments to subside before he continued.

"I know that you have all come here with certain expectations of what you will see, hear and learn, I promise to do my best to make sure you also understand when you leave. First I will explain what phase shifting is and what it does. We will have a practical demonstration of phase shifting and then a brief session for questions.

"I ask that any recording devises and cameras be shut off during the seminar since this is patented material, and that all cell phones are turned off. The literature I've given you includes general information on phase shifting that may be used for any reports you wish to give on this subject but I must ask that any quotes or specifics you intend to use be vetted by GCI public relations staff prior to their publication."

He heard eight or nine different devices being shut off. He didn't like being a suspicious man but competition for government grants and high paying private and public sector contracts could be fierce.

"Thank you all for understanding. First, I am sure you are all wondering: what exactly is phase shifting anyway?" he asked.

His eyes were drawn to the top of the stairs where a young woman with blondish hair, wearing a white peasant blouse and a long patchwork shirt with a tie died scarf tied around her middle, looking a bit like a gipsy, was standing, looking a little lost.

"Come on in, Miss, we are just getting started," said Gryphon. He grabbed another packet of information from the table and met her halfway. He continued as he was walking back to the podium.

"Phase is a *frequency* domain or *fourier transform* domain concept that is understood best in terms of simple harmonic motion. The same concept applies to wave motion, which can be seen either at a specific point in space over an interval of time or across an interval of space at a specific point in time. Simple harmonic motion is the displacement of waves that vary cyclically, as depicted here," he said as he laid a transparency onto the glass of the projector that sent a graph to the dropdown screen.

It had a sideways lowercase T, a wavy line was drawn across the body of the T and there were four words written on the chart: *displacement* was at the top of the crossed part, *amplitude* was written on the left side, *period* was written under the waves and *time* was written near the bottom of the T on the right side of the image.

"The space between the waves is the amount of time displaced and can be written as a mathematical equation." He walked to the board and wrote the formula on it $x(t)=A \cdot \sin(2\pi ft + 0)$ then he moved the piece of chalk along it. "A is the amplitude of oscillation, F is the frequency, T is the elapsed time, and zero is the phase of the oscillation.

"Phase oscillation is not an initial condition but rather one that is continuously changing. The term *instantaneous phase* is used to distinguish the time-variant angle from the initial condition, which is T equal to zero." He moved back to the projector and replaced the previous graph with another. This one looked the same as the one before except it had a second wavy line drawn on it, spaced slightly apart, one being red the other blue. He moved his finger from the bottom of the red wave to the bottom of a blue wave and said, "The area between the two waves represents a shift from zero phase, or a shift in time and space.

"The word time is often used to express the oscillation but it can be anything. Take two model trains, for example, moving around two parallel tracks at the same speed and direction but starting at different points on the tracks. They will meet at the same point, or instance in time, each pass because their phase difference is constant. If you vary the speed, their phase difference, they will no longer meet at the same place or time. This displacement is a shift in phase. Another example is how we measure the rotation of the Earth in hours instead of radians; the time zones are an example of phase differences.

"What does all this have to do with why you are here, you ask? I have invented a device that allows the phase of an otherwise static object to be shifted out of its normal variance." The sound of excited gasps made his heart beat a little faster.

"How do I demonstrate this in terms you might better understand?" he asked the room as he walked over to his briefcase, opened it and took out an aluminum can of non-alcoholic beer. "This is slightly warm and may have gotten shaken up a touch but do I have a volunteer to open it, taste it and tell the room it is indeed an actual can of beer like one you would find in any store cooler?" He wasn't surprised when several guys, sitting in a bunch near the center of the room, all raised their hands.

He knew the dean wouldn't like him using this teaching aid but he knew the only way for people to really understand was a practical demonstration and being on a college campus this was the best one to use – again, marketing 101.

"Dude, why didn't you bring a real beer?" asked the one he pointed out.

Gryphon motioned him to come forward and handed him the can, "I will not condone nor advocate drinking in the middle of the day."

This brought hearty laughs from most everyone in the room and silly giggles from the girls sitting down front, hoping to catch his eye.

"What's your name?"

"Stew," said the boy.

"Alright, Stew, open the can and take a sip. I ask you to refrain from taking more since it could diminish my demonstration and require me to get another can."

Stew nodded, tapped the top of the can, which, in theory, was supposed to stop it from exploding in a mass of froth when it was cracked and slowly peeled it open.

The distinct sound of a can being opened was heard loud and clear. "Yup, it's an actual can."

Another round of laughter erupted.

Gryphon only barely cracked a smile.

Stew brought it to his lips, took a sip of it then cringed, made an ugly face and stuck his tongue out, "Blah! It's warm as piss but it is beer."

There was another round of laughter at the look on the boy's face.

"Thank you, Stew," said Gryphon. He took the can of beer back from the volunteer and motioned for him to go back to his seat.

The scientist walked to the table then and set the can on it, beside the thing that until now had been covered with a piece of black fabric. He removed this covering to reveal what looked a bit like a laser. He flipped a switch on the side of the unit and the space between the end of it and the can kind of wavered then. The liquid that was inside the container was now floating in a can shape just beside the still intact can, on the audience's side. He heard the expected oohs and aahs from the audience. When Gryphon shut off the PSD the condensed liquid fell apart and sloshed over the tabletop. "And that is a practical application of phase shifting," he said as he looked up at the audience.

He always did this, wanting to get their reactions, which didn't disappoint this time either – as always; they ranged from sounds of awe to utter disbelief and a few swears uttered. He wasn't surprised by this, but he was surprised by something else. There was another person standing in the opening at the top of the multileveled room.

This woman had light brown hair loose around her shoulders and dressed the same as the woman in the photograph he had been staring at the day before.

Adrienne nodded to him, took a step down and sat in the last row.

Gryphon had to force his thoughts to stay in order as he went back to his talk. "The two oscillators, the can and the beer, were in the same frequency when the beer was inside the can. Now they are in different frequencies, or phases. They are now *out of phase* with each other.

"The amount oscillators are out of step with each other can be expressed in degrees from zero to three hundred sixty degrees, or in radians from zero to twice pi. If the phase difference is one hundred eighty degrees then the two oscillators are said to be in *antiphase*. If two interacting waves meet at a point where they are in antiphase destructive interference will occur.

"It's common for waves of light, sound, as well as other energy sources, to become superposed in their transmission medium. When that happens the phase difference determines whether they reinforce or weaken each other. Complete cancellation is possible for waves with equal amplitudes.

"In physics, quantum mechanics ascribes waves to physical objects. The wave function is complex, since its square modulus is associated with the probability of observing an object. The complex character of the wave function is associated with phase. The phase of particles is related to their quantum mechanics or behavior."

Gryphon could see most of the people's eyes were beginning to glaze over now so he quickly skipped ahead. "I cannot discuss how this technology can be useful in a modern application since it is classified information but as you can see it can have huge implications in the world of physics." He recovered the unit, shut off the projector, stepped back in front of the podium and asked, "Does anyone have any questions?" He was pleased to see a few hands rise and that the first one he pointed at, a man on the right side in a black turtleneck, wasn't only asking where the closest restroom was.

# 13

# Playing Games

Callie hadn't known what to expect when she arrived at the college campus, she hadn't ever even considered going to college. She had enjoyed school until she was about eleven. It was about that time she got her first menstrual cycle and began to notice she had unusual skills. After that it was like torture.

She had thought it odd at first that she suddenly found herself getting all the answers on her tests right, as did the teachers – she had been barely an average student before, this had raised questions of whether she had cheated. She started to make mistakes so teachers wouldn't get suspicious of her and quit all her extra-curricular activities, going directly home after school.

By the end of her high school years she had few friends; partly because she had told them all once too often what they were thinking before they thought and spoke it and partly because she knew what they thought of her before they thought or spoke it.

She was having trouble walking across the quad this day. She couldn't have told whose thoughts of the dozens of students and teachers around her she was getting, there was so many different voices shouting in her head that it was deafening. It was like it had been when she first started to have these skills. She had thought she had gotten these onslaughts under control years ago.

She was felling very weak in the knees when she finally reaches the building the blond boy by the coffee stand said the talk was being given in. She stepped inside and had to take a deep breath. The voices all stopped as soon as she closed the doors, which was odd. She was so happy that they had that she dismissed the thought quickly.

She walked the long, cold looking hallway slowly. There was nothing on the gray walls except a few posters of the rules of the building, the way to get out in case of fire and a few black benches between the ten doors. She moved toward a metal easel with a poster board that had a blown up version of the ad she had seen in the paper.

She could hear talking coming from the room as she got closer. She began to feel a little strangely in the pit of her stomach, like just before she would get a premonition. She wondered why she was feeling so drawn to this room; she had never wanted to learn anything scientific before.

She stepped into the open doorway and looked into the room that looked a little like an old style amphitheater with row of seats getting progressively lower until you reached the floor, which was the stage, that was about twenty feet down. She glanced around the room; it was filled with an odd mix of people. She wondered which of the people had drawn her to this seminar; which was it that she was feeling this connection with? She looked at the man giving the seminar as he said his name and knew.

The Griffin.

She was surprised when he looked at her, smiled and said it was alright for her to come in. She had thought she would be told the talk started at two o'clock not two ten, as it was now. And again when he met her halfway with a packet of information on what he was there to talk about. She forced herself not to touch him when he did, not wanting to find out whether she would get anything from the touch. With how crazy her skills were acting she might end up blowing either her or his mind.

She sat in the empty seat at the end of the fifth row down and looked at the pamphlet on top of the packet. It was for Griffin Concepts, Inc. G.A. Blake, as he was tagged in the ad, was not just a lab technician, he was the CEO of the company.

She looked at the actual man standing about twenty feet before her and could not help but draw in a breath. He had a presence even someone without her specials skills would be caught by. He was obviously passionate about his work and sounded like he knew what he was talking about. He was very articulate and spoke with ease and a quiet confidence. She could see how insecure he was underneath too, how much he wanted these people to understand him, as well. She had often wondered why the best looking men always seemed to feel inadequate and the ugliest thought they were so great.

She wasn't really listening to his explanation of phase shifting because she was being flooded with images of his youth. She got flashes of how happy he was as a child, and how safe and secure his parents and grandparents made him feel; his days at school – through the grades and here at this same college. He was popular enough, he had a good and loyal group of friends but he had always felt a little odd man out because he was so much smarter than all of them. He wasn't seen as or had ever considered himself a nerd but he would have fit the description as far as his grade point average. She saw him struggling, still, to make people believe in him and his team of crackpot scientists – believe that they were true scientists and that they could be useful.

She jolted a little as an image of a door closing abruptly and locking came to her mind then. She realized she was seeing an event that had forever changed the man before her. She guessed he was about ten. She could feel an intense fear and tightening of his chest as he realized there was no way to get out of the tiny room he was now locked inside. She heard him crying and desperately shouting out for someone named Sammy to get him out and something else... Something she remembered from her own memory... Several voices converging in a language she didn't know... and one voice clearing say, '*They come from the dark.*'

This boy, Sammy, was important to this man. She focused on that name and got an image of a boy that was slightly smaller built than Gryphon Blake, with hair slightly darker than his. Sammy was his younger brother. She could feel how much he cared for his brother and how much he still felt he needed to protect him and smiled. She saw something else then, something that made the hairs on the back of her neck stand on end, goose pimples erupt all over her body, her stomach twist up and feel like she was going to vomit.

She clasped the back of the seat before her tight as she began to swoon. She was seeing Sammy as he was today, now called Sam by all but Gryphon. Sam was older now but still just as cute. He wasn't looking so cute at that moment, bent over the toilet puking his guts up. She heard him shout out, "Shut up!" and "Go way!" to the seemingly empty room then she heard the same eerie voices speak over each other.

She felt movement around her and looked around. She realized the talk was finished and some of the people were moving down to speak personally to the man. She wondered if and how she should tell him what she had just seen. Would he believe her?

The man's brother was in trouble. She knew if she didn't say something now it would be too late; how could she not say anything?

She stood up and started toward him.

\*\*\*\*\*\*\*\*\*\*\*\*\*\*\*\*\*\*\*\*

Gryphon had tried to ignore the three girls sitting in the front row, especially when one of them pulled her skirt as far up as she could and began to play with her thighs. He had hoped they would chicken out of speaking to him with so many around but he watched them stand and start toward him. He tried to keep talking to the boy, Stew, and his friends as long as he could but he finally had to turn to them.

"Yes, ladies?" he forced a smile.

"Can we have your autograph, Dr. Blake?" asked the one that had been flashing him.

Gryphon had to fight not to groan and say no. He took the paperwork from each, quickly scribbled his name on them and handed them back.

The one who had spoken before said, "You can put your phone number on there as well."

"I am flattered, Miss, but I am almost old enough to be your father."

"That's alright with me, I think I deserve a spanking," she whispered to him.

Gryphon snorted and thought it was a good thing he hadn't taken DJ up on his offer to do the talk in his place. He realized these girls were essentially nerd groupies, meaning they got off on the thought of a man being that smart. He could just imagine what his business partner's reaction to being told something like that would have been. Unlike his younger and more brazen associate he saw no need for frivolous flings just for the sake of.

"Again, I'm flattered but I doubt my wife would be so keen on the idea."

"Oh," said the girl, looking very sadly at him. "Well, if you change your mind I live in Thomas House."

"I will remember that, thanks."

The girls left then, still giggling.

Gryphon was shaking his head as he started back to the table. He glanced up to the seats then and saw there were still two people in the room – the woman that had arrived late and Adrienne.

Both were starting toward him.

He guessed the first was like the young women that had just left, looking to get to know him better. She appealed to him more than the first three women had but he wasn't ready to get involved with anyone right now, especially right now. Adrienne he had no idea of.

He half considered pretending the former was his new girlfriend to see how the latter would react but he quickly dismissed the idea. He didn't like using people and he really didn't want to hurt Adrienne; even given all the pain she had caused him.

\*\*\*\*\*\*\*\*\*\*\*\*\*\*\*\*\*\*\*\*

Adrienne had hoped when she next saw Gryphon that he would have gotten fat or at least wouldn't still be devastatingly handsome but he wasn't the first and was all the more the second. She liked how he looked in the gray suite he was wearing and thought the pink and gray tie set off his skin nicely. She also liked how much longer he had let his hair grow out, it softened his strong features and made him look like a more relaxed person than the crew cut he'd had when they were first together. The longer hair made him look more like the mad scientist he was said by some to be, though.

\*\*\*\*\*\*\*\*\*\*\*\*\*\*\*\*\*\*\*\*

"So, when did you get married, Gryphon?" Adrienne asked teasingly as she stepped up to him and offered him her hand.

Gryphon smirked at her but said nothing. He was reluctant to take her hand, not sure he could touch her in so cold and informal a way. He didn't want to insult her either so he did.

"That was a great talk," she said as she looked over at the covered device. "I remember when you first came up with the concept for this. How excited you were, and how devastated you were when no one believed it would work. I guess you got the last laugh."

Gryphon still hadn't said anything.

"Are you going to speak to me?"

"You were the one that asked to come here, Adrienne, so cut the small talk and speak to me."

"I... I have a situation I am hoping you and your company can assist me with."

"The mummy bodies?" he asked.

"Yes. I am hoping your biochemistry lab might be able to help us come up with and pinpoint the virus."

"That's not my department."

"No, but as the owner of the company I thought it only right to ask you first before going to them. I know you have final approval of all outside contracts. I didn't want you surprised when you saw my name listed."

"I allow DJ choice of what he does, without oversight. I trust him to know what is best for GCI."

"David is still with you then?"

"Is that why you came?"

Adrienne looked at him oddly.

"You could have discussed this over the phone, Adrienne."

"I... I wanted to see you and... make sure you are alright."

"And your outfit?" he asked. He wondered if she had done it intentionally as a stab.

"I thought I would fit in with the college crowd better dressed this way, maybe draw less attention," she said as she pulled on the bottom of the tank-top.

"In that outfit you draw more."

Adrienne smiled to that. Her heart skipped a little at hearing that, it felt good to know he still found her attractive as well – though she had no idea what exactly that was good for. "So... are you all right?"

"I am, Adrienne," said Gryphon as he looked at the woman behind her, again considering using her to get to his ex and hoping his ex would get the hint he was finished speaking to her.

Adrienne did notice this. She looked behind her and saw the woman standing the second row up, trying to look as if she were waiting patiently, not eavesdropping. She wondered if she was more than just a person there to hear the talk. She felt a twinge of jealousy but tried to fight it, reminding herself she had no right to be.

"I guess... I'll give David a call on Monday then. Thanks, Gryphon."

Gryphon nodded to her. He was wishing *she* didn't still look so well. He watched her walk back up the stairs and felt a twinge of regret for how snotty he had spoken to her.

He shook his head then turned his eyes to the other woman. He hoped she wasn't like the others that had left. He was really not in the mood to deal with another drooling *fan*.

\*\*\*\*\*\*\*\*\*\*\*\*\*\*\*\*\*\*\*\*\*

Callie hadn't intended to but she couldn't stop the flood of images of the days and nights Gryphon and this woman had spent together when she looked at them standing before her. She quickly blocked out those images. She felt herself flushing a little with shame at having invaded their privacy as well as with excitement and envy at the amount of passion she had seen between these two people. It hurt her to see the look of anger in the man's eyes when he looked at the woman now, the guilt she felt in the woman's heart and the rush of desire, fear and pain see saw in both of their hearts.

She jumped when the woman walked past her, then again when she noticed, or more like felt, the man was now looking at her. His intense stare was making her a little bit weak in the knees.

"Did you have questions, Miss?" asked Gryphon. He was trying to keep his voice soft and even. He didn't want Adrienne to know how much seeing unsettled him.

"My name is Callie Summers. I run a shop on Fifth Avenue, down the alley beside the Book King, called Summer Sage."

"Yeah?" He wasn't sure why she would think he would care. He had heard of her shop before but he wasn't sure just what it was she sold there.

"It's a novelty shop of sorts," said Callie as she handed him one of her business cards.

He took it and saw the name and address of her shop and a drawing of a crystal ball, a deck of tarot cards, an incense stick giving off smoke in the shape of the yin yang sign and a black cat looking as if about ready to pounce on that smoke and smirked. He remembered the shop now, some of his younger employees had spoken of it as being a head slash magic shop of sorts. There was mixed ideas as to whether they thought she was a fraud or not.

He knew by the look she got on her face then that he was smirking. He tried hard to make his face stoic as he said, "The fay... the fortuneteller."

She had heard him thinking she was a fake even before he almost said it. It didn't really hurt her to hear, she knew many thought her such and him – being a man of true science – would think her even more of one. "Yes, the fake psychic," she said boldly.

"I am sorry, Miss, it isn't fair of me to judge a thing only because I don't understand it. I am more than just a man of science. I am a believer that a thing is no more real than false until I've been able to prove or disprove it completely. So, what brought you to my seminar?" He held the card back out to her.

"Keep it," said Callie. She knew he was only trying to smooth any feathers he may have ruffled as he put the card into his pocket. She couldn't be angry with him because she knew he wasn't the type of man to try to hurt anyone intentionally. She left the condescension in his tone alone and said, "I am truly a psychic, but... I haven't had many accurate readings lately..."

"And?"

"I had one the other night that frightened me terribly," the woman said with a very shaky voice, "One that brought me here to you."

"I am sorry, Miss Summers, Griffin Concepts is not conducting any kind of sleep studies right now but I will give your card to the head of my biochemistry department so your name can be added to the possible test subjects in case one is begun in the near future."

"You misunderstand me, Dr. Blake. I had a premonition of the couple found as mummies here in town last week... Mr. and Mrs. Stubbs... I know you read the article."

Gryphon wasn't fazed by this; it was a fifty-fifty chance that he would have so at this point all she was doing was playing the odds. "And?"

"I saw the woman being sucked dry... I saw what did it to her... to them both, her and her husband... When I awakened I had an image in my mind, an image of a Griffin. This image," she said, holding up the pamphlet he had given her with his company logo.

"We recently blitzed the media with a run of advertisements. Chances are you have seen it dozens of times and have only subconsciously interjected it into your dream, or vision, or whatever you call it."

"Premonition."

"Yeah, alright, premonition. I still do not see how I can help you, Miss Summers. If you have information on the couple's death, like who did it and their motive, you should contact the proper authorities. The police for instance," said Gryphon. He started to turn away from her, hoping she would get the hint and go away.

"Does the phrase *they come from the dark* mean anything to you?" Callie blurted out quickly.

"Wha... what?" he asked. He turned back to her and took a step back. "Where did you hear that phrase?" He wasn't sure where he had heard it or why it was affecting him so much but he suddenly felt his lungs clench. He started to reach for his medicine, thinking it was an attack coming on.

"From the Mrs. Stubbs mouth, and your mind…"

"My mind?" he asked, scrunching his face up and shaking his head.

"Also… your brother's."

"*My brother?*"

"Yes, your brother, Sammy."

Gryphon reached into his pocket then, intending to push the emergency button on his cell phone, thinking this woman was a stalker. He'd had one before, a woman who had looked him up on the web, read his bio, found out where he lived and staked it out.

That woman had broken into his home and stolen personal items more than once, then he had returned from being away to find someone had slept in one of his bedrooms though he'd had no planned guests and his staff, whom he trusted implicitly, had sworn they had not nor had they offered the room to anyone they knew. She had told the security guard at GCI, who had only just started the day before, that she was his new girlfriend and had talked him into letting her into his office. His secretary had happened to decide to choose this day to come in early and surprise him with a plate of homemade blueberry muffins but she was surprised herself. Sandra, knowing that her boss wasn't seeing anyone, had then called security, who escorted the woman off the premises. He finally had to file formal charges against her and have a restraining order put on her to keep her away from him.

"Alright, enough, Miss Summers," said Gryphon sternly. "I'm not sure how you got that name but I'm not one for playing games."

"You mean like hide and seek?"

Gryphon had to grip the end of the table then to stay on his feet.

Callie could see she was frightening him and didn't want to so she took a step back. She still wasn't sure just how he fit into whatever was trying to be heard through her but she knew that he needed to be a willing participant.

"I'm sorry, Dr. Blake. I get images sometimes... what people are thinking or of things that have happened to them in the past, sometimes of things that haven't happened yet. I don't always know which it is I am seeing. I don't mean to frighten you but... I got an image of your brother... one of him not feeling well... You haven't spoken to him recently, have you?"

"What exactly are you suggesting has happened to my brother?" said Gryphon harshly. It was one thing to threaten him it was entirely another to threaten his family.

Callie stepped back again then, the waves of love and fear coming from him when she mentioned his brother were very heartening and the anger she felt flooding from him at the mere thought of her threatening his brother told her he had a strong soul – he was the type you would want on your side in a battle. She also felt how threatened he felt and knew he was about to call and have her removed by security. She was about to try to explain herself to him when two burly looking men stepped through the door.

She saw in the man's mind that he thought he could use the men's presence, pretend they were campus security, to stop her from attempting anything with him but she knew they were really only there to help breakdown his displays. She used their arrival as the perfect opportunity to slip out before he could call actual security, which was what his mind said was the next thing he was planning to do.

Gryphon saw the men in the doorway himself. He knew they were only there to help pick up his equipment and clear out the room for the next seminar, as the dean had said, by six o'clock. He turned to them and said, "Please escort this lady off the premises."

"Excuse me?" asked the taller of the two.

Gryphon turned to point out whom he was referring to but saw she was gone. "Never mind," he said to the men, who were looking at him as if he were crazy right then. He guffawed at her audacity. "Help me get this unit crated back up," he said, motioning for the men to get the phase shifting device back into the larger crate.

While they were loading the unit he walked to the table and began to pick up and throw the left over literature into the other, not nearly as neatly as he usually would have. He couldn't stop thinking about what the woman had said about his brother. He wondered if she did have some sort of psychic connection. Was his brother ill? He hadn't spoken to him in weeks.

He pulled his phone from his pocket as the men were moving the larger crate out of the room. He pushed the speed dial number for his brother and waited, counting the rings as they chirped in his ear – once, twice, three times… After the fifth ring the beep of the answering machine kicked in and his brother's voice spoke to him. "Hi, you have reached the home of Sam Blake. I am unable or unwilling to come to the phone right now. Leave your name and number and if you are someone I wish to speak to I will return your call as soon as I am able to."

"Shit," said Gryphon. He waited for the beep then said, "Sammy, haven't heard from you in a while. Wondering if you wanted to meet tomorrow for lunch? Call me as soon as you get your ass out of bed." He hung up the phone feeling only a little less comfortable than he had before.

# 14

# A New Project

"You didn't call me," said DJ as he knocked on Gryphon's door and stepped in, not even waiting to hear permission to do so, Monday morning.

Gryphon was sitting in his chair, his back to the door, looking out the window at the snowcapped mountains on the horizon. He spun the chair around and said, "Sorry, I was a bit wrecked when I got home so I just took a shower and went to bed. I spent most of Sunday there as well."

"Alone?" asked DJ with a wicked glint in his eyes. He knew, from the few talks he had gone on, with and without Gryphon, that there were always groupies hanging around that were more than up for the chance of having some fun with a man that was as brilliant as they were. He personally saw it as all being in the name of science.

"Yes, alone, DJ."

"Bummer... So... how did it go?"

"Lost a few at the end, as usual, but overall..." said the man, sounding more than a little preoccupied.

He was. He had been about to try his brother's number again. He had called him twice more after leaving the campus and four more times over the course of Sunday, only getting his voice mail each time. It wasn't like his brother to be out that long and not return his call quicker.

"Did... anyone... anyone interesting stop by?"

"You mean like a strange thinks-she's-a-psychic woman that tried to tell me about some boogey men coming out of the woodwork?" Gryphon asked sarcastically.

"Excuse me?" asked DJ. He was about to ask the man to share whatever he was on.

"There was a woman at the talk who claims to be clairvoyant. She said she had a... what did she call it... a premonition? Yeah, a premonition, about the bodies that have been cropping up. Said she got an image of this," Gryphon held up the coaster under his glass of whiskey, with his logo on it, "and thinks I am somehow involved in all this."

"Okay, gives ya' the heebie jeebies, don't it?"

"Is that who you meant?" asked Gryphon as he drained his glass and started for the bar to refill it.

Gryphon knew whom it was his friend meant but he wasn't ready to face having seen her just now, which was why he was the other reason why he was refilling his glass with alcohol in the middle of the day.

DJ was about to ask if he really thought getting drunk before noon was the way to deal with it but he didn't. He knew how badly Adrienne leaving him, especially the way she left him, had hurt his friend.

"I won't help her if you don't want me to."

Gryphon was still facing the bar as he said, "We have never before refused a lucrative venture and being a government facility they will likely be willing to pay top dollar. If it will save anyone else from having to die the way those other people had to, then so be it." He turned back to his friend with a now full glass of whiskey and added, "I don't care to have any updates on your progress and I'd prefer you handle delivering any findings to her either at her office or over the phone."

"Gryphon," said DJ, "It's been six months... I really think she is trying to make... I don't know, amends maybe?"

"I need to make a phone call, DJ, so," he said, pointing at the door.

"Gryphon."

The man gave him a nasty look.

DJ knew that look. He nodded, turned around and walked to the door.

He looked back as he reached it to see Gryphon pouring himself a third drink, or the third he had seen him pour himself anyway – he hoped it was only his third. Even only three was excessive for the man doing it. He hated to see his friend like this and he didn't know what to do to make it better. Part of him wanted to walk over, take that drink from him and dump it but he only shook his head and closed the door.

The biochemist walked back to his office, which was on the same floor but the opposite corner of it, wishing there was something he could do to help Gryphon and Adrienne both, since he cared for them both, he thought they were good together; he had no idea what he could do though.

He opened the door and was only slightly surprised to find Adrienne standing before his bookcase looking at photos of him and Gryphon taken the last time they went kayaking, a few months before, in the Rockies. He cleared his throat and felt a little guilty when he saw her jump.


\*\*\*\*\*\*\*\*\*\*\*\*\*\*\*\*\*\*\*\*\*\*


Adrienne hadn't intended to get nosy but she was having a hard time containing herself. She knew DJ had gone to see Gryphon, to make sure it was alright for him to offer her the services of GCI. He had said before DJ chose his projects but she knew the younger scientist enough to know in this, he would seek his boss' approval.

She had only been inside this building twice. The first time was about six months before they broke up. He had brought her in to show her the building. He had helped design it especially for his employees, so each had just what they needed to reach their full potential. She remembered how happy and proud it had made him to be making them all so happy. He wanted her to help him choose which office he should take as his own.

The one she was currently in had been the one he had planned to take, it had a nice view of a meadow of wildflowers and a stand of trees, but she had preferred the one he had ultimately taken. The view of the mountains with the sun setting behind them was framed perfectly by the window in the back of the office.

The second time he brought her here was after his office had been decorated, which was about five months before they broke up, to get her opinion of it. They had made love on the new suede couch he'd had delivered only about an hour before.

She glanced around her and thought, as she had so many times before, how different the two men were. She had always wondered what it was that had made them so close.

Gryphon's office, when she had last seen it, had been quite stately, with rich dark wood paneling, fine antique furniture, expensive sculptures, knickknacks and artwork. She wondered if it was still the same as her eyes took in the exact opposite of it before her.

She saw a well-stocked chrome and glass bar with a lit Budweiser bar sign over it. Two of the walls were decorated with chrome framed posters of science fiction and horror movies; some were signed by the actors in them. The third wall had two chrome book cases with scale die cast cars, trophies and framed photos. The fourth wall was a huge picture window. A large metal and glass desk with a mess of papers was set in the center of the room with a black leather executive chair setting askew behind it – left that way when DJ had left it to see his boss. She found herself smiling as she remembered how Gryphon always pushed his chair in before leaving, even if only for a few seconds. Two chrome chairs were set before the desk, for visitors, one of which she had just been sitting in, and two lounge style chairs with black cushions were set in front of the windows – where DJ and Gryphon often sat and brainstormed.

Her eyes stopped on the chrome bookcases and went to the framed photographs. She could see one of them was of DJ and Gryphon. She walked over to the case for a closer look. She smiled, then frowned.

It was of them in kayaks in the white water rapids of a river. Both had huge smiles on their faces. Gryphon looked like he had been laughing as well; she liked how much his eyes were sparkling. The only times she had seen that look on him was when he had gotten the results he had wanted from an experiment he had performed or after having really good sex.

He was showing only from the waist up, the lower half under the rubber gasket to keep the water out of the hull of the craft. He was wearing a lifejacket with no shirt underneath so his fine chest muscles and just the right amount of chest hair were showing around the edges and he had a baseball hat turned backward on his head. His longer and damp hair curling up around the edges and the boyish smile made him look a lot younger than he was.

She wished she'd seen him like that more often and was very jealous that he had allowed DJ and whoever had taken the photo see it. She started to bring a finger up to touch the picture; she jumped and quickly put it down when the door behind her opened.

"You look like you were having a great time."

"We were," said DJ slowly, not wanting to hurt her but not wanting to lie either.

"When was this taken?"

"About four months ago."

Her hand and heart clenched, that would have been about two months after they split up. He had told her not more than three weeks before that he had no time for a vacation. "Who took the picture?" she asked, hoping it was a man. She wasn't sure she could take him looking that happy and smiling that brightly at another woman so soon after their breakup.

"Sam."

"I'm glad he and his brother are still close." She hoped she hadn't sounded as anxious to the man standing in the door as she had to her own ears. "How… how has he been, David?

"I prefer DJ, Dr. Ivekio."

"All right, DJ, and you know me well enough to call me Adrienne."

DJ nodded but said nothing.

"Gryphon said he was fine at the college but…You know as well as I do… he is too stubborn to admit it aloud if he was a wreck. Is he really alright?"

"I am sorry, Adrienne, I don't mind offering you the use of my staff and lab but I'm not sure I'm ready to be friendly and I'd prefer not to talk about Gryphon."

Adrienne picked up how tense he was and knew he was taking Gryphon's side. She supposed she shouldn't have been surprised, she knew the two of them had an almost brotherly connection since soon after they met. "I didn't mean to hurt him, DJ… I was tired of waiting for him to find me as interesting as he did this company."

DJ knew his friend had taken her for granted but he still thought she had handled it wrong. "I've decided to offer my department's services. When will we be getting the first tissue samples?" he asked, wanting to keep on the subject she was actually there for.

"I will send them over by courier later today. We're performing the first autopsy today, later this afternoon. You will not inform the public or media of this, of course?"

"We handle lots of hush-hush projects here, Adrienne. We will tell no one but you the results."

"Thank you again, DJ."

He nodded then walked her to the door. He closed it behind her then walked to the shelf and looked at the photo she had been looking at. He set it back as he'd had it then sighed.

\*\*\*\*\*\*\*\*\*\*\*\*\*\*\*\*\*\*\*\*\*

Gryphon drained the third glass of whiskey then pushed the blue intercom button on his phone. His secretary's soft voice came through seconds later. "No calls from my brother?"

"No, I'm sorry."

"Alright. Can you let DJ know I'm going to take off for the day and ask Jacob to bring my car around?"

"Yes, sir."

He could hear the concern in her voice but it really didn't help. He set the glass into the sink on the bar, grabbed his coat and briefcase and walked out the door. He had a sinking feeling in the pit of his stomach that was getting worse with each step – the so-called premonition of the so-called psychic from the seminar was itching at the back of his mind.

He walked to the elevator and started to push the down button then shook his head and went to the door to the stairwell instead. He was out of breath when he reached the bottom floor but it was only because he had all but run down them. His Magnum was sitting out front, idling, and Jacob had his newspaper waiting for him as usual. *At least some things never change,* he thought.

# 15

# Emergency

It seemed to take hours rather than minutes to Gryphon before he reached the high-rise his brother's apartment was in.

He was about to buzz the security door when he saw a young woman, who had been standing at the mailboxes, stepped toward it. She knew his name and greeted him as she opened it for him. He felt a little bad that he could not remember hers. He greeted her kindly though and held the heavy door for her then went inside.

Sam's apartment was on the third floor. He started to step into the elevator then stared into the seemingly smaller-than-the-last-time compartment. He really didn't want to climb the narrow stairs but he could not do the elevator. He turned, opened the door to the stairs and, with a heavy, tension releasing, sigh, started up them. He was a little winded as he walked up to the door with the number thirty nine over the peephole but at least he wasn't having an asthma attack.

He took a deep breath and held it as he tapped on the center of the door with the knuckle of the middle finger of his right hand. He waited a count of ten and knocked again, a little louder and with all his knuckles. He heard someone coughing but he wasn't sure if it was coming from Sam's apartment or the one across the hall, behind him.

He reached into his pocket and pulled out his key chain then. His brother had given him a key to his apartment last summer so he could stop in and water his plants while he was gone to the Bahamas with his then girlfriend; he hadn't had a chance to return it yet. He inserted it into the lock and slowly opened the door, calling out, "Sammy?"

He heard someone grunt what sounded like "In here" but he wasn't sure if it was his imagination. Louder than usual music was coming from the stereo in the living room so it might have been the lyrics from the song currently playing. He walked along the hallway to the living room, dining room combination and found every light in the room on, as were the ones in the kitchen. All the curtains had been pulled off the windows and the shades were drawn up all the way. The rods on two of the windows were hanging from only one side. The curtains were lying in piles on the floor below each window. They looked as if they had been pulled down by force… or in anger.

He walked to the stereo and turned if off then called out again, "Sammy?" He heard another grunt but couldn't make out what might have been meant to be uttering. "Sammy?" he said again. A little bit of fear was creeping into his voice as he stepped into the bedroom.

It was all lit up and the curtains and shades were all ripped down in this room as well. The bed sheets were in a shambles and there were several spots on the sheets and carpets that looked like vomit, in various stages of dryness. Gryphon threw his hand up to his nose and mouth before he added some of his own. The smell of that and body odor was heavy in the air. His brother would never have let his room get this bad unless something was seriously wrong with him.

"Sam!" he called out more pointedly. This time he distinctly heard a cabinet door closing and the sound of water running. He walked into the bathroom off the bedroom and froze.

Sam was leaning over the edge of the tub, in the middle of several more spots of vomit, looking very fresh and tinged reddish with blood. He was pouring water over his face and hair and was trying to cover himself with a towel at the same time.

"Oh, God, Gryph, no... Please, go away... don't want... not you... Please... Don't want them to get you too!"

"Sam," said Gryphon. He stepped over the piles of vomit to get to his brother. He started to take hold of him but stopped when he saw he was trying to back away from him.

"Please, Gryph, go away... Please," said the man desperately. He was trying to cover his gaunt and colorless face with the towel as if ashamed.

"Sam, let me help you," said Gryphon. This time he did take a hold of his brother. His heart sank at the feeling of him, he was clammy and cold to the touch and he weighed nothing. He had been a touch overweight all his life but now his bones were clearly showing in his arms and he could feel the others through his clothes. He seemed unable to struggle though he had always been quite strong. He had been a star on the wrestling team through high school and the first couple years of college.

"How long have you been sick, Sam?"

"I don't know... I... What day... How long?"

Gryphon didn't like how cloudy his brother's eyes were, how dilated the pupils were or that he seemed unable to focus them. They were darting back and forth quickly as if looking for something. He hoisted him into his arms, carried him into the living room and laid him down on the couch. He started to reach for the light beside it, intent on turning it off, watching him cringe and squint his eyes from the glare in the room.

"**NO!** *They come from the dark*!" Sam started to stand up and fell over, into the coffee table, knocking the compote and magazines off it.

"What?!" said Gryphon. He felt all the blood rush out of him. "What did you say?"

"They come from the dark, Gryphon. Out of the shadows... Don't go near any shadows... They keep trying to get me, can't close my eyes... so tired... can't sleep... Can't let myself... Please, don't let them get me." He was gagging and his face was screwed up but no tears seemed able to come from his red, swollen eyes.

"Sam? Who is trying to get you? Sam? Sam!" Gryphon just barely caught his brother as he started to keel over; he would have fallen through the glass top of the coffee table. He laid him back on the couch. His eyes were now rolled back in his head and he was barely breathing. He grabbed his phone then and dialed 911.

Gryphon was beside himself as he watched the emergency technicians working on his brother. They had a hard time getting him to lay still long enough to get him strapped to the stretcher, one of them sustaining a nasty bruise from a punch the thought to be weak man was able to throw. Gryphon finally had to help them calm him down, promising his brother they were not the things from the dark.

Two of the men quickly took his brother out the door, heading him for the elevator; the third, the one with the bruise, walked over to Gryphon.

"Is your brother on anything? Any medication… or… do you know if he takes any kind of recreational drugs?"

"My brother is not a drug addict," snapped Gryphon. He had to admit it did look as if he was going through a withdrawal of some sort. "I don't believe so," he said then, though it broke his heart.

"Can you look through his belongings… we need to know what he might have taken," said the man, looking as if he wished he didn't have to.

Gryphon only nodded.

"Take anything you find to the hospital," said the man then he ran out the door.

Gryphon stood staring at the room, trying to fight the tightening he felt in his chest. The last thing he needed right then was to have an attack. He took a deep breath, and tried to steel his heart and soul for what he might find as he walked into the bedroom again. He brought his hand up to cover his nose and mouth again. He prayed he wouldn't find anything incriminating.

He remembered his clean cut brother had quit the wrestling team, meaning he had also had to give up his full scholarship, because his coach had insisted he take steroids to build up muscles – thoughts of him making the US Olympic team in mind. He didn't want to think he could have changed so much.

The brothers had always been very close, speaking at least once a week – even if only to say hi and wish each other a good weekend. It had been almost three weeks since they had last spoken. He couldn't think of why that should have been so… He supposed they had both started to take each other just being there for granted.

He walked over to the most recent looking expectorant and forced himself to look at it. He took a pen from the bedside stand and pushed it around a bit. He saw several small capsule shaped gelatin bits in it.

"God, Sammy… why didn't you tell me you needed help?" said Gryphon through a tight throat.

He went to the kitchen, grabbed a handful of zippered sandwich bags and a spoon then went back to the room and scooped up some of the bodily release from various piles. He stood up and went to the sink. He needed some cool water, feeling like he was going to be sick himself. He caught his reflection in the mirror as he did. He was white as a ghost and his red eyes looked twice their normal size. He had no idea how he was going to tell his parents... especially since he really didn't know what it was his brother had done. He shook his head and turned off the light.

As he started out of the room he froze. He heard whispering voices, like the ones he had heard in the attic closet so many years before. He tried to tell himself it was only what his brother had said getting his hackles up but he knew better. He ran from the apartment then, slamming the door shut behind him.

# 16

# A Living Host

DJ was just pouring himself a third, or was it a fourth, cup of coffee when the phone on the corner of his desk buzzed. He walked to it and set the cup down beside the phone, it was still too hot to drink just then anyway. He pushed the answer button and said, "Yes, Bethany?"

"Dr. Ivekio is back," said his secretary.

"That was fast. Send her in," said the chief of Biochemistry.

There was a soft knock on the door.

"Come in," said DJ, as he lifted the cup and began to blow over it.

"Hi, DJ, I hope you don't mind that I came right back. The autopsy was done when I got back to CMC. I wanted to bring the report and tissue samples over right away."

DJ took the vials from her and set them on his desk to take to his lab and look at under the microscope then took the reports she was holding and looked them over. There was one hundred and fifty of them; this surprised him, the papers had only reported a dozen cases.

Knowing what the look of surprise was for, Adrienne explained, "We have asked that the number be kept low so as not to cause mass hysteria."

DJ nodded and mumbled, "Yeah, probably better that way."

They were a wide range of ages, race, living conditions and both genders so there seemed no obvious or immediate connection, other than their manner of death. He then looked over their findings.

Toxicology came up with just the usual; the youngest males had slightly elevated alcohol levels but nothing a few beers wouldn't have come up with. One colored woman showed positive for Ortho Tri-cyclen, which was a popular birth control pill, and the older and elderly victims had various fifty plus medicines in their systems. None of the readings explained the reason for their similar deaths.

He looked over the tissue report and was more than a little shocked at the findings, and the conclusions that had been drawn from those findings. He guffawed as he read it out loud, "Homeostasis; impairment of water in the body or extreme dehydration? That's just a wee bit vague. Is that seriously all they could find?"

"That is partly why I have come to you. It doesn't make sense, DJ, something had to have caused them to lose all the fluids in their body but we cannot pinpoint a cause."

"I thought you had some of the most brilliant doctors in microbiology on your team?" he said a little curtly.

He had never told Gryphon that she had called him shortly after accepting the position at CMC and asked him to join her as her head laboratory technician. He had said no instantly. The position held no desire for him for three reasons: he couldn't imagine leaving Gryphon, part of him wondered if she was only doing it in an attempt to hurt his friend, and he didn't like army green.

Adrienne gave him a look to say she wasn't in the mood for his being curt or cute.

He remembered Gryphon telling him, on more than one occasion, that when the woman got this look it was better just to humor her. "So they think that excessive dehydration made their bodies withdraw water from their cells and blood vessels in order to compensate for the loss in intravascular water?"

"What else would have caused them to become so massively dried out?"

DJ shook his head and went back to the report. "There was no noticeable change to their lymphatic systems, hearts, kidneys or adrenal glands, which rule out Cholera and Shigellosis. There *is* an increased level of neurotransmitters, primarily adrenaline and serotonin, and lower than normal levels of melatonin... which suggests elevated levels of stress... But from what?"

"We are leaning toward Yellow Fever," said Adrienne as she rubbed at the bridge of her nose. A habit Gryphon had told DJ she did when she was frustrated. "It would account for this excessive dehydration and the speed of it."

"Your report says no necrotic masses were found in the cytoplasm of the hepatocytes, which would imply it can't be Yellow Fever," said DJ, sounding much more like the doctor he was rather than the wise-ass he typically acted like.

"It may be a new strain, or a mutated one... The normal incubation for Yellow Fever is only three to five days, perhaps this strain is even faster moving, meaning no masses had a chance to form. There has been an elevated level of mosquitoes this year."

"Sounds a bit like you are grasping at straws, Adrienne... You will want to be certain. If this is a new variety of the virus we will need to get vaccines out to all hospitals, and information to environmental agencies suggesting they begin to exterminate the mosquito population... and you need a way to contain the masses of hypochondriacs and crazies that will be sure they have it. I would suggest you start with a list of some of the possible symptoms."

"We aren't sure of them though, since we have no living host."

"You're a doctor, Adrienne, what're the symptoms of normal Yellow Fever? They'd be pretty much the same... High fever, chills, vomiting?" started DJ.

"Dehydration... headaches, sores, bleeding from the skin, rapid heartbeat, back pain, constipation, weakness and in extreme cases – delirium."

DJ was about to make a curt comment about it sounding like a real blast to have when a male voice came over the emergency scanner behind him. It had been relatively quiet most of the day, couple that with him being more than a little keyed up from reading the autopsy findings, made him jump.

"R One to Biscayne ER," a deep male voice said.

"This is Biscayne ER, go ahead R One," a female voice answered him.

"We are about twelve minutes from your facility with a male patient in his early thirties found by a relation in extreme distress. Vitals are as follows: pulse of one twenty and thready, blood pressure by palpation is ninety over seventy, respiration is thirty and shallow, we have him in a mask on ten liters per minute. He has a fluctuating temperature, with a reading of 103° when we arrived, dropped to 99° when checked upon strapping into rig and is now back up to 101. We attempted to establish an IV but were unable to due to the condition of his veins. His skin is pale, cold, clammy, no elasticity and is a bit leathery. He is disoriented and was combative at scene. Patient had vomited and appeared to have blood in the vomit. Patient's relation on scene states no known illnesses, no medications, ETOH or illegal drug use. Do you require any other information at this time?"

"Nothing at this time. Take the patient direct to CC2. What is your ETA, R one?"

"We are ten minutes out."

D.J and Adrienne looked at each other. Both of them jumped as the phone beside them rang.

DJ grabbed the handset and said, "Yes?" He expected it to be his secretary.

"I am on my way to Biscayne General," said Gryphon's voice.

"What?" asked DJ, A sense of foreboding was creeping into his usually skeptical bones.

"Sammy is in trouble," said Gryphon.

"Sammy?" asked his business partner.

"What's the matter with Sam?" asked Adrienne hearing the way DJ said his name.

"I need to make a stop. Can you go over there and sit with him until I get there… I don't want him to feel like he is alone right now," said Gryphon.

The frantic sound of his best friend's usually calm and collected voice worried DJ more than having just heard what he now guessed was the description of Sam's condition. He whispered a curse then said, "I'm on my way, Gryph." He hung up the phone slowly and looked up at the woman behind him. "Sounds like you may have your first living patient, Dr. Ivekio."

"Oh, God," said Adrienne.

# 17

# Sharing a Premonition

Gryphon walked fast down the dingy alley to the shop called Summer Sage. He wasn't sure just how to approach this, all he knew was this woman knew something that he hoped would help his brother – that was all he was focusing on right then.

He stepped up to the door and smirked at the piece of plywood duct taped over the lower portion of it. He wondered if someone had kicked it in after getting a reading they hadn't liked. He reached for the handle and slowly opened it. He was almost afraid of what he was going to find inside. He jumped when a small bell rang over his head.

He supposed he had half expected to walk in on a group of witches dancing naked around a smoking cauldron or maybe a goat being sacrificed to make it rain but it looked like a typical head shop.

There were psychedelic posters, tapestries with Celtic knots, a black and white photo of Stonehenge at dusk, shrouded by wispy fog, black lights, and a rack of incense sticks and candles in every possible scent. Some of the former was burning in a holder beside it, which was making his nose and eyes burn and was giving him a headache.

He saw various size pots or cauldrons, he supposed they were called, wooden and papier-mâché decorated boxes of every size and shape, charms on black and brown leather cords and crystal balls in various colors and sizes, some on plain wooden stands others on intricately carved bird talons. There was a whole shelf of different shaped bottles with different colored liquids and powders inside them, each with a label before it. He saw love and luck and health potions, headache tinctures, cold and cough remedies, generic healing potions, protection spells, hair tonics, male and female body enhancement potions and other homeopathic remedies.

Another shelf had bottles of things he guessed went into making spells. He smirked at some of the labels: various animal tongues, penises and testicles, dried fly, bee and bat wings, snake and lizard skins, scorpions, chicken feet, rat tails, plant seeds and pollen and potpourri looking concoctions.

A rack of books on everything from astrology to magic tricks was near the back of the shop, as was a doorway with black curtains draped to each side of it and a sign over it that read *fortunes told here*.

He didn't see the woman in this first room so he started toward the doorway. He jumped when he heard her voice. It sounded strangely like it was coming from all around him at once, which was disconcerting to say the least.

"You are safe here, Dr. Blake."

"Pardon me?" he asked, taken a little off guard. He wasn't sure where she was so he just stood still.

"I am not a crazy stalker, obsessed with you and looking to take up residence in your home."

Gryphon started to snigger at that then realized there was no way for her to have known that was what he was thinking unless...

"Yes, I can really read minds," said Callie as she stepped from the room with the black curtain blocking it from the rest of the shop. Images of the man before her having just come from finding his brother flooded into her mind as she said this. They made her dizzy. She stumbled to the counter and said, "He is not on drugs, Dr. Blake."

"What!?" Gryphon stumbling a little himself.

"Your brother. He is not on anything other than energy pills to keep himself awake," said Callie.

"He said he... he said he needed to stay awake, that *they* were trying to take him. Who is *they*? Who is threatening my brother?" said the man. He was rubbing at his nose hard, which was really burning now. He was trying to make himself sneeze.

"I am not sure who or what they are but I know they are not of this world," said Callie. She went to the incense stick, wet her fingers and touched them to the smoking part of the rod. "Is that better?"

The inside of Gryphon's nose was still irritated but the pungent smell had more or less dissipated already so it was more out of nervousness now. "Yes, thanks. What do you mean *not of this world*? You mean like aliens?" he asked, wondering again if she was crazy.

"I don't know... maybe."

"This is crazy," said Gryphon. He started to turn to leave, deciding he was better off just going to the hospital and seeing what the doctors had to say.

"I can show you what I mean," said Callie.

Gryphon turned back to her and gave her a look to say he didn't understand. "Show me?"

"At least I think I can. I have never actually tried it. I have some sort of connection to you and your brother... I know you think I'm crazy and I know it sounds that way but... I was honest with you when I said I hadn't had a premonition in weeks. Not until the night I got an image of your company logo... I didn't enjoy

166

watching the couple in the article in the Gazette, the Stubbs, die but I did and I saw what did it to them."

"Then go to the police," said Gryphon as his chest began to tighten.

"And have them take me away, put me in a rubber room, slap a straightjacket on me and pump me full of mind altering drugs? You are a man of science and you don't believe me, how do you think they would react?"

Gryphon had to nod in agreement. At the same time, looking around at the shop, he had a hard time not wanting to call and have her taken away himself.

"I know that you have been questioned by the scientific and academic communities, Dr. Blake, you know how hard it is to make people believe what you say is true sometimes."

Again Gryphon had to nod in agreement. He had been called a mad scientist and told he was crazy by several people in and out of the scientific and academic communities. He really had no right to judge her without evidence. "What exactly are you suggesting?"

"I've never tried to share a premonition with another person but I know some who have … If you are willing, if you will trust me, I think I can show you what your brother and I have seen and you have been hearing most of your life."

Gryphon wanted to laugh but he could see that she honestly believed she could do this. The scientist in him was interested in finding out if this was actually possible, wanted to either prove or disprove this. His methodical mind was thinking up dozens of uses for this skill if it was real. He did want to see what it was that had affected his brother so severely and what exactly it was that had haunted him for so long and might have given him his claustrophobia and asthma. "How?"

"Did you ever watch Star Trek?"

"Yeah, when I was a kid."

"It's kind of like a mind meld of sorts," said Callie. She saw how skeptical he was but also how much he really wanted to believe this was possible. He had to believe in this if it was going to work. "Are you willing?"

"What do I need to do?" he asked. He was expecting the next words out of her mouth to be how much money she would need to reach this altered state properly; still thinking this was some sort of scam.

"I don't want any money for this, Dr. Blake."

"All right, Miss Summers, you apparently do have some skills. I don't want to believe I am this easily read by just anyone and everyone. I suppose, since you seem to know all of my deepest darkest secrets you may as well call me Gryphon," he said as he took his jacket off and loosened his tie. He pulled it off and stuck it in his jacket pocket then draped the jacket over his arm and unbuttoned the top three buttons of his dress shirt.

"I don't know all of them. I have learned to block out a person's most intimate details... for most people," she said, blushing and flushing a little. She was remembering what she had seen of him and the pretty woman after the seminar.

"But you do know some of them?"

"I didn't mean to, I was a little stressed, which can counter my usual blocks. I wasn't as in control of my abilities as I normally am... I saw bits of... I know you and the woman, Dr. Ivekio, were lovers," said Callie, looking away from him. "That you were in love."

Gryphon of a few days ago would have been very angry at this invasion of privacy but the one in the shop this day couldn't be. Whether he liked it or not he found the woman before him believable and he found himself unusually comfortable with her. "All right, Miss Summers, what do we do?" he asked tentatively.

"First, please call me Callie. When this is done we will both know each other quite a lot better," said the woman as she stepped to the door and locked it.

"All right, Callie," said Gryphon.

She walked over to the booth she had come out of when he first arrived and motioned him to enter it. "Come in and sit down."

He followed her into the booth and immediately felt his chest tighten, not only because it was a small space but also because it was so dark. He didn't hear the voices he often heard in the dark but he didn't feel comfortable either.

"It's all right, Gryphon," said Callie. She sat down and motioned him to do the same, her hand touching his bare forearm.

He instantly felt calmed by that touch. He took a deep breath, put the jacket over the back of the chair, rolled his sleeves up to his elbows then sat down.

Callie lifted the crystal ball from the center of the table and set it on a small stand behind her then she set her elbows on the table and asked him to do the same and to lean forward. "I need you to relax all of your muscles, Gryphon. I need you to clear your mind," said the woman in a musical voice.

He took several deep breaths, trying not to laugh. He told himself this was for his brother... and science.

She placed her hands on his temples and began to rub them gently in circles with the tips of her index and middle fingers, first in one direction then in the reverse direction. "Focus on the movements of my fingers," she said slowly.

He did. He began to feel a little dizzy and like he was falling. He grabbed hold of the edge of the table and started to pull away then.

"Keep still. You will feel a little fuzzy and dizzy, it's supposed to happen. It'll feel weird to you when our minds connect but I need you to try your best to remain perfectly still. Some have severe headaches and vomit when they pull out too quickly. Do you understand?"

"Yes," said Gryphon.

"We will both be able to see into each other's minds when I do this… you aren't trained to block out my memories, as I am yours… so I am going to try to keep you to the ones I want you to see but…"

"I promise to respect you in the morning," Gryphon teased, flashing her a charming and boyish smile. That smiled faded quickly.

She hadn't told Gryphon how quick the connection would be made so he jolted a little when he was flooded with images. He guessed it was the woman across from him as a young girl. She was playing wildly on a playground with other children about her age, laughing and having fun. This made him smile unconsciously.

He saw her going through the awkward years of adolescence and how much her body changing had affected her… He relived the first time she read someone's mind, her mother's. She was seeing her true feelings for her father, which were less than kind… Next he went on her first date. Hearing what the boy's mind said he had in mind for her sickened him – the boy had essentially planned to force himself on her so he could tell his friends he had *done the freak*. He started to pull away again, feeling that this was wrong when he heard her soft voice speaking.

"Don't move, Gryphon. I am trying to direct you but it's hard for me to do as well," said Callie. Her voice was shaky and her head was getting fuzzy from the effort of trying to coax his mind to the place she wanted it to go and keep hers own out of his.

Gryphon could hear her voice still but it sounded like it was coming from a long ways away. Everything got black for a moment then he jumped again as he saw into the booth they were sitting in except he was on the other side of the table, in the place she was sitting. His body felt different, smaller and softer, he looked down and saw he had breasts. He was surprised that he could feel the shivers running up and down his body, even out to the tips of the nipples on those breasts. If he hadn't been doing this for a particular reason he wouldn't have minded experiencing this a bit longer. He realized he was seeing out of Callie's eyes and it was her body he was inside of. It was a strange thing to imagine even for his somewhat skewed view of physics and the natural order of things.

Gryphon watched an older woman's head come into the booth, the woman whose picture had been in the paper two days ago. He could see her lips moving and could feel Callie's moving but he didn't hear what was being said. Everything moved in slow motion then it was in fast-forward, back and forth, making his head spin.

Suddenly he was outside the shop, above the alley, but not on a cat-walk or fire escape... more like he was floating. He felt weightless but he was also paralyzed, he couldn't move anything but his head. He looked down and saw the old woman running away from the shop below him, looking over her shoulders as if she was being chased by something, then he was suddenly inside of her, inside of Callie, and was seeing through Callie's eyes, through the old woman's eyes.

He saw three grayish humanlike forms with no real features, only ear and nostril holes and short stubby arms with three fingered hands step out of the deep shadows at the end of the row. They weren't running, more floating a few inches off the road and they didn't cast shadows. The scientist's always-methodical mind was trying to come up with how they'd managed this trick. He was thinking it had to be a magnetic resonance device of some sort set in the roadbed, the polarized magnets pushing away from each other, or forced air making them appear to levitate.

He could feel how frightened Callie and the old woman were and was a little surprised he was actually more intrigued than afraid. Though he began to get a little of the latter as he felt the woman stop and saw the things come up to her. He felt pain and tightness in his chest when the deathly cold grip of their three fingered hands closed over the woman's arm. It was a tight grip and it felt like they were burrowing into his skin. He felt like he was being tugged at and could feel Callie was as well. They were being pulled out by that grip. He started to get more than a little scared then.

That coldness spread out from those tight grips and engulfed the woman's, Callie's and his bodies. He heard the old woman, Callie and himself screaming then he felt Callie being ripped out of the woman's body and could see her floating over them.

He was still inside the older woman's body and he had no idea how to get out of it. He tried to call out to Callie to help him but couldn't make his mouth move. Everything went dark then.

Gryphon opened his eyes and could see he was in a bedroom, one the woman recognized – her bedroom. He realized there was someone in the bed beside her – her husband. He knew that she knew he was dead. He could feel the pain in her heart at this realization and felt warm tears coming to his own eyes.

He saw Callie's ethereal body floating over the woman's bed. He forced his eyes away from her because she was completely naked. He wondered if it was really her or just his mind projecting what he thought she might look like naked. Either way, he knew it wasn't proper so he forced his eyes to the corner of the room. He would have rather remained staring at the naked woman because he then watched three beings like what had been chasing them step from the deep shadows of the corner – out of the shadow.

Gryphon watched them float to the old woman's side, watched through her eyes as they raised their stunted arms over her and heard them begin to chant in a language neither he nor she could understand. He felt the woman's back arch as if it was his own and twist up, this way then that, as if huge invisible hands were ringing out a washcloth. He again tried to scream but he couldn't get his mouth to open.

He felt something he hoped he never felt in his life again then, his and the older woman's soul leaving her body. He watched one of the beings take out what looked like an urn, take off the cover of this vessel and the woman's soul get sucked inside it then he saw them turn toward his ethereal form and heard his name spoken by three different voices, one from each of the forms before him, he guessed. He began to panic then as he felt his own soul being pulled inside the vessel. He tried yet again to scream and realized he couldn't breathe now either.

Gryphon pulled out of Callie's grip then. Hard. He fell back, nearly knocking the chair and table over with the force of it. His right hand went to his throat and his left went to his chest, pushing and pounding on the center of it. His airways had constricted on him before but they had never closed off completely.

His mind was slow and fuzzy, the blood pumping through the veins leading to it was pounding hard and fast – partly from the thing the woman had just done to him, partly because he still felt like his soul was being tugged at, partly at the terror of not being able to breath and partly from the lack of oxygen to his brain. He wasn't gasping because he couldn't even get enough air into his lungs to do that and he was turning blue.

"Dr. Blake? Gryphon?" Callie shouted. She knew he couldn't answer with his mouth but he had with his mind. She grabbed his jacket, reached into his pocket and pulled out his inhaler. She shook it a few times then stuck it into his mouth and pushed it together. She could smell the menthol scent of the medicine telling her it hadn't gone into his lungs. She set the thing down on the table then laid him down on the floor and began to message his chest and throat. When she began to hear deep wheezing she grabbed the breathing medicine again and again shot it into his throat. She hit him with it a couple more times then sat back.

He had lost consciousness, which was actually a good thing because it made all his muscles, including the ones that were exacerbating his chest tightness, loosen up. She held her breath as she waiting for his breathing to become more normal.

It was several minutes before Gryphon awakened, to a dry and raw throat and a splitting headache. He jumped, not recognizing where he was, then fell back. The sudden head rush made his pulse jump, which made him dizzy and made his head hurt even worse. He relaxed, a little, when he saw Callie sitting beside him holding a goblet with jewels along the rim. "What... what happened?" he asked. He knew it was his voice but it sounded so distant to him right then.

"You had an asthma attack."

"I... I thought I was dying," said the man as he tried to sit up.

"You tried to. Here, drink this; it's a chamomile and lavender tincture. It's like tea but it's a little thicker than you are likely used to. It will help to soothe your throat and calm your nerves," said the woman as she held the goblet out to him.

Gryphon took it and drank the purplish liquid without question. It was a little bitter tasting but it did help his dry throat and he immediately felt the calming effect of the herbs. "Thanks."

"I didn't think it would be that traumatic for you, I'm sorry..." said Callie. A shiver ran up her spine, "the bit at the end..."

"Is that what made you think there was a connection between us?"

"No, that didn't happen."

"What do you mean, didn't happen?"

"That part was new... That wasn't part of my original premonition... That wasn't there before," said the woman. A more violent shiver racked her body, visibly shaking her and leaving goose pimples behind on her arms.

"Then... how did they know I was there... How did they know my name?"

"I don't know..." said Callie.

Gryphon handed her the brew and watched her drink some then got on his feet, less than gracefully. He felt like he had been hit by a fast moving truck. He grabbed his jacket and said, "I have to get to the hospital to see my brother... I... Do you want to go with me?"

Callie was already reaching for her coat and purse.

# 18

# The Fourth Floor

Gryphon and Callie walked into the emergency room and waited for the receptionist to acknowledge them. She finally looked up from her computer screen and asked, "Can I help you?"

"I want to see my brother, Samuel Blake. He was brought in by ambulance about an hour ago."

The woman at the desk punched the buttons on her keyboard. "What is his date of birth?"

"May Third, 1974."

"He was transferred immediately to CCU, on the fourth floor."

Gryphon had to grab the edge of the counter to keep from falling over. The fourth floor was where his grandfather had been taken to so long ago and again just about a year ago when he had his final, and mortal, heart attack.

Callie saw this in his mind and helped him to a seat. "Do you have a water fountain close by, Nurse?"

"Just a moment," said the woman. She returned a few moments later.

"Thanks," said the man, feeling pathetic just then.

"It's alright, Gryphon," said Callie.

In this case he believed he did not need to explain. He guessed she had seen everything he had been through in this hospital so she knew why his brother being here, on the fourth floor, would have upset him so much. A few hours ago he would have sworn there was no such thing as a psychic but then a few hours ago he had not been shown what she had shown him. He stood up and offered her his hand. "I cannot handle the elevator right now. Go on up and I will meet you there?"

"I can do the stairs. I don't get enough exercise."

"Thanks for... I'm sorry I was so rude to you before, Miss Summers," said Gryphon. "I'm not always the fastest on the uptake in all things social and polite but I do usually get there."

"I know you are not the type of person to be that way normally."

Gryphon tried to let that make him feel less guilty but it didn't. He had never suffered normal people well.

It took three times longer to get to the fourth floor than it would have taking the elevator and they were both out of breath but they were alive. Gryphon quickly went to the nurse's station and asked which room his brother was in then started toward it. He had expected to see DJ already there waiting for him but there was no sign anyone else had arrived. He stood in the doorway of the room for several seconds, trying to breathe.

It was a large room with three large windows but it felt like it was very, very small to him right then. Between the tightness in his chest, the pungent smell of medicine and harsh cleaners, the beeping of the monitors on his brother and other patients in the vicinity and the sucking and thudding sound of the breathing apparatus set up beside his brother, feeding him oxygen, he was feeling very overwhelmed.

He suddenly realized just how mortal his brother was. As well as every other person he cared about. It took all his willpower not to turn and run away.

"I can go in and sit with him if you want to get some air?" said Callie.

"No… my therapist says I have to confront the things I fear… I need to do this," said Gryphon.

Callie sat down in the chair just outside the door knowing the man would want his first moments of seeing his brother this way to be private. She knew he was not a man to show his emotions easily to anyone let alone her, who was in essence still a total stranger.

Gryphon had been trying to prepare himself for how his brother was going to look as he was climbing the stairs, memories of his grandfather flooded his mind, but he still wasn't ready for what he saw. It took effort but he managed to stifle the sound of shock and horror he so wanted to emit in case his Sam was awake. He didn't want to scare him more than he already was.

His brother looked only about half the size he had been when he had last seen him. He was thin and his cheeks were gaunt and sunken in. His skin was a pale yellowish and looked too big for the body wearing it. His hair was dull, greasy and longer than when he had last seen him and was even more disheveled than the sometimes-lax man would have ever let it get. He had more than a week's worth of growth on his always clean-shaven face. The quasi-beard made him look thinner and older than he was; it had way more gray in it than Gryphon would want to see on his younger brother.

He forced his eyes away from Sam's unpleasant visage; what they took in next was little better. There were several tubes running from his frighteningly thin arms. He watched the fluids drip from the bag for a moment, trying to fight back the well of emotion and fear tightening his throat. His eyes followed one of the tubes down to the port. There were ugly, deep purple, bruises around the entry points from the trauma of trying to find a viable vein to get the vital fluid into him. He had other bruises over both his arms from him fighting the ambulance drivers as they tried to get him strapped to the gurney. The last time he had seen him this badly bruised was after a particularly intense wrestling meet between their high school and their closest rival school.

The sound of the blood pressure cuff kicking on brought Gryphon's eyes to the monitors across from him. It took much longer than it should to fully inflate because his arm was so thin. He jumped again as the pressure cuff began to deflate, a little at a time, trying to get a reading. He didn't breathe until it had deflated fully. He shook his head and expelled an upset sigh when he saw how low it was. He continued to stare at the machine for several minutes after; mesmerized by the jumping line that was his brother's heartbeat. Even though he wasn't that type of doctor, he knew it was far slower than should be.

"God, Sammy. Why didn't you call me?" He slowly stepped back and felt his legs give out on him, luckily there was a chair below him that he, less than gracefully, fell into.

# 19

# Slap of Reality

Gryphon was holding Sam's hand tight but his brother wasn't reciprocating. He jumped as he felt a hand on his shoulder. He looked back, expecting it to be Callie, and found DJ looking worriedly at him as well as his and Sam's regular doctor, Doug Parsons. It was DJ's hand he had felt. "Hey." He almost looked around to see who had said this, it hadn't sounded like his voice.

"I stayed with him for close to an hour... I stepped away to talk to Doug."

"He opened his eyes when I first came in but I don't know if he realized who I was," said Gryphon, the pain in that admission was clear in his voice.

"He is incoherent still; partly because of the medication we have him on," said Dr. Parsons.

"What is wrong with him?"

"We aren't certain yet. We are treating him an antipsychotic and an electrolyte solution."

"What for?"

"The first because he appeared to be suffering from hallucinations and said he was hearing voices, the other is for Hypernatremia."

"What is that?"

"Extreme dehydration. He is going through water intoxication; his body is essentially stealing water from his organs in order to keep hydration in his blood. We run the risk of doing damage if we push too much fluid into him but we risk organ failure if we don't. We also... Due to the condition he was found in and suspicions of the EMT's that brought him in... We ran a tox screen." He had known the Blake boy's since they were in diapers so it was very hard for him to think or even suggest such a thing to either of them about the other.

"What did you find?" asked Gryphon, steeling himself for the answer. Part of him almost hoped to hear his brother was on something, still having a hard time believing the things Callie had shown him were real.

"We found nothing in him to suggest that he was having an adverse reaction. There were no elevated levels of any known narcotics or alcohol to suggest he was in stages of withdrawal."

"Any steroids?" asked Gryphon tentatively. He half expected, and was ready to hear the man say yes. Again, he wanted to and did not want to.

"No," said the doctor. "The psychosis may be a chemical imbalance brought on by the dehydration."

Gryphon sighed then he drew in a breath. He remembered DJ telling him just the other day about the results of the tests his staff had been conducting in his lab the last couple months, the effects of synthetic growth hormones on rats.

His brother had stopped in to see them at the office about a month ago to give them copies of the photos he had taken of them on the kayaking trip. DJ had told him later how interested his brother, who had hated science in school, had been in the tests. He didn't want to believe his brother might have stolen any of the unsafe drugs but he had to at least field the question. "Did you find anything unusual? Anything unexplained?"

"No. Only a slightly higher level of caffeine than I would like to see."

Gryphon sighed and nodded. He was relieved to hear this. He didn't want to believe Callie was right, that his brother was being drained by these eerie monster things of hers. He didn't want to think what this might mean… If she was right then no one was safe.

"I also took the liberty of phoning your parents."

Gryphon had hoped to find out what was wrong with his brother first and only involve them if it was required, not wanting them to have to see Sam in this condition. He knew, like him, his brother wouldn't want to worry them needlessly nor would he want the embarrassment of having to explain why he was like this. He knew too that they would have been quite angry with him for not telling them as well so again he only nodded. "Thank you, Doug."

"I'm just down the hall if you need anything, Gryphon," said the doctor. He touched his shoulder and squeezed it gently then mouthed to DJ to keep an eye on him as he left the room.

DJ nodded to the doctor then turned to his best friend and said, "You want me to get you anything, Gryph?"

"No, Callie went to get coffee," said the man.

"Who?" asked DJ.

"Half regular, half mocha, and a touch of cream."

DJ spun around, wondering who, other than him, his friend's ex-girlfriend, his friend's brother, his friend's secretary and his friend's head chef knew that was how Gryphon liked his coffee. He drew in a deep breath and let it out slowly when he saw what looked like an angel standing framed in the doorway.

"And a French Roast with three packs of sugar for Dr. Wright," said the woman, smiling.

"Who's that?" asked DJ asked.

Without looking away from his Sam, Gryphon said, "DJ, this is Callie Summers. Callie this is my business partner, DJ Wright."

"Did you tell her what kind of coffee I like?"

"No. She's the psychic that came to my phase shifting talk."

"You mean…" DJ whispered to him.

"Yes, Dr. Wright, I am the crazy psychotic woman that thinks she can read minds," said Callie, giggling to herself. "And, in answer to your questions: yes, I am a natural blonde, I'm a thirty four C and I prefer it on top."

"What?" She had just answered all of DJ's immediate thoughts.

"She really can read minds." Gryphon shrugged.

"It's a strange thing, actually… I've been having trouble doing it for nearly three months but I am able to somehow read the two of you and his brother easily."

"Is this a good thing?" asked DJ.

Gryphon sniggered, "Depends on what you are thinking about, which, in your case, is probably not a good thing."

This made Callie giggle as well. "I can block out most minds and will yours if you prefer, Dr. Wright."

"Call me DJ, Miss Summers. I have been told, by more than a few, that I have got multiple personalities, what's one more in there?"

"Callie," said the woman as she handed him the cup coffee then walked over to Gryphon and held his out to him. "I will wait outside, DJ has something to discuss with you, Gryphon, and Gryphon has some-thing he needs you to run tests on, DJ."

Gryphon looked up at his business partner quizzically and DJ looked at his equally as.

The head of Biochemistry for GCI watched the woman leave then he turned to his boss and friend and said, "Damn, she is hot! Are you interested in her?"

Gryphon shook his head, both to answer the man's question and at how rude he could be.

"You don't mind if I have a go at her then?" DJ smiled when he saw his friend shake his head again. "I am not sure I like anyone knowing what I am thinking," he added, with a shake of his own head.

"Including yourself," said Gryphon. It felt good to jest a little, relieving some of his built up tension.

DJ gave him a snotty look then said, "And before I even have a chance to enjoy thinking it myself. She said you have something you want me to run tests on?"

"Yeah," said Gryphon as he pulled the bag of bits he had taken from the vomit in Sam's apartment from his pocket. "I need to know if there is anything in this."

"Where did you get this?"

Gryphon only looked at his brother.

"Okay."

"What was it you needed to discuss with me?" asked Gryphon then.

"Adri… Dr. Ivekio brought the tissue samples and autopsy reports from the first cases."

"Decided to help her then?" asked Gryphon. He hadn't intended the angry tone in his voice but he knew DJ would understand where it was coming from so he didn't apologize for it. He had known DJ would help her, just for curiosity's sake if nothing else.

"Did you really want me not to? I can still turn her down, no contracts have been signed and no price has been negotiated yet."

"I told you when I made you head of chemistry that you choose the projects for your department. As long as she pays the bill I could not care less."

"I… She saw the picture of us kayaking."

"Probably pissed her off a touch. She had been begging me to go on a trip with her but I kept saying I didn't have time… I wish I…" He swallowed down what he was about to say, he wasn't ready to face that their breakup had been mostly his own fault yet.

"She said she liked how happy you looked, that it had been a long time since you allowed yourself to go like that."

"The findings?"

"They think it's a new strain of Yellow Fever,"
"We have plenty of vaccine in Cryo, don't we?"

"Yeah. They have tried their own supply on the tissue and it's had no effect... Of course it might be because it was already too degraded... If they had living tissue to test it on..."

"Do they have anyone with this disease that hasn't died from it yet?"

"Sort of..."

# 20

# **Tensions Build**

Adrienne and the colonel that had spoken at the news-briefing stepped into the room as DJ said this.

Gryphon's ex-lover had her hair pulled back from her face in a French braid; a few loose strands curling along her cheeks and the light make-up she was wearing helped to soften the angular shape of her face a little. She was dressed in blue jeans and a soft pink wrap around sweater with a darker pink tank top layered under it.

Part of him was angry at her gall – the fact that she was dressed in such casual attire and that she had the soldier, who was a stranger to him in every sense of the word, with her only exacerbated this. He was about to ask her what she was getting out of coming to see him during so private and personal a moment as this but she spoke first.

"Hi, Gryphon, how is Sammy?"

"He's been a whole hell of a lot better," he barked. He watched the colonel's hand go to the woman's shoulder, as if guarding his property. He knew instantly there was more between them than just a professional relationship. He tried to deny the knot that suddenly formed in his stomach was from jealousy.

Callie, who was standing in the doorway, backed out of the room, the flood of feelings and images she was getting was overwhelming. She had seen the relationship between the woman and the colonel too. She had seen it in vivid images rather than just body language. She was gladdened that she didn't see the passion she had seen between Gryphon and the woman though. She knew how much he still loved her and could see she was confused about her feelings for him. She hoped they might have a future together though right then she didn't see one. She could see the flairs of jealousy shooting between the men and those shooting from Adrienne to her as well.

Adrienne remembered the woman standing in the doorway from the phase shifting talk and now guessed she *was* someone Gryphon was seeing. It hurt her to know he was dating again but she knew she had no right to say anything about it since she was as well.

"Hello, DJ."

"Uh... hi, Adri... Dr. Ivekio," said DJ, acting usually shy.

"How many times have I told you to call me..."

"What are you doing here, *Adrienne*?" Gryphon asked sternly, having recovered faster than DJ had.

Adrienne ignored his tone and the glare. "This is Colonel John Graham. John this is Dr. Gryphon Blake, head of Griffin Concepts and Dr. DJ Wright, head of its Chemistry department."

All three men only grunted.

Adrienne put her hand out to the woman, who was now standing in the hallway, "I am Adrienne Ivekio."

"Ca... Callie Summers, I'm a friend of ... Just friends," said Callie. She could see the threat clearly in the woman's eyes and her body language.

"*What* are you doing here, Adrienne?" Gryphon.

Adrienne turned to face her former lover with a sweet and slightly sad smile on her face. "I had hoped we would get to see each other again very soon after hearing your talk the other day. I would have liked it to be under better circumstances." She looked at his brother, lying still on the hospital bed and asked, "How long has Sammy been like this?"

"Answer the question, exactly why are you here?" asked Gryphon again. He could see how tense his tone was making the colonel but he didn't care.

DJ motioned to Callie then and signaled for her to follow him into the hallway.

She nodded and followed him out.

"Governor Price has asked me to lead a panel to discuss possible causes of this outbreak and how we might counter it before it causes mass hysteria."

"Outbreak?"

"We have three hundred and twenty five reported deaths now," said Adrienne. "One hundred of those in just the last twenty-four hours. At that rate it will reach thousands in less than a week."

"I'm sorry to hear that and have no doubt you will do all in your power to solve the problem, but this brought you here, to this hospital, for what?"

"I'm here to assess Sam. Viral infections are my area of expertise, if you remember?"

"Sam isn't suffering from a viral infection."

"I believe he is, Gryphon," said the woman as she walked over to the sleeping man and gently pushed the hair off his forehead. "Has DJ told you we think it is a new strain of Yellow Fever?"

"He did," said Gryphon, getting agitated.

"Your brother is suffering almost exactly what we suspect are the symptoms of what affected those people."

"What?" asked the man; completely taken off guard. "My brother doesn't have Yellow Fever."

As if not hearing him, she continued, "We are hoping we can now let the media know what is happening and be able to provide the proper vaccine within days; hopefully before anyone else has to die."

"This is not an outbreak," barked Gryphon.

Adrienne gave him an odd look. She wondered if DJ had held back information, which he had told Gryphon, hoping the two of them could cash in on it and make a hefty profit.

"I don't know what they're called but they come at you from the dark and take away your soul. They apparently drain the body of its fluids in the process. I don't know for what purpose other than possibly as some form of food," said Gryphon so clearly that it made Adrienne step back and the colonel actually laugh a little.

"I see your years of therapy have worked," said the doctor, just under her breath.

"Meaning?"

"I thought you were convinced what you thought happened in the closet when you were ten was just childhood ramblings?" Adrienne realized as she said this that she sounded sarcastic and condescending but it was too late to take it back.

"Fuck you, Adrienne," said Gryphon.

"I think we started on the wrong foot, Gryphon…"

"No, we ended on the wrong foot."

"That was as much your decision as mine."

"How is coming home from a conference to find your bags packed and half the furniture in a moving van as much my decision as yours?"

"This is not the time nor place," said Adrienne.

"Yeah, never was one for confrontations were you," sniffed the man.

She turned to the other man in the room and said, "John, can you go for a walk? Get us some coffee or something? There is a cafeteria on the second floor."

"I will be in the hall if you need me," said the colonel. He was obviously quite upset that he was essentially being dismissed.

Adrienne didn't respond to the man. She turned back to her previous lover and said, "I don't want to fight with you, Gryphon. I didn't want to leave you. I was so deeply in love with you it hurt. I asked, no I begged you to go away somewhere with me, to get counseling with me, to do *anything* with me but you were too busy at your office… You spent more time with DJ than you did me the last six months we were together."

"You knew how important my work was. We were just moving into the new building and I had to be there to supervise… I always supported you when you wanted to take a class for your medical degree, you never once even tried to support me," said Gryphon, showing just how upset he still was about the way it had ended.

"My medical degree wasn't more important than we were. Can you say the same about your work? And apparently you found the time for a vacation after we separated."

"What?"

"Kayaking."

"I had to get away then, I was going crazy."

"I was as well," said Adrienne.

"I'd rather not do this right now, Adrienne," said Gryphon then, seeing his brother beginning to shift, likely feeling the tension in the air.

Adrienne sighed, took a deep breath and said, "You're right, as I said before, this isn't the time or place." She stroked Sam's forearm and he settled back down. "I came here to ask you if you and DJ would sit in on the briefing."

"What for?"

"Just humor me."

"Fine. When?"

"In half an hour. The conference room on the second floor."

"Fine, we will be there."

"Thank you," said Adrienne curtly. She looked back at Sam and said, with far more compassion than she had shown moments before, "We will figure out what is happening to him, Gryphon, I promise."

Gryphon knew she and DJ would stop at nothing to figure this out he only hoped it was before it was too late for Sam.

# 21

# Willing Chances

"We have to get to the briefing," said DJ.

Gryphon nodded but he made no sign of planning to stand any time soon.

"Gryph?" said DJ.

"I can sit with him if you like," said Callie. She came up behind him and gently placed her hand on his shoulder.

Gryphon's hand went to hers and squeezed it softly, "Call me immediately if he awakens."

"I will, Gryphon."

The man saw movement behind him. He turned and watched Dr. Parsons, Adrienne and Colonel Graham step through the door. He couldn't miss that the colonel now had an AK47 rifle hanging off his arm. He wondered if the man thought they needed the added incentive or if he just needed the weapon to feel more like a man – he suspected which it was.

He took a few steps away from his brother's side but he was still reluctant to leave the room entirely. He was turning to go just as a nurse was stepping in with an IV bag to replace the almost empty one dripping into his brother's veins.

He stopped and watched her switch the bags then walk over to the window to close the blinds. The sun was shining brightly through them and the rays were slowly moving up from the foot of the bed. He guessed she was doing this because in a few more minutes the sun would be shining on his brother's face.

He watched all this in his mind in slow motion and felt himself tensing up with each step closer she took to the window. Just as her fingers touched the string he shouted out. "Leave them alone!"

This startled her as well as the others in the room.

"I… I am sorry… I just… thought it might be easier on Mr. Blake if he wasn't blinded by the sun if he awakens," said the nurse.

"Darkness is where they come from!"

"What?" asked the confused nurse. She looked at the man then at the doctors.

Adrienne shook her head then nodded.

She nodded back and quickly left the room.

Gryphon said, "Thank you," to Adrienne. He knew she too thought he was losing it but he appreciated that she was humoring him.

He finally started for the door but he stopped again when he reached the casing of it. His eyes went to the light switch on the wall, his methodical mind could see someone coming in the room and doing the opposite of what the young nurse had done – turning it off out of habit as they left the room, or thinking the man in the bed would sleep better in the darkness.

He turned to Dr. Parsons and asked, "How long does it take for the backup generator to kick in when a circuit breaker is popped?"

The doctor looked at him oddly and said, "I am not certain… about thirty seconds or so, I would guess."

Gryphon nodded, took one step sideways, grabbed the rifle from Colonel Graham's hands and smashed the butt end of it into the light switch box. There was the sound of the gun hitting it, a loud pop, then sparks flew out of it. The electricity coursed down the metal gun body and numbed his fingers, hands and arms up to his elbows, making him drop the rifle, but he had accomplished his task.

The monitors began to beep frantically and lights in the room went dark briefly, the first stopped and the second flickered and came back on; they were now slightly dimmer but they still gave off enough light to keep the shadows out of the corners of the room.

"What the hell were you thinking?" asked Dr. Parsons, DJ, the colonel and Adrienne at the same time.

Callie was the only one who didn't look surprised, knowing why he had done it – *they come from the dark.*

"You coulda' electrocuted yourself!" shouted DJ.

"Chance I was willing to take, DJ," said the usually very cautious scientist. He leaned over, picked up the rifle and handed it back to the stunned soldier then nodded to Callie, who nodded back, and walked out of the room.

# 22

# Bargain Made

Gryphon still had no idea why exactly he and his business partner were being asked to sit in on this briefing, except maybe because of DJ's involvement, and because they thought his brother was the only living case of whatever it was killing these people. He remembered saying to Callie just a few hours before that she should go to the police and tell them what she suspected and how she had reacted – after how Adrienne had reacted to him saying it he had to admit that sadly, she was right.

"DJ," Gryphon touched the man's arm and motioned for him to fall back a step with him.

"You okay?"

"I am not sure anymore… I need to talk to you about what is doing this."

DJ looked at his friend funny, "Yeah, it's a virus, Gryphon, and we will now know for certain which one."

"How is that?"

"A live specimen."

"A what?"

"Your brother," said DJ, smiling.

"My brother is not a *specimen*!"

"I didn't mean it that way, Gryph," said DJ, he had realized how it sounded as he was saying it but it was too late to take back.

Gryphon stormed ahead of him then.

The man of science burst into the conference room. He was only slightly surprised, but not deterred by, the number of people he found there already, or by who was there. There were several men and women he guessed were hospital staff, some from the one they were currently in and some from CMC, several in army uniforms and the governor of their state. He slammed his fists down on the table making more than a few of them jump and said, "My brother is not a fucking specimen."

"Of course he isn't, Gryphon," said Adrienne, "but he appears to have the symptoms we suspect would have preceded this. If we can figure out what is causing it in him we can hopefully stop or contain... whatever it is."

"He will not be a guinea pig either, Adrienne."

"No, he will not be."

Gryphon felt all his frustration leave him in a flash then. His knees started to buckle as all he had been through crashed down on him and the adrenaline he'd been going on went away in a rush.

DJ and Adrienne both saw this and reacted at the same time. The former grabbed a chair and the latter helped him to it.

"Dr. Blake, as Dr. Ivekio said, we do not intend for your brother to be a guinea pig or a specimen but we do wish to run some tests on him," said Governor Price. He had been a medical doctor for forty years before going into politics.

"I already know what is doing this," said Gryphon under his breath. He took the glass of water Adrienne had brought him and drank nearly half of it down in one gulp. He didn't want to say what he believed before all these people, knowing he would find himself being carted away, so he held his tongue, sat quietly and just listened.

"Dr. Parsons is treating Mr. Blake for dehydration and mental psychosis, he isn't treating the underlying cause," said a short, red haired man with round-rimmed glasses. The CMC nametag read Dr. M. Updike.

Adrienne waved the man to silence, "We're going to begin by taking blood and tissue samples from your brother and run tests on them. See if there is any response to any of the known vaccines for Yellow Fever, as well as some other viruses that present similarly."

"You said Dr. Parsons is treating Mr. Blake for mental psychosis, I take it then he too was seeing... beings... for lack of a better term?" asked the governor.

"Beings?" DJ guffawed.

Gryphon sat up straighter to this. He had known the older woman he had seen in Callie's premonition had seen something and Sam saying the ominous phrase that had haunted he himself most of his life, having it always in the back of his mind, implied he had too but he hadn't known others had as well. A part of him had still been trying to explain away what Callie had shown him; this seemed to imply there was more than a little truth to it.

"People suffering from severe dehydration can have bouts of delirium," said Adrienne.

"But not typically all the same thing," said the governor, suspiciously.

"It's likely they had all recently seen a similar movie or TV show and their fevered brains worked the ominous images into their psyche," said Dr. Updike.

"It is actually not unheard of for an illness to present itself with similar hallucinations," said Adrienne.

"Where? In a science fiction book?" asked DJ.

"The virus may have affected them all in the part that affects vision. The damage may have made them all see what would seem to be shadows coming to life," said Adrienne, "which is why I want to schedule Sam for a P.E.T. scan and an M.R.I. as soon as possible." She looked at Gryphon to make sure he was not against this, not wanting him to fight her. Seeing he didn't seem ready to act she added slowly, "As soon as Dr. Parsons says he is stabilized we will transport him." She was the only person in the room that wasn't surprised by what happened next.

This snapped both Gryphon and DJ to attention. "Excuse me? Transport Sam where exactly?" asked the first one, anger creeping into his voice then.

"We need the patient close to us to be able to perform required tests and administer any treatments," said Dr. Updike.

"He is not just a *patient*," said DJ, making air quotations with the first two fingers of each hand.

"He is to us," said Dr. Updike a little snidely.

"He is not just a patient, to us either," said Adrienne. She could see the situation from both sides, having known Sam, but ultimately he was just a patient. She knew there was no way to make Gryphon and DJ see this that way though.

"The situation requires containment, the CDC can offer that," said the colonel.

"I thought you said this wasn't contagious," barked Gryphon. He was now sitting straight backed and stiff.

DJ, beside him, was in about the same stance.

"We're no longer confident of it," said Dr. Updike.

"If it is Yellow Fever, unless a mosquito bites him then goes on a spree across the hospital it will not spread," said DJ.

Dr. Updike sniffed and said, "Be that as it may, Dr. Wright, we are required by rules and regulations, to take him and quarantine him until we know for certain."

"He is not leaving this hospital," said Gryphon, through clenched teeth.

"We can take him by force, if we must," said Colonel Graham, getting just as stiff and through clenched teeth as well.

"Over my dead body," said Gryphon, standing up.

DJ also started to rise, "Mine as well."

"Gentlemen," said Governor Price. "We are all only trying to look out for your brother, Dr. Blake. Our ultimate goal is the same."

Gryphon guffawed and said, "I know how government hospitals work, Governor Price. The end goal for you all is not to save the one, *him,* it is to save the masses. For all normally I would be for that, normally it isn't *my* brother that is being made the means to that end. The goal of this hospital's staff is to save the one, him, which is why he will not leave this facility.

"The staff at CMC will do all in their power to keep him alive, Dr. Blake. We have to be realistic, without some kind of treatment his chances are not good," said the governor.

"Your staff could not care less whether he survives the treatment or not. In fact, you hope he doesn't. We both know the only real way for you to know what is doing this is with an autopsy. My brother is not nor will he ever be treated as a fucking lab experiment."

"Of course not, Gryphon." Adrienne could see the pain and fear in his eyes, behind the anger, and felt her heart clench. She had forgotten how passionate he could be when he was fighting for something he strongly believed in.

"We have jurisdiction, Dr. Blake. We do not need your permission to remove him," said Colonel Graham.

Gryphon locked eyes with Adrienne, and said, "You know I do not advocate violence, but I am telling you, here and now, anybody even gets near my brother with the thoughts of moving him for anything other than a test that can be performed in this same building will find themselves in a room of their own healing from a whole lot of hurt and a few broken bones."

DJ nodded and added, "More than a few."

Adrienne was torn, she knew it would be harder to get accurate and timely results if they had to transport the test samples between the two facilities but she didn't want to harm Sam or hurt Gryphon either. She looked at the governor and said, "You said I am the head of this?"

"You are."

"So it is my call?"

"It is."

"Then Sam will stay here; on one condition, Gryphon."

"Name it."

"We are allowed to set up a lab at GCI. I am afraid the samples could get compromised if we have to transport them any farther than that."

"Done."

"Adrienne?" barked the colonel.

"That is ill advised," said Dr. Updike.

"It is my call and I have made it."

"Thank you, Adrienne," said Gryphon.

The woman still wasn't sure she had made the right decision but it was done. She nodded to him then looked at the governor to be certain she hadn't overstepped her boundaries.

"Are we done here then?" asked Gryphon.

"We are," said the governor.

"DJ will help you get set up at GCI," said Gryphon as he turned and left the room.

"When do you want to move in?" asked DJ.

"We will bring the equipment down tomorrow," said Adrienne, her eyes on the door.

"Give me a list of the equipment you need. We likely have some of it already, will save you the hassle and time." said DJ, then he too left the room. He said,

"Have a nice day," to them as he went through the door, intent on finding his friend.

Once the door was closed, the governor said bluntly, "I understand you and Dr. Blake were once in a relationship."

Adrienne really didn't feel it was any business of his, or the other people in the room, but she knew there was a small conflict of interest if anyone wanted to push the issue. Deciding it would hurt her, Gryphon and Sam more to deny it than admit it, she said, "Yes, we were seeing each other for almost four years. It ended just before I took the position at CMC."

"I know you aren't the type of person to let that former relationship and familiarity to the patient cloud your judgment, Dr. Ivekio. I know also that I don't need to tell you, if it becomes essential that the patient be brought in for quarantine you will do it no matter how, what or who Dr. Blake threatens, yes?" said the governor. His fingers were steepled before his face and he was looking down his nose at her pointedly.

"Of course, Governor Price," said Adrienne, realizing how thin a thread she was walking then.

"Very good, I need to get back to the capital. Please keep me informed of your findings," said the governor as he stood.

"I will, Governor Price."

The governor left the room then.

"We will see about getting a list to Dr. Wight and getting the equipment CGI doesn't have packed up," said Dr. Updike, shaking his head.

"Thank you," said Adrienne; this left only her and the colonel in the room.

The woman walked to the wall of windows and looked out across the sea of vehicles in the parking lot. She was trying to decide if she had made the right decision or had let her heart make it. She jumped when she felt hands come down on her shoulders. She knew whose hands they were because they were kneading her muscles roughly; she so missed the gentle massages Gryphon used to give her when she'd had a rough day. She squirmed out of reach of his touch by taking a step closer to the windows. "Not now, John."

John smirked and sniffed, suspecting why she had done this. "The man has no idea the risks or the danger he is causing."

"The man is thinking about his brother, John."

"The needs of the many outweigh the needs of the few."

"*It's his brother*, John," said Adrienne.

John knew there was no way to win this argument so he said, "Let me take you to dinner, then we can go back to our place and make love."

She didn't want to tell him she had never once made love to him and was only with him because it was easier than trying to start a real relationship. Deep down she knew it was because she was still hurting from the last one but she wasn't willing or ready to face that just yet. "Not tonight, John."

John was starting to get upset but he didn't want to start anything where they were. Instead he nodded and said, "I will go help coordinate the move then."

"Please." The woman turned back to the windows.

\*\*\*\*\*\*\*\*\*\*\*\*\*\*\*\*\*\*\*\*\*

DJ caught up to Gryphon, who was headed into the reception area outside Dr. Parson's office. "You okay?"

Gryphon ignored his friend. He walked up to the soda machine in the corner and pounded his fist into the front of it, which cracked the plexiglass near the edges. He then kicked it hard with the side of his foot, which knocked the unit onto its back legs, made it hit the wall behind it and left a dented line in the plaster. These hits rattled the machine's internals making it spit out a can of cola and several dollars in quarters.

"I could have loaned you a dollar, you know."

Gryphon was opening and closing his fingers to be sure he hadn't broken any of them and was smirking as he turned to the man. "I really am not in the mood for your being cute just now, thank you, DJ."

"Come on, Gryph, you need to lighten up a bit. We *will* find out what is going on with Sam and get him better, you have to have faith."

"No medicine that is going to do that, DJ."

"Excuse me?"

"The people that have died, and Sam, are not just having mass hallucinations; they're being haunted and attacked by things that are taking the fluid from their bodies, leaving them as dried up husks when they are finished with them."

"Excuse me?" asked DJ. He started toward his friend then, wondering if he now had the virus as well. "Do you need to sit down?"

"*No, DJ, I do not need to sit down.*"

DJ noticed how pale Gryphon was, how drawn and gray his skin looked and thought he looked as if he had lost some weight, "We may be able to keep you from getting to the point Sam is at if we can start now, Gryphon," said the man.

Gryphon pushed the man away from him and said, "I'm not sick, DJ and I'm not going crazy either." He stomped past his friend and walked fast down the hall toward his brother's room.

# 23

# Glimmer of Hope

Gryphon heard his mom's voice, asking where her baby was, long before she came around the corner into the room, and felt his heart sink further.

Gloria and Bruce Blake weren't jetsetters but they did like to travel and had an active lifestyle. They had been on the final leg of a cruise of the Mediterranean when they got Dr. Parsons' call about Sam. Needless to say they had gotten off at the next port of call and immediately booked a flight home.

"Oh, my God, Gryphon… What happened?" cried the woman. Gloria Blake was a healthy sixty-eight. She admittedly colored her hair back to the amber of her younger years but it looked good on her. She was still in good shape and was normally always put together but this day her hair was flat and dull and all her makeup was gone, telling her son she had been crying all the way to the hospital.

Bruce Blake was a young looking seventy-two. He looked like an older version of his oldest son, graying hair on his head and a few more wrinkles on his face and hands the only differences. He wasn't crying; like his older son, he didn't people seeing him that vulnerable. He was obviously shaken though. "Are you alright, Gryphon?" Bruce stepped up to his oldest son and placed his strong hand on his shoulder.

"I'm sorry I didn't make the call," said Gryphon. He was holding Sam's hand again and didn't want to release it, even to hug his parents whom he hadn't seen in more than a month.

"It's alright, son, Doug told us how you didn't want to leave Sam's side."

Gryphon looked over at Dr. Parsons, who was standing in the corner of the room, with Adrienne, and mouthed, "thank you," to which he got a simple nod.

The two doctors walked over to them then.

"Sam is suffering an extreme case of dehydration. We are unsure of the cause of it but we are running tests to determine it."

"He looks so thin," said Gloria. She didn't see her youngest son as often as she did the older one. It had been almost two months since she had last seen Sam and he had been a touch heavy then. "Was he on a diet?" Her eyes went from Dr. Parsons' face to the person beside him with surprise. "Adrienne?" she asked. A spark of life lit her eyes as she looked at her older son, wondering what this might mean.

She had told Gryphon, many times since their breakup, that she had liked him and the young doctor as a couple and had hoped to be picking out a dress and helping to plan a happy occasion very soon. She had been very upset when he told her they had ended the longtime relationship.

"Hello, Mrs. Blake," said the woman. She stepped forward and took her offered hand. She had always liked Gryphon's parents as well. "I am sorry this is how we got to see each other again." Her eyes unconsciously went to Gryphon then went to the floor quickly.

Gloria saw this and looked at her older son again herself then, with hope in her eyes.

Gryphon had seen both of these looks. He wasn't certain about Adrienne's – other than worry for his brother – but he knew his mother's. He shook his head at her quickly, hoping to stop the thoughts she was having before she ran with them.

"I will give you some time with your sons." The female doctor. She stepped around the bed and touched Gryphon's shoulder quickly as she left the room.

"As will I," said Dr. Parsons, who shook the elder Mr. Blake's hand before going.

Forgetting Sam for a moment, Gloria looked at her first son and said, "Are you giving it another try?"

"No, Mom."

"Then why is she here?"

"Because of Sam."

"I saw how she looked at you, Gryphon; it isn't just because of Sam."

"Not now, Mom," said Gryphon. He stood up and had to grab the rail on the edge of the bed.

"Gryphon," his mother cried out.

"Son," his father said, "when was the last time you left this room?"

Gryphon looked at the clock on the wall and shook his head, "I don't know."

"It will do Sam no good if you get sick as well."

"I know, Dad, but... I just want to be here when he wakes up... I don't want him to think he is alone."

"Your mother and I will sit with him for a while. Go home, go to the office, go for a drive," said Bruce.

"I don't want to be that far away, Dad."

"Let me see if Doug can find a room for you to lie down in for a few hours then," said Bruce, his hands taking his son's shoulders. He could feel how tight they were getting and added, "We will get you if there is any change, Gryphon."

Gryphon sighed; he was tired. "Alright, Dad."

The father and son walked out of the room and started for Dr. Parson's office. They came upon DJ and a young woman sitting together in the small reception area before it.

"Hello, DJ," said Bruce.

"Hello, Mr. Blake," said DJ. He stood up and shook the man's hand then turned to the woman and said, "This is Callie Summers, a friend of ours." His eyes went to his best friend then, unable to hide the worry and concern there.

"Hello, Miss Summers," said Bruce.

Callie stood as well and said, "Very nice to meet you, Mr. Blake." Her eyes went to the man's son too, filled with worry and concern as well.

Gryphon didn't notice this; his eyes were looking up the hall toward his brother's room half expecting to hear alarms going off and people running into the room because he had let his guard down for even a moment.

"We are hoping to find a place for my son to rest for a bit, since he refuses to leave this building," said Bruce. He sounded very much like an older version of the usually quite sensible Gryphon.

Dr. Parsons stepped from his office, having heard this, and said, "He can use my private lounge, Bruce. No one will disturb him there."

"Unless there is a change in Sam's condition," said Gryphon pointedly.

"Of course, Gryphon," said the doctor, DJ and his father at the same time.

"We will find you, we promise," said Callie.

"Thanks," said the man. He took her hand in his, squeezing it slightly and kissing the top of it. "Thanks, DJ," he said as he hugged his best friend to him. "Dad," he said, hugging him tight as well. "Thanks, Doc," he said finally, then he allowed him to lead him away.

Bruce and DJ had both felt how tightly the man, who was normally not nearly so openly affectionate, had held them. Both were now looking worriedly from each other to the door of the doctor's office and back.

Callie was wiping her eyes as she excused herself.

Bruce watched her go then looked at DJ and said, "She yours or Gryphon's?"

"Neither, but I am hoping I have a chance."

"Adrienne and my son?"

"I think they both still want to be together but neither is willing to make the first move," said DJ.

"How long has Sam been ill?"

"Gryphon found him three days ago but he said he hadn't spoken to him in almost a week so... Somewhere between four and seven days ago."

Bruce rubbed his eyes and motioned DJ to follow him back to Sam's room.

# 24

# Suppressed Feelings

Gryphon stood inside Dr. Parsons' lounge room unsure what exactly to do. His mind was running a million miles an hour in a million different directions, he wasn't sure how or if he could shut it down enough to allow himself to relax. He was certain sleep was so far out of the question to even be considered.

It was a comfortable looking room. A double size bed was set in the far corner, with soft cotton sheets, not the starched hospital stock, a fifty inch flat screen TV was mounted on the wall across from it. A small stand with a lamp, remote for the TV and alarm clock was beside the bed. He looked around and saw there was no phone. Dr. Parsons would have his pager on him in case he was needed; otherwise he was in the room himself to relax.

He pulled his shirt over his head as he reached about the center of the room and dropped it to the floor then kicked his loafers off, left them beside the shirt and added his pants to the pile. He pulled the bed sheets halfway down, sat down and sighed loudly. The mattress wasn't as firm as he was used to but he supposed he could get some rest on it – he truly doubted he would find any sleep though. He was about to lie back when movement across from him caught his eye.

He looked up to see his reflection in the full-length mirror on the inside of the door. He barely recognized himself. His eyes looked bloodshot, he was pale, his hair was dirty and disheveled and he had about two day's growth of beard on his face. He was like his mother in that he didn't like going out of the house without feeling and looking put together. Sam, like their father, could throw on a pair of sweats and a t-shirt and be perfectly comfortable at a black tie event. "God, Sammy," he said aloud to the room.

That was all it took. All the fears and emotions he had been bottling up for three days came rushing to the surface and there was no way to stop them. His face met his hands as the tears began to flow. He was so caught up in the flood of feelings that he didn't hear the door open or notice that someone else had stepped into the room.

Adrienne watched Mr. Blake helping his son out of the room and knew he had managed to talk him into getting the rest he desperately needed but had refused to let himself have. She guessed Dr. Parsons would give him the use of his personal lounge. When she saw him leading the man inside his office she knew this was right. She waited for the doctor to leave his office then stepped in and opened the door to the back room. She had nothing in mind except to offer the man inside some support, guessing he would finally break down once he was alone.

Gryphon was sitting on the edge of the bed in the corner with only black boxers on. The rest of his clothes and shoes were lying in a pile on the floor, about halfway across the room. She remembered again how fine he looked when he was naked but she put the thought to the back of her mind, feeling it was wrong given the current situation. His face was in his hands and his shoulders were shaking, telling her he was either laughing or crying. She knew it was the latter, which made her heart clench. All the feelings she still had for the man flooded back in at full force. She fought her own tears back, knowing right now he would need her to be strong, and stepped up to him. She was surprised he didn't seem to have noticed anyone had entered the room. He was usually so observant. Many had joked the man would be a perfect criminologist because he could see details even an expert would miss. She sat down next to him and gently touched his shoulder. She jumped when he jumped. The tears she had been fighting began to flow when he looked at her, seeing how destroyed he was.

Gryphon jumped when he felt the mattress shift beside him and a hand touch his shoulder because he had thought he was alone. His heart stopped for a split second, thinking something had changed in Sam's condition already and he hadn't been there. He saw Adrienne sitting beside him. He choked back his tears and started to stand up, not wanting her, of all people, to see him this way.

She stopped him with a hand on his arm. "It is alright, there has been no change. It is alright to show you are human, Gryphon. No one will think you any less a man for it."

Gryphon again started to rise then a fresh wave of emotions, this time the ones he had suppressed since the day she had left him, came to the surface. "God, Adrienne... I... What am I... what am I going to do if he doesn't make it?"

"I'm so sorry, Gryphon," said the woman despondently. Her tears were for him and Sam both. She threw her arms around him and he turned and wrapped his around her.

They held each other tightly and both cried into the other's shoulder for several minutes then they separated and wiped their faces.

"I am sorry, Adrienne... I..."

"There's nothing to be sorry for, Gryphon. I know how much you love your brother and how hard it is seeing him in this condition with nothing to do but watch and pray." His love for his family was one thing she had never questioned about him.

"I mean... I am sorry for how I treated you... I... I know I took you for granted," he said, his hand came up then and gently brushed the hair that was stuck to her wet cheek away then the tears that had stuck them there.

"I let you, Gryphon," she said, doing the same to his face. "I am at fault as much as you. I should have told you I was leaving in a different way."

"I shouldn't have said what I did to you then... I didn't mean it... I never... I never told you... what I really wanted to say." A fresh wave of tears started down his face and his chest hitched with the pain of not being able to take a full breath. He whipped the wetness away, angry at their betrayal.

"Told me what?"

"I never told you how much I… how much I liked you around, in my life… I never told you how much I… how much I loved you, Adrienne," said the man. He was having trouble breathing now and it had nothing to do with his asthma this time. "How much I still do."

Adrienne was suddenly aware one of her hands was on his bare chest and that she had unconsciously began to slowly move her fingers over his skin. She liked the feeling of the muscles shifting with his movements as he fought to breathe and could feel his heart beating under her palm. She felt it speeding up and felt her own doing the same, matching his beat for beat. The fingers of her other hand, which had been on his cheek, wiping the tears he missed, moved to trace his lips as she looked into his beautiful blue gray eyes. She liked what she saw in them.

This look, his words of a moment before and his hand moving to her cheek and caressing it then was what made her do what she did next. She leaned forward slowly and brought her lips to his. His hand moved through her hair to cup her head while the other went to the small of her back and pulled her closer to him.

The kisses started out slowly, tentatively, gently. Neither was sure the other wasn't going to suddenly realize what they were doing and push the other away.

Once they both realized that neither was going to they began to kiss harder and their hands began to roam.

Adrienne's hands were already on his bare chest and back so she had nothing in the way of her caressing and kissing his heating skin. His hands began to pull her sweater and the tank top underneath it off to give him skin to caress and kiss.

They had to separate a bit in order for him to do this, at which time both looked into the other's eyes, both still red from having been crying moments before, both still trying to gauge the other's reactions not wanting to make a mistake.

Gryphon's eyes moved over Adrienne's body slowly, as he dropped her tops to the floor beside his. It looked even better than he remembered it. She was wearing a light pink bra that was essentially nothing but lace and was quite see through. She didn't need it for support, her breasts were quite firm, she wore it for security – it was considered very unprofessional to have erect nipples in a meeting with high government and military officials. He could see she was more than a little aroused at the moment – it was far too warm in the room for her to have been cold – which made him aroused. He leaned forward and began to kiss her neck then the exposed sides of her breasts.

She leaned her head back and moaned, digging her nails into his back. His hands moved up from her waist then; feeling the skin of her stomach twitching made him smile. He cupped her breasts and his thumbs rubbed the erect nipples, which got larger still. He remembered how sensitive they were; hearing her moan and feeling her arch her back toward him told him they still were. He reached to the center and unclasped the fabric, exposing her breasts fully to him then brought his mouth down to the right one, which he knew was the more sensitive, his fingers were still playing with the left.

Adrienne's mind was screaming that she should stop him but her body wouldn't let her. She had been having sex with John for about three months but it was more just for release, for her at least. He wasn't much for foreplay and she rarely climaxed with him. Gryphon enjoyed foreplay as much as she did, often bringing her to orgasm several times before finally entering her and giving her more that way. He was now doing all the things he had then, making her feel good and very lightheaded. She knew this wasn't fair to either her current or her former lover but right then she knew it was something her former lover and she needed so she lay back on the bed and allowed him to lay on top of her, hoping he would do more to her now.

He did with eagerness.

His hands squeezed at her waist, making her skin tremble with pleasure. Lines of heat were moving over her body, every nerve ending was awake with the rush of feelings and goose pimples were rising all over her, making her quiver. She thrust her head back, arched her back, closed her eyes tight and took her lower lip between her teeth as her body began to shake uncontrollably.

She hadn't been this aroused since before they broke up. Near the end of the relationship their love-making had begun to consist of essentially quickies wherever they could fit them in.

Gryphon felt her starting to shake and smiled to himself as he unbuttoned her jeans then pulled them open. She arched her back and helped him slide them and her panties down then he reached between her legs and began to move his fingers over her, quickly bringing her to another climax. He began to kiss down her body as he did this. Her skin was quivering under his lips as he moved his mouth down her stomach, along her pelvis to the insides of her thighs then went to work on her with his tongue, bringing her to orgasm again.

He was smiling as he stood up, watching her twitch, bite and chew on her lower lip and breathe hard from that one. He had always found satisfying her equally as satisfying as having an orgasm himself. Knowing he had the power to make the very controlled woman lose control for a moment, or several, was exhilarating.

He was now more than a little bit aroused himself so he removed his boxers, moved over her and entered her gently.

Adrienne was seeing stars as she felt him go inside her, bringing her to orgasm again. He had always fit her so well. She let him move in and out of her for a while, giving her yet another, then she pushed him over so she could get on top.

She remembered what he liked as well. She began to do it now, moving her hips slowly, in a circular motion. She felt him arch his back and his hands squeeze her hips hard. His face got very calm then and his grip on her body softened. She smiled as she felt him reach an orgasm himself.

She leaned forward, twisted her hands in his hair and brought her eager lips to his equally as, sucking on his lower lip and tongue as he began to caress her back and hips. She slowed the movements of her hips for a bit. When his hands went back to her waist and tightened their grip again she began to move faster, feeling him stiffening up again.

Gryphon rolled Adrienne over, lifted her right thigh, set it against his chest and began to thrust harder, making her cum again just before he did again as well.

It was several hours before they falling apart, completely spent, and just lay in each other's arms.

# 25

# The Day After

Gryphon opened his eyes and looked around, unsure where he was at first. He didn't feel frightened just uncertain. The room was still a little dark but he could make out the lamp beside him. He twisted the knob to turn it on and looked around. He remembered his father making him leave Sam's room and Dr. Parsons bringing him into his personal lounge, which this was, so he could get some rest. The rest of it, what he and Adrienne had done, he was trying to tell himself had not been only a dream.

The fresh scratch marks dug into his chest told him it had been real. He and Adrienne had really made love for hours, like they used to when they first started dating. He smiled then frowned, he had enjoyed it but he didn't want to think it had essentially been sympathy sex. He stood up, pulled on his clothes and left the room deciding staying there wasn't going to answer any of the questions he had.

He stepped into Sam's room, hoping to find Adrienne there. He wanted to see if he could get a reading of how she felt about last night. She wasn't. His mother and Callie were. They were playing a game of rummy on the table in the corner.

Gloria smiled at her older son, oblivious of the happenings of a few hours ago, and said, "Sam seems to be sleeping soundly, dear."

"Thanks, Mom. Where's Dad?"

"Your father went to your house to get some rest and DJ went in to the office. He said something about needed to oversee Adrienne's crew setting up their equipment."

"And, Adrienne?" He doubted his mother had guessed anything by the question but he knew Callie knew by the look on her face – caught halfway between joy and pain. The fact that she was blushing and how quickly she looked away from him confirmed this.

"We haven't seen her this morning yet. I would guess she is with DJ, getting things set up."

"Likely right, Mom. Why don't you get your-self some breakfast, I will stay until you get back, then I need to go into the office myself."

"Alright, Honey. Do you want anything?" she added, looking from her son to Callie and back.

"I will get something on the way to the office," said Gryphon.

"No thanks," said Callie.

"Alright, I'll be in the cafe if you need me then."

Gryphon as he kissed her on the cheek. As soon as he was sure she was out of earshot he turned to Callie, put his hands on his hips and gave her an expectant look.

The woman started to blush again. She hadn't intended to invade his privacy; she had been worried about him and had reached out for his mind, just wanting to be sure he was alright. She had seen Adrienne enter the room through his eyes. She left his mind soon after the clothing came off but she knew that she had stayed longer than he would have wanted her to.

"I am not angry with you, Callie. I cannot say how I might have reacted only a week ago to the invasion but the last few days I have found myself rethinking a lot of things."

"You are strong, Gryphon, though I know you don't see it."

He only nodded. "Any insight?"

"I had seen that both of you still had a lot of feelings for each other, tension between you, but as to whether she was only there to offer sympathy and took it a step over I can't say. I can't see into her head as easily as I can yours and DJ's."

"I'm very sorry for you then, on both accounts. They can't be the most enjoyable places."

The woman giggled a little. "You are not all that frightening, Gryphon. In fact you are one of the sanest people I have ever had the pleasure of reading. I really don't mind most of what I have seen there…" Her smile deepened as she added, "DJ… I'll give you, has some dark thoughts. I don't like to lie to people but I told him I couldn't read him as well as I can…"

"He really is a decent guy; he just has some strange thoughts, beliefs and opinions."

"I can tell that about him, if only in that he has your affection. I also see what he thinks when he looks at the pretty nurses that come in here to check Sam, and what he wishes he could do to me, which doesn't particularly scare me but does worry me some."

Gryphon sniggered and said, "He's all talk, or thought, in this case, I think you'll find. I'd be willing to bet he would run away screaming if someone actually offered to do some of the things he comes up with."

"I sense you are right there."

"So, you like him then?"

"I'm… interested," said Callie, blushing a little.

Gryphon walked over to his brother and moved the hair that had fallen onto his forehead back.

"Your mother is a wonderful woman."

"That she is."

"And your father. They both are so proud of you and Sam both."

Gryphon tried to let the words sink. He still hadn't forgiven himself for not knowing Sam was in trouble before he got as bad as he was. He was just starting to sit down when his father stepped in.

"Good morning, Miss Summers."

"Please call me Callie, Mr. Blake."

"Very well, Callie, I am Bruce then," he said smiling to her. He still didn't know exactly what her relationship to his son and his friend was but he found he liked her very much; she was very intuitive.

Callie nodded then walked to the table to pick up the cards she'd been playing with the man's wife.

"Good morning, Gryphon. You need a shave and shower still but you are looking much more like my son."

"Hi, Dad. Yeah… Think maybe I'll slide home and get cleaned up a bit before I go into the office. Did you find everything you needed there?"

"Yes. Abigail made me a huge breakfast. I know I thought the house was far too much for you when you first showed it to me but I must say now that you have made it very comfortable."

"Thanks, Dad."

"Your mother?"

"She went to the cafe to get some breakfast."

"Very good."

"I need to go to my shop for a bit and run some errands. Can I get a ride with you?" asked Callie.

"Of course," said Gryphon.

He smiled at his dad then his eyes went to his brother. He still didn't want to be away from him but he needed to at least make an appearance at the office. "Call me if there is any change?"

"Of course, Son."

\*\*\*\*\*\*\*\*\*\*\*\*\*\*\*\*\*\*\*\*

Aggie, Jayne and Jerome were on the steps of the house when Gryphon arrived home. He guessed the butler had called the ladies out as soon as he heard the gates release; likely guessing it was him coming home. He knew they all only wanted to console him, chances were his father had told Aggie about his other son's condition and she, in turn, had told the other two, but right then he didn't want to be reminded that this was all really happening.

"About your business," he said to them.

"Have you eaten yet?" asked Aggie, ignoring the dismissal.

"I am not sure I could do any of your fine fare any justice, Abigail," said the man flatly as he walked past them and bounded up the stairs two at a time without waiting for her response.

Gryphon peeled his clothing off as soon as he reached his bedroom, not even bothering to close the door. He walked into his bathroom, got into the shower and sank to the tiled floor, knees to his chest. He let the water from the shower mix with the tears flooding from his eyes and mask the sounds of his sobs.

# 26

# Watercooler Gossip

DJ never got involved in and didn't usually even stop to listen to the *water cooler* gossip in the office but he couldn't help but hear what the topic of conversation was this day – the headlines of all the local newspapers. He had stepped into the cafeteria to refill of his coffee cup, the fifth time that morning, this time. The fact that the whispers stopped as soon as he was seen told him at least some of it had been about him or someone he was close to.

In this case someone they were all close to. It seemed someone at Biscayne General had blabbed to the local gossip columnist that the brother of the head of Griffin Concepts Inc. was in fact a patient there and was believed to be one of the few that had so far survived whatever this *plague* was that was hitting the area.

A part of DJ wanted to confront them but he knew that would only give validity to their thoughts. Instead he stood in his best Gryphon Blake stance and said, "How many lab techs does it take to empty a water cooler?"

Two of the people before him actually looked like they were trying to puzzle out this question, thinking he really wanted an answer. The others knew he was making a point. They quickly scattered

DJ walked over to the pile of newspapers left there by the gossipmongers. He flipped through them slowly, reading snippets of each story and getting more and more heated. One op-ed claimed there was anywhere from several hundred to several thousand that had now died or were *infected* and was warning that no one should try to make contact with anyone that even looked like they may have contracted this mystery disease, since it was not known yet how it was transmitted. Another said people were swearing off everything from liquor to shampoo, in fear it might be a contaminated product doing this. Some were saying it was aliens, others said that this was the angels of death come to take the souls of those that had sinned. Only one of them was even close to having the right information: that this was thought to be a stronger than normal strain of yellow fever.

He found the one that made mention of his best friend's company and took it with him, reading it as he walked down the hall to the labs they had set up for use of the CMC. He guffawed aloud, wrinkled the paper up and tossed it into the rubbish bin just inside the doors of the lab, spouting, "Not even worthy of lining the cages of my lab rats!"

The articles were all quickly forgotten as he pulled rubber gloves over his hands and grabbed a vial of blood from the last known death. He used a pipette to take a drop out, set the drop on a glass slide, placed a cover slider over it and moved it to the closest microscope.

"Anything, DJ?" asked Gryphon. He sounded very much like his old self as he stepped through the sliding glass doors into the clean environment of the man's main laboratory.

The head of GCI's chemistry department looked up at his boss and best friend a little bit funny. He remembered his crazy rant from the day before. The man had shaved, washed up and donned clean clothes so he at least looked like his normal self again. He seemed to be in his right mind again but he wasn't about to test this just then. DJ wanted to shrug it off as just stress and anxiety over his brother's condition but he knew Gryphon wasn't one to normally crack under pressure. His mind replayed his friend telling him of the *premonition* Callie had somehow shown him of things from some other world roaming free on theirs, taking victims at random and were feeding on them. He knew there was no way he would joke about a thing like this – putting his brother's life at risk if they didn't treat him – but if they both had seen these things, as the other victims seemed to have, it likely meant they both had been infected. This thought scared DJ.

"Well?" Gryphon said.

DJ shook himself out of the malignant thoughts and said, "I ran tests on the pill remains you found in Sam's apartment."

"Anything odd?" asked Gryphon. He knew the fresh vomit would have more of a chance of showing them if there was any in his brother's system than his blood work, which had been diluted by time.

"No. I did find residue of Niacin, Caffeine, Yerba Mate, Ginseng, Kota Gola Leaf, bee pollen, barley, wheat grass, Calcium Carbonate, Magnesium Carbonate, Potassium Citrate and Gingko Biloba though."

"I didn't pay much attention to that part of my science classes, DJ, which is why you are the head of this department, not me. What does it mean?"

"All common ingredients in many over the counter energy drinks and pills."

"Callie said that was all he was taking," said Gryphon. He wasn't so sure he was happy to hear that. A part of him still wanted to believe Sam was only suffering the effects of withdrawal or was sick with a curable or treatable virus. He didn't want to believe there really were monsters lurking in the dark.

DJ saw how disappointed Gryphon looked and figured it would be easier to tell him the rest of his findings while he was already down. "The blood samples we took from Sam so far aren't responding to any of the vaccines... not as they should be. I don't get it. If it is a virus it should have done something ... even if only to mutate..."

Colonel Graham, who was standing silent in the corner, *overseeing the project*, huffed then.

"Into something different," the biochemist finished his thought.

The colonel sniffed arrogantly again then.

"Excuse me?" asked DJ just as arrogantly, turning to face the officer. "Do you have something to add to this conversation?"

"Cover-up."

"What?"

"We know what is really going on, Mr. Wright."

"That is *Doctor* Wright, *Colonel* Graham. I have more than one plaque in my office to say that is my correct title as the bars on your uniform name yours."

"Sorry, *Dr. Wright*. Your title changes nothing about what is truly happening here," said John.

"I am not sure what you mean."

"Your company's involvement in developing questionable chemical agents is well-known," said Colonel Graham.

"I'm uncertain of your meaning," said DJ. He set the clipboard down and tensed his body.

Gryphon put his hand on DJ's arm and said, "Care to clarify that remark, Colonel?"

"I am only quoting from military intelligence we have received on your company and its habits."

DJ guffawed and said, "Military intelligence?" He was getting very red faced now. It was his side of the business that handled chemicals so these accusations were essentially being directed at him.

"If you have an accusation to make, Graham, come out with it," Gryphon spat as he stepped up to the man.

The colonel crossed his larger arms over his larger chest and smiled.

The only slightly smaller built scientist didn't back down or step back, not the least bit intimidated by the man being almost twice as wide as him. His blue-gray eyes were boring into the colonel's hazel eyes with no fear in them.

"I am suggesting that your facility accidentally released a toxic agent into the local air or water supply and now you have no idea how to contain it. Or, you did it intentionally so you could *all of a sudden* find the answer and look the heroes."

"Excuse me?" said DJ.

"You cannot deny your company has been under investigation before, *Dr*. Blake."

"No formal charges were ever filed," said Gryphon.

"That doesn't mean…"

"Because there was nothing to find!" barked Gryphon, balling his fists up.

"Ah yes, because it was these *boogeymen* you say are coming to get us, right?"

Gryphon only shook his head to this.

"Trying to blame this on something other than your company's malpractice is absolutely ingenious," said the colonel snidely. "You are good at hiding your tracks. And I'm guessing you are used to getting your way…"

"Meaning?"

"I know of your past with Adrienne. I have seen how you look at her, still. I am guessing you are hoping to win her back by playing your sympathy card but you will lose there. She and I are very happy together."

"I am not playing any sympathy card!" said Gryphon, his voice getting deeper.

"Yeah, like your brother being in the hospital isn't the ultimate ace of hearts?"

"Are you seriously suggesting that I would use my brother being sick to further myself?" asked Gryphon angrily. He had never once been this insulted, which said a lot, given some of the things that had been said about him being a mad scientist over the years.

"I believe you are a shrewd enough business person to use whatever resources you have to further your goals."

"I have never used anything to further myself except my principles, Colonel Graham. I would not consider using even a perfect stranger to further myself."

The colonel only sniffed at that.

"I would appreciate it if you would take your leave of this building right now, Colonel Graham," said Gryphon, as he turned toward DJ, about to tell him to call security.

"I am with you that your brother is not sick with this virus," said the colonel, continuing to stab. "For all it helped cover the truth quite nicely."

"What truth might that be?"

"That he is nothing but a druggy. There is no helping him because he has fried his brain."

"My brother is not a drug addict. There were no narcotics found in his system."

"Because he puked them all up before you found him."

Gryphon wasn't one to anger easily but when he did it was justified. The man before him had just bounded over the line. "*Accuse my brother again*," he said. He started to bring his fisted hand up to punch the colonel if and when he did. This time it was DJ's hand on his arm, stopping him.

The man didn't say any more, feeling he had gotten his point across already.

None of the men moved when the door opened.

"DJ, can you verify these readings?" said Adrienne. Her eyes were on the clipboard in her arm, holding the top paper up, as she stepped into the room so she was surprised when she looked up to see Gryphon was there. Her heart skipped a beat, she felt her neck and cheeks getting flushed, a quivering in her belly and a smile coming to her lips as her mind replayed what they had done the night before as their eyes met. He had cleaned up, changed his clothes and shaved, which made her smile more. She watched him look away quickly. She wondered if he was mad at her for last night or... she guessed that he was confused by it, as was she.

She knew he liked to wake up beside her after they had nights like that while they were together, so waking up with her not there had probably bothered him. She had fully intended to stay with him; she had always like waking in his arms. She had awakened at five o'clock, as she usually did, he didn't typically get up much before six thirty. She had watched him sleeping for quite some time; happy she had helped him to be able to. When she caught her reflection in the mirror across from them she felt guilty and hypocritical. She had gotten up then and quickly left the room, knowing he would be waking up soon.

Part of her hoped he was there to discuss what last night meant for them but knew it was only to see what they had learned about his brother's condition and go to work. She saw the looks going between the three men, especially Gryphon and the colonel and DJ appeared to be holding Gryphon back and knew something was happening, and it was bad.

She walked over to them quickly and put a hand on her former and current lover's chests, hoping to get in between them, "What is going on here?"

"This..." Gryphon started, he didn't want to respond to the accusations of what the man said Sam was involved in and that he was trying to use his brother to try to win her back so instead he focused on the malicious accusation that his company had been involved in criminal activities. "The colonel is implying that GCI was involved in chemical weapons testing that went bad and it was this that has killed these people."

"The truth does hurt," said the colonel.

"We do not believe that, Gryphon," said Adrienne, looking pointedly at the colonel.

"I will show you hurt," spat Gryphon, taking a step closer to the man.

"Please, stop this, John. This will not help your brother, Gryphon," said Adrienne as she looked from one to the other.

Gryphon nodded. He took a step back.

"I can see why she left you," said the military man just under his breath, starting to turn away. "No fucking backbone at all. You needed a real man, didn't you?"

"John, please don't say anything more," said the woman.

"Why not?" he barked. "Look at him; even now he is wimping out."

"Some men don't need guns to make them feel like men," said DJ, rolling his eyes.

The colonel turned back then and started to take a swing at DJ.

Seeing this, Adrienne stepped forward and again put a hand on each man's chest. The colonel took her hand and pushed her back. Not expecting this, she was caught off guard. She stumbled into the desk behind her and took the corner of it in the thigh, which made her cry out. She had hit the desk hard enough to knock the stack of reference books off the corner of it and smash three brand new beakers.

DJ and Gryphon both stepped forward, both intending to punch the man out for laying a hand on the woman. Gryphon got there first. He took the man on the end of the chin.

The colonel fell back a step then he lunged forward and punched Gryphon in the stomach, which, given his asthma, made it even harder for him to breathe, the colonel hit him in the face then, cutting his eyebrow with the edge of his ring and blackening his left eye instantly.

Gryphon swung again himself; taking the larger man in the cheek and stomach himself this time.

Adrienne came forward again then, again getting between them. She pulled the colonel around. "Stop this, John!" she shouted at him. Reason returned to the Colonel as he saw the look on her face. "Let's go," he barked.

"She is not going anywhere with you, Asshole," said Gryphon. He was wheezing and holding his ribs, trying to catch his breath. He needed his medicine but he would not use it in front of this man.

"Go, John," said Adrienne pointedly. "GO! I will see you later."

DJ had called security in the middle of all this, so two men as big as the colonel, their hands on their tasers, were standing in the hallway now.

Gryphon was trying to speak between fighting for breaths, "Ge... the... man..."

"Get this man out of here," DJ finished for him. He followed the men out to make sure the colonel was tossed out completely.

Adrienne went to the sink, pulled a cloth from the cabinet over it, wet it and went back to Gryphon. She waited for him to take two hits of his medicine then stepped forward again, intent on cleaning the blood off his face.

"Back off, Adrienne," snapped the man.

The woman ignored him, knowing he was just as upset that he had been forced to come to fisticuffs as he was about the accusations made against his company. He had always prided himself on not reverting to violence and he had never taken well to his company's image being blemished. "Shush, Gryphon," she said as she took his face in her hand and looked at his nose and fast bruising eye.

He jumped and hissed as the cold cloth touched his heated forehead and the stinging pain of the fresh cut being touched.

"Easy," said the woman softly.

"How long have you and the colonel been together, Adrienne?" asked Gryphon gruffly. He was remembering that she had secretly been at the army hospital for several months before they had broken up, meaning she could have been with the colonel during that time.

"It doesn't matter, Gryphon," said the woman. She didn't want to speak about the man, whom she was quite upset with; especially not to the one currently before her.

"The hell it doesn't. *How long*?"

"About four months," she said quietly. She knew it would hurt him to hear it – it meant she had only waited two months after their break-up. The Colonel had been asking her out since he first saw her ten months before, four months before she had left Gryphon, but she had refused him.

"And you are still with him?"

Adrienne didn't answer this question. She turned his face a little so she could finish looking at his nose to make sure it hadn't been fractured by the larger man's fist.

Gryphon pulled his face out of her hand then and pushed the one holding the wet cloth away gently. "I am guessing that means last night was just for sympathy?"

"No!" she said quickly then she shook her head and said, "I don't know… I think it was something we both just… just needed."

"I didn't need that, Adrienne. I said things last night…"

"That was part of why I did that."

"If the next word out of your mouth is closure," said Gryphon, just under his breath. He hadn't wanted her to know how much her leaving him had hurt; didn't want her to know he was that weak. He pushed past her then and walked out of the room.

"It wasn't closure... I did it because I liked what you said." Adrienne said to the now empty room. She waited a split second then followed him.

DJ was still fuming as he walked back to his laboratory, even after having the pleasure of watching the idiot colonel being tossed out. He wished he'd gotten to hit the man a few times as well. He was very much looking forward to asking Gryphon how good it had felt; he knew the usually calm man would still be fuming as well. He also wanted to be sure he hadn't been injured himself in the fistfight.

He stepped around the last corner and saw his boss stomp out of the lab and walk fast toward the warehouse. Adrienne was right behind him. He followed as well.

# 27

# The Voice of Truth

"Son of a bitch, not now!" said Gryphon as he began to wheeze again. The colonel was right, he was a wimp. He couldn't even get into a fight without having an asthma attack anymore. He thrust the doors of the storeroom open so hard that they splintered around the top hinges and stormed into the middle of it, his hands still clenched in fists as his sides. He set his head back, ready to scream. He couldn't though because he couldn't get enough air into his lungs to do it, which only fueled his rage.

The cavernous room was deathly quiet and made the sound of his heavy and thick breathing and the echoes of it even more pronounced, and made him even angrier – feeling like it was mocking him. He whipped his breathing medicine from his pocket, shook it and pumped a hit of it down his throat, then another. He needed a third but he refused to take it, even knowing it would make it better. He threw the thing hard into the far corner of the room. He smiled sickly as he heard it clinking on the cement floor then jumped as he heard the door open behind him. He turned and swore under his breath when he saw it was Adrienne.

"John was out of line, Gryphon," said the woman. She knew he was still upset so she ignored the swearing.

"No... he was right *in line*, Adrienne..." he began to wheeze again. "He isn't as dumb as he looks... Have you come to give me... another sympathy bone," he finally managed to gasp, starting to unbutton his pants.

"*That* was out of line, Gryphon."

"*John* is... *fucking* right... Adrienne..." He was getting even angrier because he could not say more than a few words before he had to fight for air. "I am... such a fucking wimp... that you... had to fuck me... to get me back right..." he gasped. He had to force himself to pause so he wouldn't pass out. "You really are... a great doctor... to know just exactly... what a person needs... to get better... I applaud you... for how well... you do it." He was pressing on his chest, trying to force air to move down his shrinking bronchial tubes.

"I didn't make love to you last night for sympathy, Gryphon."

DJ was stepping through the door just as this was said.

Gryphon whipped around, to see who it was. "Yeah… *fucking great*… timing, DJ," he barked through the worsening wheezes. He was now bending over and looking very peaked.

The interruption was just the opportunity Adrienne had been waiting for. She quickly ran to the corner of the room where Gryphon had thrown his medicine. She knew he would have stopped her out of hurt pride.

DJ turned around then, realizing this was a conversation he really didn't want to be in on. He had intended to turn and quietly take his self away but he stumbled on a low box on the floor as he did. The biochemist cried out, "Shit!" loudly as he fell forward. He tried to catch himself but there was nothing but the phase shifting device before him to stop his fall. Gryphon had not had a chance to crate it back up for storage yet. He tried to catch it as he and it fell forward, not wanting to damage the quarter of a million dollar piece of technology, but it was too heavy.

It crashed loudly to the floor and kicked on.

"Shit!" DJ barked again, just under his breath.

The beam hit the dark corner of the room and a funny lightshow bounced back at him, which made him squint and throw his hands up to block his eyes. His eyes widened when he saw the boxes and metal racks before him were all gone and there was now an opening in the side of the building. He guessed he was seeing the sky. If it was then an ugly storm had moved in quickly because it was blood red. The man of science wasn't sure what exactly he was seeing next.

There were three human shaped things about his height but very thin on the other side of the opening. They had no apparent eyes but DJ got the impression they were looking at him. They didn't have any mouths or noses either, but there was two holes in about the place a nose would sit on their faces.

He stared at them with wonder for a moment then he jumped as he saw one of them reach through the opening. Its three fingered hand gripped the broken edge of the wall then it stepped through, followed closely by its two friends. DJ was frozen in place as he watched them move toward him, very slowly but far faster than he would have liked them to be. Their feet were pointed downward, like they were wearing ballet slippers, but their toes didn't touch the floor and their legs did not move. They were floating about three inches off the tiles and they weren't throwing any shadows in the overhead lamps.

He turned around to see if Gryphon and Adrienne were seeing the same thing. The latter was trying to get the former to take more of the medicine and the former had his head back and his eyes closed, taking slow and loud breaths. "Gryphon?" DJ asked slowly.

"Give him a minute," said Adrienne, not looking at him. Her hands were pushing the hair from Gryphon's forehead back. "Take slow and steady breathes."

"Um, Gryphon," said DJ more pointedly, ignoring her. He was backing himself past them now, pointing away from him.

Gryphon was still trying to get his breath back fully, his head still back and his eyes still closed, trying to swallow the tears he was fighting back, so he didn't see this.

Adrienne did. She wondered what was wrong with DJ. She didn't want to believe he would be crass enough to pick now to attempt a practical joke. She turned and looked where he was pointing and saw the three things coming toward them. It took a moment for it to fully register that she was really seeing what she was seeing. When it did, it came in a rush of panic making her jump and scream.

Gryphon looked down then and immediately wished he hadn't. It took a moment for him to realize he really was seeing the things before him as well. "Oh, God, no!" he said. He was instantly sorry for speaking. The things shifted their thin bodies from being aimed at DJ to being aimed at Gryphon then. The scientist was fixed in dread as he watched them raise their arms. He saw one of them was holding an urn-like vessel, like the ones he had seen in Callie's premonition. He wanted to tell the other two to run but he could not get the words to come to his mouth.

They all jumped when they heard the things' voices. They could only guess how this was being done since the things did not have any apparent mouths. *"Gryphon!"* was repeated over and over again, sometimes in only one voice, sometimes all three in unison sometimes one said slightly after the other, after the other, in a sick song sung in the round.

The man whose name was being said so terrifyingly was knocked for six. He felt like he was ten years old again and he suddenly couldn't breathe again.

"What are those things?" asked Adrienne.

"How do they know your name?" asked DJ.

Gryphon finally found his voice. "You... you see them?" he asked, swallowing hard, "You can hear them?" He realized Adrienne was standing in front of him, meaning they would reach her first. He pulled her to him then pushed her behind him, there was no way he would let them take her. He moved several feet to his right, to the middle of the room, set his legs and said, "You want me, I am right here."

He had no idea how they did their deed, other than the little bit he had seen in Callie's premonition, and he didn't by any means want to find out, but he couldn't risk

DJ or Adrienne's lives. He hoped he could keep them busy long enough for them to get away. Seeing them moving in his direction told Gryphon he now had their full attention. "Get out of here," he shouted to his best friend and ex-lover through clenched teeth.

"No," both said in unison.

DJ saw they were now moving toward Gryphon and acted without thinking. He moved around behind them, back to the phase shifting device, and saw it was still on, the beam of it still aimed at the corner. He had no idea whether it would make any difference or not but he didn't know what else to do. He shut the device off and watched the hole in the corner of the room kind of blink then it began to shrink. He breathed a sigh of relief when he saw the three forms were being pulled backward, toward that shrinking hole.

Gryphon and Adrienne watched this as well, shocked beyond words.

DJ turned to the other two once the things were gone and the wall in the corner of the room was back to normal, he was white as a ghost – as were they. "What... what the fuck were those things?"

"They come from the dark," said Gryphon, as his legs gave way. He fell back onto the crate behind him and grabbed at his chest, which was constricting painfully again.

Adrienne shook Gryphon's medicine and held it up to the man again.

He let her shoot it into his mouth and held his breath.

"Are those what you think is trying to hurt Sam?" asked the woman.

Gryphon was still holding his breath, letting the medicine soak into the fibers of his throat and lungs. Finally he breathed out and nodded. "They took them all."

"Them all who?" DJ asked then.

"They suck the souls out of people… they took all their souls."

"What?" asked Adrienne; she wanted to say that was crazy but then what was it she had just seen. "What do you mean?"

"Callie is a psychic. She saw the couple in the first news article, the Stubbs, getting taken… It was after the fact so it was too late to help them and she knew no one would believe her… She came to see me at my talk to tell me she had also gotten an image of my company logo. She had no idea how I was connected, just that I was. She showed me what she saw… Those things suck the life out of their victims, literally."

"You mean leaving them…"

"Leaving them like mummies."

"Are they what you saw inside the closet at your grandparent's house when you were ten?" asked DJ. He felt horrible now for all the things he had thought about his friend when he had finally told him the story. He was thirty-three years old and was scared shitless by what he had just seen, he could not imagine how he would have handled seeing them at ten years old.

"I didn't see them but I heard them…"

Adrienne fell against Gryphon's chest, shaking and fighting tears of her own. His arms went around her without giving it a thought that a moment ago they were shouting at each other.

# 28

# Phase Shifting 102

"You have got to be joshing me," said Colonel Graham as he stood by the doors of Gryphon's office.

Adrienne and DJ were sitting in chairs before the large desk and Gryphon was standing framed by the large windows that created the corner of his office with his arms crossed over his chest. John was staring from him to Adrienne to DJ and back. All three of them had the same look on their faces, telling him they didn't think they were, or, if they were, they were running the joke perfectly.

"I saw them, John. I did. I would never have believed it myself, but I did," said Adrienne, shivers ran up and down her spine and a wave of nausea made her stomach twist up painfully as she remembered it.

"There are a lot of drugs that cause hallucinations and have suggestive qualities. Drugs these men have access to, Adrienne. Think hard here, have they offered to get you coffee or a drink or anything you wouldn't normally have asked for?" said the colonel.

"I am not drugged," said the woman, getting very perturbed now.

DJ looked equally as upset and Gryphon looked ready to give him a repeat of their earlier confrontation for the new accusation.

"Then perhaps you're getting the virus yourself. You said that it may affect brain tissue and make you think you see…"

"I'm perfectly healthy, John. I was given all the current vaccines for all known viruses before I was accepted to the position at CMC and was quarantined for two weeks to be sure I didn't have anything incubating," said Adrienne.

"You said yourself this isn't responding to any known vaccines," said the man, still not believing them.

"The only way he is going to believe us is to show him," said DJ.

Gryphon had a feeling the man would still claim it was somehow a trick but he nodded. He was still more than a little sore with the man for what he had said earlier, maybe he could accidentally throw him in the things' paths and he could see firsthand what they were.

He wasn't the type to sacrifice a human life, even for science, and even if he was an asshole, though. "Fine," said Gryphon. He walked from his office, leaving his door open.

"Can we show you, John?" asked Adrienne, for all she was still very upset with him for what he had done earlier to Gryphon and DJ and the bruise she had on her upper thigh thanks to him, she didn't want him to do this unless he was certain he wanted to.

The colonel had a look on his face halfway between wanting to laugh at how ridiculous this all was and disbelief that they could truly show him anything like a monster. He shrugged, nodded and held his rifle tighter to him. "Anyone comes near me with any sort of syringe is going to get the end of this in their ass."

DJ gave the man a look to say he might find that not so easy an endeavor.

Adrienne was only shaking her head. She was wondering how she had ever thought she might have a future with the stiff man.

Gryphon was already in the warehouse, staring white faced at the spot of the building that had opened to the world of the hideous haunts and three of them had come out of, trying hard to fight the tightness building in his chest, when the others walked in. DJ was visibly nervous as he stepped into the room. John was shaking his head, knowing somehow he was about to be the butt of a joke. Adrienne was shaking slightly. She didn't want to see them again herself but she needed to in order to prove to herself that she had actually seen them as well.

She started quickly for Gryphon's side, wanting to be near him for comfort and safety. She remembered John was there; with reluctance, she stepped over to him instead.

John saw her hesitate, which made him shake his head harder.

Gryphon was oblivious to all this – he was still trying to come to terms with the fact that the things Adrienne and his therapist had been telling him for years were only manifests of his subconscious mind were real and were really killing people.

The owner of the building was standing beside the phase shifting device. He had no idea it could be used for this sort of application. Any other day, and in any other setting, he would have been fascinated by this discovery and would have wanted to learn more about it…

DJ stepped up to his best friend and said, "Let me do it." He jumped when Gryphon jumped. He put his hand on the man's arm to steady him and said, "For whatever reason, they seem to have focused on you. No point in giving them a chance to get you."

"I don't want you taken either," said Gryphon.

"Don't worry, I can run fast," said the younger man. "And I don't have the slightest desire to be a hero."

Gryphon wanted to say no, he didn't want to risk anyone else that he cared about but he knew his friend was right on both accounts. He nodded and stepped back to where Adrienne and John were standing then nodded again to his business partner.

DJ took a deep breath, held it a moment then blew it out slowly. He flipped the switch and took several steps back. He didn't want to be close to the opening but he didn't want to be too far from the unit so he could reach it and shut it off before the things could harm any of them if needed.

John's instincts were telling him to walk out of this room right now. He didn't even like to watch other people having practical jokes played on them. He wanted to be able to prove to the woman beside him that these two men were frauds though. He was getting un-comfortable with the looks she and Gryphon were giving each other. He watched DJ walk over to his rival, who was standing next to a unit that looked like a stupid movie prop. It looked like a laser used in many action flicks he had seen, to shoot at and down various crafts. He wanted to laugh but the tension in the air was too thick now. He watched the man nod to whatever the other doctor had said then step back and slowly walk over to where he and Adrienne were. He watched his eyes connect with hers and saw some sort of mental message go between the two. His attention was drawn away before he had a chance to comment on the look by a strange zipping sound, which had come from the direction of the unit.

The four looked at the wall opposite the end of the device, they watched the items on the shelves shifting slightly but nothing unusual happened.

John audibly breathed out then got his angry face on again as he growled, "You satisfied now?" He looked from the doctors to the woman and back. "I'm not sure how they convinced you to join in their shenanigans, Adrienne. I truly do not want to cause you any harm but you are fast forcing me to contact the governor and tell him you have been compromised."

"You do what you feel you must, John. I stand by what I saw," said Adrienne, stepping closer to Gryphon.

DJ looked over the unit as this exchange was going on. He turned it off then on and off again, wondering what had changed. As a scientist exact recreation of an experiment was crucial to prove the results. He scratched his head as he replayed the previous experience. "Duh! I had to reset it. I had knocked it off frequency when I knocked it over." He turned the small black knob on the side of the unit back to the space between twenty eight and twenty nine megahertz then flicked the switch again. This time the opening did reappear though none of the creatures were there immediately. The other three were busy arguing so none of them had seen this.

"I am going to rake you and this joke of a company over the coals until I find out what you did to hurt these people, Mr. Blake. I know this is something your company did."

"Gryphon," said DJ behind the colonel.

"You will find nothing criminal done here, Colonel Graham," spat Gryphon.

"This is not anything Gryphon or his company has done," said the woman who was positioning herself between the men again.

"We shall see. I can have you so deep in shit and red tape that either way this think tank of yours will be flushed down the tank."

"Gryphon!" DJ said more adamantly.

"You do what you think you can to me," said Gryphon, balling his fists up.

"*Gryphon.*"

The hairs on the back of Gryphon's neck instantly stood up, his stomach twisted into a knot and all the color drained from his face as he turned his head.

"Gryphon," Adrienne said then, turning toward the things that had said this, touching his arm.

Gryphon looked to the side and breathed out a sigh – in relief as well as hopelessness. He had still hoped somehow they weren't real. There were only two of them this time but that made them no less eerie.

Colonel Graham turned then too, with a smirk on his face. He was thinking they were now lowering the joke boom on him. He jumped when he saw the things floating toward them then laughed and said, "Great Halloween costumes."

"Those are not costumes," said DJ as he started toward the unit, not wanting to take the chance that he might not be able to send them back if they got too far into the room.

The doors beside the things opened then. One of DJ's staff, Roland, stepped in with a bankers box in his hands. He had been emptying a file cabinet of old projects that were now completed and were being moved to storage.

He stopped when he saw the things moving before him. His eyes took in his boss, his boss's boss and the two that had come with equipment from the army hospital in the room. "Dr. Wright?" he asked, more than a little confused.

DJ and Gryphon both shouted for the man to get out of the things' paths but it was too late.

They turned to face Roland, who had dropped the box but seemed to be frozen in place. One of them raised one of its short arms and a beam of light left the end of it and connected with the center of the man's forehead. His eyes rolled back in his head and his mouth opened as if he was going to scream but nothing came out except a line of drool. His body slumped, falling over the box.

"What is this?" John barked. He started toward the two things he still thought were only men in costumes. "I will get you for harming this man as well."

"Don't go near them, Colonel Graham," shouted Gryphon.

The four in the room were beyond horrified as they watched the two beings step to either side of the twenty something man, who had never been sick a day in his life. One of them had an urn-like vessel before it now. The things raised their arms and began to chant in their odd language then Roland's body began to shrink up as if he was turning into a raisin.

"Wha... How... How did you do that?" demanded John. He stopped halfway between the scientists and doctor, the now drained man and the beings. He turned back then and froze.

The one holding the vessel removed the lid and a bright sparkling cloud formed around the body of the drained man then it rose off the floor slightly as if it was being physically pulled out of him. It wisped in the air for a bit then was drawn into the urn.

*"You will add to our proviso."*

John flipped the safety off on his rifle, aimed it at the beings and shouted as he opened fire on them. The bullets and the sound of the discharge ripped through the building. They went through the beings as if they weren't really there and lodged themselves into the boxes, shelves and wall behind them. "What the hell?"

"Shut the unit off, DJ," shouted Gryphon and Adrienne at the same time.

DJ came out of the stunned trance then and jumped for the device just as the dark things turned to him, the next closest human to them, and moved in his direction. He flicked the PSD off and held his breath as the hole into the things' world began to shrink back as it had before. He was smiling as he turned to look at the beings, waiting for them to disappear as well. It faded when he saw they hadn't. "Fuck!" he shouted. The things were still there and were still moving toward him even after shutting the unit off.

Gryphon ran to the doors. He jumped over the now withered body of his employee and slammed into the wall beside it. He flipped all the switches up, flooding the room with bright light from the halogen fixtures overhead.

The things raised their arms as if trying to block their faces to that bright light then they kind of just winked out.

"What the hell were those things," asked John as he watched Adrienne meeting Gryphon by the body of the man he had witnessed be murdered just moments before. He watched her bend over and put her hand to the man's throat, shake her head to Gryphon then look back at him and DJ.

"He's dead," she said.

"*What the hell were those things*," John repeated, anger and fear making his voice deeper than usual.

"We don't know what they are, Colonel," said Gryphon. He pulled his cell phone out of the holder on his belt, intending to call security to get the body. "Did Roland have anyone he wanted called in case of an emergency?" he asked DJ.

"Yeah… um, I think his mother is listed as his emergency contact."

"Can you see to that for me?"

DJ was still a little stunned; it was one thing to hear Gryphon tell him this was what the things did, it was entirely another to see the things actually drain a victim. He stumbled over the man that had worked under him for over two years and left the room.

Gryphon turned to Adrienne, "Think it's fair to say you can quit searching for a vaccine."

# 29

# A.S.P.

"Thomas just buzzed me to say the governor has arrived," said the animated voice of Gryphon's secretary through his intercom.

Gryphon pushed the answer button, "Tell Mr. Hill to send him up to my office, Sandra." He looked at the others in the room. DJ was shaking his head with an odd smile on his own face; Adrienne had an unusual look on hers, not quite jealousy more uncertainty; and the colonel had a disgusted look on his, but then his always looked that way.

DJ started to make a nasty comment about how it would do his secretary a world of good if the man would take her under his proverbial wing and show her the ways of the adult world but thought better of it, since the man's ex-lover was sitting beside him, looking as if she was wondered if Gryphon hadn't already and it really wasn't the right venue for such – given who else was in the room. He shook his head quickly and scrunched his eyes and nose when he noticed Adrienne was looked at him, letting her know nothing had happened between Gryphon and his secretary.

There was a knock on the door seconds later.

"Enter," said Gryphon strongly.

Sandra stepped halfway through the door and said, "They're at the end of the hall, Dr. Blake."

"Show them in directly, please, Sandra."

"Yes, sir."

It was only a few more moments before the door opened again, this time with Sandra as well as Governor Price, several secret service men, Dr. Updike, an unknown man in a suit and two of DJ's lab techs, Julia and Derek.

"Would you like me to have coffee or tea brought in, Dr. Blake?"

Gryphon did a quick sweep of the room then said, "No thanks, Sandra. Please hold all my calls for the next hour as well."

"Yes, sir."

As soon as the door closed the governor spoke, "Why is it again that you have called this meeting, and at this location instead of on the base?"

"I assure you this facility is just as secure as any of your military installations, Governor Price. I think you will find most of the technology you rely on for security was patented here, in fact," said Gryphon.

The governor looked uncertain still but finally nodded and took one of the chairs that had been brought in to accommodate the added guests.

Neither Gryphon nor DJ was entirely happy to see Dr. Updike among them. Neither had particularly liked him from the meeting at Biscayne General. Both were looking a bit odd and questioningly at the new man, recognizing him as the prominent astrobiologist, Richard Kearns. Both had read the man's theses and several articles on him in the science journals but neither had ever met the man before.

Seeing them looking at him, Dr. Kearns, who had also read their theses' and articles in various science publications before and had wanted to meet them as well, stepped forward and held his hand out. "Dr. Blake, Dr. Wright, it is a pleasure to finally meet you both. I am a fan of your... of some of your work."

Gryphon shook his hand but didn't speak.

DJ shook his hand too and said, "Same to you."

"I asked Dr. Kearns to join us... as he is an expert on... unusual terrain and conditions," said Adrienne.

Obviously getting impatient, Governor Price then said, "Tell me why you've asked him and the rest of us here, Dr. Ivekio?"

"We have discovered… an aperture… a doorway, to another world… We aren't sure if it is another dimension or another planet or… another reality…" Adrienne realized herself how crazy she sounded but it was fact. "There are… beings in this other place… that we believe are crossing over into our world and… they are the cause of the deaths."

"Are we back to this being some sort of creature doing this?" asked Dr. Updike, looking at the colonel, knowing him as a man that would not fall prey to allegory.

"I didn't want to believe they were right in this either, Dr. Updike. I am still not certain that it is legit but I did see something that I could not explain… I cannot see how they could've faked what I witnessed."

"So, why is it we are here," asked Governor Price.

"We want to see if it is possible for a human to cross into this other place, to study it and determine how and why these things are doing this," said Adrianne.

Gryphon cut over her then, "We want to see if we can find a way to stop them and seal off their method of entrance to our world."

"And how exactly do you propose to do this?"

"Send someone across," said the colonel, pushing his chest out. He was the most obvious candidate for this mission, and he was ready and eager to prove that – feeling more than a little inadequate given every person in the room was far more educated than he was.

"And you want me to tell you if this other place can sustain human beings?" asked Dr. Kearns.

"Yes."

"I would suggest we send over an unmanned probe first," said the man.

"Already had that figured," said Gryphon.

"A.S.P?" asked DJ excitedly.

"A.S.P," said Gryphon smiling. He knew his friend had been anxious to play with the oversized remote control toy but he had refused to let him, not wanting the expensive equipment destroyed so the man could peak in windows or dive bomb unsuspecting pedestrians.

"ASP?" asked the colonel.

"Arial surveillance plane," said Gryphon.

He produced a poster board with an artist rendering and full schematics for an unmanned flying device that looked well-suited to military intelligence gathering. This was the prototype of a project for that very purpose that GCI had received government grants to design and had a lucrative contract to fulfill the orders of. The design had been modified since, the rights to the newer designs were now held by the Department of

Defense but the obsolete design was still GCI's to use as needed.

"It is equipped with regular and infrared cameras, microphones, atmospheric, gravity and radiation sensors and sample collectors," said Gryphon. He could see the colonel, governor and astrobiologist were all trying hard not to be impressed.

"Will it work?" asked the governor.

Dr. Kearns stood, walked up to the drawings and looked them over carefully then he turned to the governor and said, "This seems to be adequate."

"Does this ASP thing need to be built?" asked the governor.

"Already waiting in the warehouse," said DJ.

"When do we do this test?" asked the governor.

"As soon as we get the okay from you to proceed, Governor Price. There is no way to tell how many of the things there are, how many are able to cross to our world or how many more people might succumb to them if we wait too long," said Gryphon.

"You have it."

"I suggest we head down and get this party started then," said DJ.

# 30

# Foreign Landscape

The group of scientists, the doctors, politician, security men and the soldier stepped from the office and followed DJ toward the warehouse where they had the ASP set up and where they intended to again open the rift to the other realm.

Sandra sat up as they walked past her. She looked at each of them then at her boss, expectantly.

"I will have my cell phone on me, if my parents, Callie Summers or anyone from the hospital calls regarding Sam, otherwise DJ and I are unavailable, Sandra."

"Yes, sir," said the woman, settling back in her seat. She was staring holes in the back of the beautiful woman walking beside Gryphon, wishing it were her.

The attendees all moved into the back of the open area of the warehouse floor, across from what looked a bit like a miniature rocket launcher with a miniature plane. It was set at a forty five degree angle, aimed at the corner of the chamber. Also aimed at the corner of the room was a device that looked like a prop laser out of any of a dozen science fiction movies and TV shows. A desk with what looked like a video game console on steroids with a keyboard, joystick, five monitors, several printers and various gages was set to the side.

The governor, secret service men and medical doctors all looked uncertainly at these devices then at the others; half expecting to see the cameras of a movie being shot around them or the people before them to suddenly yell, "April fools!"

DJ stepped up to the phase shifting device and nodded to Gryphon as he, Adrienne, the colonel and Dr. Kearns stepped to the front of the group.

"What do we do if the creatures come out as well?" asked John, remembering the AK47 on his shoulder had no effect on them. He couldn't believe how easily and seriously he had asked that, still not wanting to believe this was truly happening.

"They disappeared as soon as you turned the lights on full," said DJ, looking at his best friend.

Gryphon nodded and walked to the wall with the light switches. He flipped them all on. The room that had been half hidden in shadows was now flooded with warm light in every corner. Bright enough to make more than one in the room squint until their eyes had adjusted.

"This is for?" asked the governor, shielding his eyes with his hand.

"The things seem unable to exist in the light," said Gryphon, ignoring the snorts and looks of disbelief before him then. The governor actually more only looked confused by this response.

"Ready?" asked DJ as he watched Gryphon walk back to Adrienne and the colonel.

Gryphon looked at the people behind him and knew there was no way that they could be. They had no idea what they were about to see. He looked at Adrienne and John; both of them nodded so he nodded to DJ.

"I accidentally knocked the unit off its base, which knocked it off frequency and flipped it on," said the man as he checked to make sure the dial was still set to the frequency that had opened the rift the last two times then turned it on. "And this happened."

The beam hit the corner and a small round opening appeared. It began to expand out to about a five foot circle and, as before, showed a strange landscape of huge black rock formations and a blood red sky.

"My God," said more than one of the people in the room, including the governor.

The astrobiologist stepped forward; completely flabbergasted, more than a little intrigued and excited. He had studied many of Earth's unusual and inhospitable places, trying to find if any sort of life was sustainable in them. He had been thoroughly surprised and pleased by the results. He had also conducted several studies of other planets, using images and sensor readings from the surveillance satellites as they skimmed their atmospheres, offering glimpses of what kinds of conditions each might have and what would need to be present to allow life as they knew it to thrive. He had wished there was a way to prove his theories but had thought there was no way he would ever be able to visit any world other than their own. It seemed he was looking at one now. It didn't look like anywhere on Earth he had ever seen, but if it wasn't on their planet, where was it?

"Don't get too close, Dr. Kearns," said Gryphon.

"I do not need to be babysat, Dr. Blake," said the man, looking back at the assembled men and woman behind him.

"What in the hell is that?" asked the governor suddenly, pointing at the opening.

"Get back, Dr. Kearns," Gryphon, Adrienne and DJ said at the same time.

Strange whispering sounds were coming from the opening, sounding like more than one voice talking over each other in a language only four of them had ever heard before.

Richard, hearing these voices now, turned back to the opening and froze stiff. There were three things in front of him, looking at him through that opening. At least he thought they were looking at him. He couldn't say for sure because they had no visible eyes. He saw them start forward, as if about to step through, then back away as if frightened to.

He jumped when he felt something touch and squeeze his shoulder then felt himself being pulled backwards. He looked over his shoulder and saw it was only Colonel Graham. "What… what are those things?"

The colonel only shrugged and shook his head.

"Why aren't they coming through the opening?" asked Richard.

"The lights," said Gryphon as he fought to keep his lungs from closing off. "They don't seem to be able to exist in the light."

As if to test this theory the colonel and security men all turned on their flashlights and aimed them at the things in the opening. They let out what might have been a scream of pain, or rage, and backed away.

"Before they learn a way to exist in the light let us get this underway," said the governor. He had moved himself behind his security men, who had their hand-guns in their hands and were aiming at that opening.

Gryphon said, "I agree. Launch the unit, DJ."

DJ nodded and moved to the control console.

The youngest scientist put the headset on then told them all to stay back. He waited for the colonel and astrobiologist to move back before hitting the ignition. The jet engine on the aft end of the plane fired up and blazed hotly. He let it burn until it turned bluish white then punched the button to release the clamps holding the A.S.P. to the launch pad and the vehicle shot forward. There was a brief flash as it passed from the warehouse through the rift opening then it was soaring over the unworldly landscape. DJ motioned for Gryphon to shut off the PSD unit then.

The governor, doctors, scientists and the colonel all stepped over to the console – all eager to see what exactly this other place was. DJ was operating the controls of the unit so he had to keep his eyes on the monitor showing the landscape through the camera and the radar screen. Gryphon, Adrienne and John were watching the monitors, Dr. Kearns and Dr. Updike were watching the sensor readouts.

The cameras showed a landscape of rugged terrain: huge towers of rocks, long mountain ranges and odd cloud formations. They saw no signs of water, foliage or civilizations – at least not as we know it – and all they heard was white noise.

"Are the speakers working?" groused the colonel.

"They worked when we tested it this morning," was DJ's snide response. He turned the volume up but still all they heard was static.

"Shouldn't there be engine noises?" asked Dr. Updike.

"It is intended to be unheard, Dr. Updike. Kind of hard to conduct recon missions if it announces its arrival," said Gryphon, with as much bitterness as DJ had answered the colonel. "Can you bring it closer to the surface?" asked Gryphon, pressing on his chest with a grimace.

DJ nodded and sniggered as he said, "I told my mother the hours in the arcade would pay off," as he moved the joystick forward to send the unit down.

Gryphon and Adrienne were the only ones that smiled to this.

"There, what's that?" asked Adrienne as what looked like a lake came into view.

DJ nodded and moved the camera over the feature then set the unit to hover. He typed new instructions into the keyboard then moved back to the joystick that was now operating a small arm. It extended out from the body of the vehicle. It had a test strip on the end of it, which it slowly lowered to the surface. They all jumped as they heard a very loud slurping sound when the strip broke the surface.

"The speakers are working just fine," said DJ. He turned the volume back down a touch.

It was a liquid substance but it was thick and dark.

"Definitely not water," said Gryphon.

They all looked to the astrobiologist then.

Richard looked at the sensor readings and said, "It's almost pure methane."

"Don't think I will be drinking any of that," joked DJ. "Where to now?"

"See if you can make it over the mountains. There has to be some place that those things live in, some form of structure or cave maybe?" said the colonel.

DJ nodded then typed the directions into the keyboard. The unit began to climb again.

"It's all so barren," said Adrienne plainly.

That it was. There was mile after mile of the same kind of landscape, the change in shape and color of the rock the only difference.

DJ was about to turn the unit when both he and Gryphon said, "Whoa." The former swung the joy-stick back to the previous place. The latter said, "What was that?"

The ASP had been moving over what looked like just another rock formation from the air; several tall, thin spires, set close together. As the unit moved past it they saw something that wasn't natural, or at least wouldn't have been natural on Earth. The formations came into view again. They were definitely not natural; openings were cut into them at far too even of intervals.

"Can you get any closer?" asked Gryphon.

The other doctors and the governor moved over to see what they had found.

DJ typed the command to set it to hover and zoomed in on the closest spire. He was just getting the lens to focus in when a loud screaming sound came from the speakers, making them all jump and slap their hands over their ears.

DJ reached up quickly and turned the knob for volume down a little further then looked back at the monitor and said, "Shit!" The image was spinning, now, meaning so too was the plane. He was typing frantically trying to get the unit back under control. It did stop but it was nothing DJ had done to make it.

One of the things was in the center of the screen. They watched a bright beam of light leave the center of the thing's forehead then hit the camera lens. There was a loud squeal, like microphone feedback, the monitor went to snow then went black.

"Did we lose it?" asked Gryphon.

DJ didn't answer, except to repeat the last thing he had said over and over again. He was still typing at a feverish pace.

"What happened?" asked the colonel.

They all jumped when a loud explosion came from the speaker.

DJ jumped back and let out one final expletive then shook his head and said, "Yes, we lost it."

# 31

# Sustainable To Life

"Were we able to get enough data before it went dark?" asked the governor as he took one of the chairs before mahogany desk and took the glass of whiskey one of his service men had poured him.

They had returned to Gryphon's office, which was more comfortable and farther away from the device that opened a portal to another world.

"Yes," said Dr. Kearns.

"Can a human survive in those conditions?" asked Adrienne.

"The atmospheric sensors showed infrared and ultraviolet levels at very low, there is no sunlight to speak of. The percentage of oxygen is one point three bars, a normal level is one bar, there are higher concentrations of helium, sulfur, methane and carbon dioxide, which is not surprising, since there doesn't appear to be any kind of vegetation to consume the latter and produce oxygen. The gases are unpleasant but not toxic. Radiation levels are elevated but not high enough to hinder a human, as long as they limit their exposure. The temperature is high, averaging a hundred five degrees, with little variation, and it is extremely dry. It is an unpleasant environment to say the least…"

"So, can a human survive?" asked the colonel.

"Technically, yes, but I wouldn't recommend anyone go across," said Richard, looking pointedly at Gryphon.

"How long, Dr. Kearns?" asked Adrienne.

"Maybe five or six hours," then he repeated, more pointedly, "but I wouldn't recommend it," looking at the governor this time.

"I suggest we send another, or several other, ASPs, equipped with weapons, to destroy the structures we saw," said the Colonel.

"Yeah, sure, cause that won't piss 'em off much," said DJ.

"Each one of those units costs two million dollars, Colonel Graham," said Gryphon. "I am not sure about our state budget but I am pretty sure it doesn't have enough to front another one, let alone several."

"Don't you have more of them?" asked John.

"I cannot afford to send another over either."

"What is it you are suggesting then?" asked the governor.

John, wanting to steal the scientist's thunder and look the braver man, said quickly, "I am suggesting we send a troop, under my command, over."

"There is no way to know what effects long term exposure to that climate could have," said Adrienne.

"There is no way for us to stop those things if we don't send troops over there," snapped Colonel Graham.

"Is there a way for a human to cross through that opening?" the governor asked then.

All eyes turned to Gryphon and DJ.

"The same way the ASP went through," said Gryphon as if that should have been obvious.

"It was hundreds of miles over any solid surface when it went through, Gryphon. How can we be certain anyone that crosses over won't end up in midair, falling to their doom?" asked Adrienne. She couldn't believe the always totally rational man would even be considering this absurd action.

"If they have jetpacks on…" started the colonel.

"You would be willing to risk yourself and your men that way?" asked DJ.

The colonel looked like he wasn't so sure of that.

Gryphon shook his head and said, "There is no need for jetpacks."

"You want us to fall to our doom?" asked the colonel.

"We would walk in on foot." They all looked at him like he was crazy, including DJ. "It is just a matter of finding a place that opens to a solid surface," said Gryphon as if this explained it all. Everyone looked confused by this answer, except DJ this time. "The phase shifting device will open a rift to their world from anywhere we turn it on to, not just the corner of the warehouse. It's the frequency the device is set to that is making the connection. We only need to find a place where the opening is on solid ground on their side of it," said Gryphon.

The simplicity of this had never occurred to any of the others, except DJ, all with so much education between them – at that moment the others all felt very stupid.

"We'll begin to test different locations first thing in the morning," said Gryphon.

"I have a troop ready for as soon as that happens."

"No one is going through that rift until I am certain it will not cause lasting harm," said Adrienne.

"How do you test that?" asked the governor.

"We can send a dummy rigged with life sensors over; it should show definitively whether the conditions are harmful to a human," said DJ.

"How soon could we schedule this?"

"I can have a unit ready within a few hours."

"I will not approve anyone crossing over unless they're in peak physical condition. There may be need to climb over the terrain. The low quality of air, being so hot and dry, could affect a person's respiratory system, meaning they'd have trouble with overexertion," said Adrienne.

"As I said, I have a troop, that are in peak physical condition, ready as soon as word is given," said John.

"I am the only one going through the rift," said Gryphon plainly, as if there was no room for discussion.

"You can't go, Gryphon," said Adrienne, her voice teetered between fear and worry. She didn't want to embarrass him before the men so she didn't elaborate.

"The PSD is mine, as is all the other resources of this company. No one else is going to use them," said Gryphon. "I will not allow anyone else to be put at risk."

"You can't go alone, Gryphon," said DJ suddenly. Even though he was essentially the one to discover the rift – though purely by accident – he still hadn't fully accepted what they had seen as real. Hearing his best friend saying he was going to go into the place they had just seen alone was far too painful a slap of reality.

"I will not allow anyone else to be at risk," said Gryphon again, more pointedly.

"It is getting late. We will hold this discussion until tomorrow evening," said Governor Price. "After we are sure this can even be done."

"Good idea," said Gryphon.

DJ, John and Adrienne didn't move with the others as Gryphon showed them to the door and wished them all a good evening. He turned back to them and had to physically and mentally force himself not to order the colonel out of his office.

"You are not trained for this kind of recon mission," spat the colonel.

"And you are?" asked Gryphon.

"I'm trained to be deployed in a moment's notice anywhere our forces are needed, Dr. Blake."

"On *this* planet," said Gryphon.

"Neither of you is going," said Adrienne then.

"I'm not arguing, Adrienne, I'm going."

"Gryphon…" started Adrienne and DJ in unison.

"As the governor just said, it's getting late." Gryphon stepped to the door and opened it, looking pointedly at the colonel.

Getting the hint, John looked at Adrienne and said, "Are you coming?"

The woman looked torn. She finally shook her head and said, "I will see you tomorrow, John."

The colonel didn't look pleased but wasn't going to start anything with her ex-lover and his friend in the room. He sniffed and stomped through the door.

"You too, DJ and Adrienne," said Gryphon.

DJ looked at him worriedly.

"I am right behind you," said the man.

"See you in the morning," said DJ, his eyes shifted from his best friend to the doctor and back. He guessed she wasn't going to give in quite so easily. For all a part of him wanted to stay and be included in the conversation he was certain was to follow him leaving, he knew it was none of his business.

Gryphon left the door open, knowing Adrienne wasn't going to leave quite so easily. Part of him was warmed by her fighting him so hard on this; another part was annoyed by it. He started to walk around the room, collecting the mugs and glasses left by the people that had been in the meeting.

"Gryphon," said Adrienne, watching him act as if nothing unusual was happening.

"You will not talk me out of it, Adrienne. Those things have some sort of connection to me – not DJ, not the colonel, not a perfect stranger – you heard them, they were calling *my* name. Callie said I am the key, that they and I are connected in some way."

"Do you realize how you sound right now?"

"I am not crazy," said the man.

"Is being the hero that important to you?"

Gryphon looked at her sternly after that remark.

"I didn't mean it that way," said Adrienne in earnest. "I know how often you have put yourself in harm's way to test one of your theories because you didn't think it right to ask anyone else to do it and how often you came home with the burns and bruises to show for it. This time it will not be just burns and bruises."

"I can't allow those things to take my brother... What if they decide DJ is there next victim or my parents or... you..." The man's voice hitched at that.

"I don't need to remind you that you suffer from acute asthma, Gryphon. The conditions over there may damage your lungs beyond repair."

"The conditions over there will give a person asthma, Adrienne," said Gryphon as he set the last cup into the sink of his bar.

"What do you mean?"

"How many children do you know of that have gone from being healthy ten year olds to having the lungs of a cancer victim overnight?"

"You think you were exposed to their atmosphere when you were in the closet at your grandparents' house?" asked the doctor, unable to hide how absurd she thought this was.

"Yes, I think I have a piece of their world in my soul, how's that for crazy for you?" he started past her then but her hand on his arm stopped him.

"Gryphon… I don't want you to be hurt… can't you get that?"

"I don't want anyone to be, can't you get that?"

"I…" said Adrienne.

Gryphon wanted badly to take her in his arms and kiss her but he knew where it would lead. He didn't want another round of sympathy sex. "It really is getting late, Adrienne. Can we hold off on this until morning?"

She knew once he had decided on a course there was little she could do. Reluctantly, she nodded and started for the door. She stopped about halfway to it and said, "Shoot! I rode over with John."

"I can give you a ride to your place."

"I… I don't want to go to my place."

Gryphon looked funny at the woman then; he had never known her to be so vague.

"I…" Adrienne wasn't sure how to say what she was about to say other than to just come out and say it. "I moved in with John a few weeks ago."

"I see," said Gryphon. A part of him wanted to ask her again why she had slept with him just two nights before if she was in a committed relationship with the colonel.

"I… I did it more for the convenience, Gryphon."

"Yeah? Is it?" he asked, thick with sarcasm.

"I really don't want to be around him right now," said Adrienne. She took a deep breath as she said the next, unsure how he would take it, "Would you mind if I stayed at your place, in one of your other bedrooms?"

Gryphon's pride was screaming for him to say no, that it could only lead to trouble; his mind was saying it would bring more heartache but his heart was telling him to say yes. "No, I don't mind," he said as he motioned her to walk out of the office with him.

# 32

# So Familiar

"I only have my bike," said Gryphon as he and Adrienne walked through the parking garage. Normally he would have the valet bring it to the front door for him but the man had gone home two hours before.

"I haven't ridden on a motorcycle since..." Adrienne didn't want to finish.

Gryphon only nodded; the photos of the day still as fresh in his mind as the memories. He passed her his helmet and offered her a hand getting on then pulled on his gloves and climbed on the front.

Adrienne started to wrap her arms around him then forced herself to place her hands on his sides only.

Gryphon was acutely aware of those hands as he revved the engine of the Dyno Super Glide and moved them out of the building. He rarely rode without a helmet, partly because of how tangled his hair got afterward, but he had to admit he could see why the purists only rode that way. The feeling of freedom, the wind whipping past his ears, mixed with the sound of the engine, was mesmerizing. All made even more enjoyable by the feeling of the woman's body pressing against his back as he increased the speed a little.

Gryphon slowed them down as he reached the gates and pulled up to the security panel set into the stone column beside them. He knew there was no one in the house at this hour so he didn't bother to hit the call button; instead he punched in the code to open them. He stopped the bike beside the front doors, helped Adrienne off and handed her the keys then continued down the driveway to the garage, entering himself through the doors off the back of the kitchen.

Adrienne stepped through the front door and smiled. It all looked just as it had the day she left it. She wasn't surprised; she knew the man liked his routine. She looked into the parlor and through it to the arboretum, which had several plants in full bloom and could see beyond that to the pool. She would have loved to take a swim but wasn't sure she dared impose on the man more than her being there would be. She wondered if coming here had been a mistake. What was she hoping for? Why had he agreed so quickly? What was he hoping for?

She slowly walked along the hall and peered into the kitchen, she knew the door to the garage opened to that room so she wasn't surprised to find the man standing by the refrigerator. She saw the tie he had been wearing on the counter beside him, that he had untucked his shirt and had rolled his sleeves up to his elbows. When he turned to face her she saw that he had about half the buttons of the shirt undone, showing most of his chest, as well. The wind tousled hair on his head and the way the moonlight was reflecting through the skylight over their head made him look like one of the men drawn on the cover of a steamy romance novel – it took her a second to catch her breath.

"I don't have much ready-prepared in the fridge right now but I can whip up something or we can order in if you're hungry," said Gryphon, having seen the woman enter the room in the reflection of the stainless steel door.

"Actually, I've been having a craving for Chinese lately," she said, surprised at how suddenly comfortable she felt. She walked over and sat down on one of the stools at the counter behind the man.

He passed her the portable phone and a menu for the local takeout place. "You still aren't much for beer, are you?" he asked as he started to pop the cap off the bottle he was holding.

"No," said the woman. She was about to say a soda would be fine when he set the beer down, leaned down and pulled a bottle of merlot from the cooler before him then went to the drawer to find a corkscrew.

"Yes, sir, I would like to place an order to be delivered…" started Adrienne. She watched the muscles of the man before her working, showing clearly through the thin shirt, as he twisted the screw end into the cork in the top of the bottle then pulled the thing loose. Her eyes stayed on him as he turned and took two wine glasses down from the rack over his head. She felt a flutter in her stomach – that wasn't anything to do with being hungry.

Gryphon could feel her eyes on him, which was warming his blood. He poured a small bit of the wine into one of the glasses, swirled it around and passed it to her to taste and approve. "Yes, we would like a number one, number three and number five, and make number five Yu Hsiang style," she said as she took the glass. "85 Helsing Ave, 555-4581. Have the man buzz the house to be let in. Thank you."

Gryphon was leaning on the counter now, just watching her.

Adrienne set the phone down and drank the small sip in the glass. It was smooth, rich tasting and didn't leave an unpleasant taste in the back of her throat. "This will do just fine," she said smiling as she passed the glass to him for more.

He poured them each a decent portion then took a sip of his own. He usually only drank wine when he had company but he did like the taste of it, especially of this one. "Did you want to take a shower or a swim before the food arrives?"

Adrienne got stiff then. "Gryphon… I…"

He heard the change in her voice and saw the change in her body language and followed suit. "I'm only trying to be cordial to my guest, Adrienne," he said just as stiffly, turning away from her. He wasn't really sure what he was actually trying to be.

"I shouldn't have asked you to bring me here, it sent mixed signals…"

Gryphon didn't respond to that, he only took the bottle of wine and the glass and started out of the room.

She looked up at the skylight and shook her head then took her glass and followed.

Adrienne found Gryphon in the sitting room, one foot on the coffee table before him the other bent up on the cushion beside him, in the corner of the couch. One hand was holding his tangled hair back – it was a position she remembered he got in whenever he was frustrated. She sat down opposite him and said, "I'm sending mixed signals because I'm mixed up right now."

Gryphon only nodded to that.

"The other night wasn't just for sympathy, Gryph, and it wasn't planned. I just... Being near you again awakened feelings I thought I was over." She was looking at the top of the wine glass, not wanting to see how hurt or happy that would make him.

Gryphon wasn't particularly hurt or happy to hear it, more just numb.

"I am not in love with John and I truly don't think I ever will be, but... he makes me feel safe... He doesn't expect more from me."

"And I did?" asked Gryphon.

"We both did, but not the same things."

"Do you know why I bought this house?"

"Because it spoke to you," said the woman, taking a drink of her wine.

"Because it gave me a glimpse of what the future might hold for me," said the man.

Adrienne looked at him strangely, uncertain of the meaning of the statement.

"I have no need for six bedrooms by myself and I do not have guests over enough to need them," said the man, hoping he wouldn't have to say more than that.

Adrienne thought she was getting his meaning but she wanted to hear him say it to be certain. Her heart was beating faster as she looked at him quizzically.

"You're going to make me say it, aren't you?" he said just under his breath. He closed his eyes and said aloud, "I was hoping to have a family in it, Adrienne."

Adrienne's throat constricted, her heart skipped a beat and her stomach fluttered as he said the next.

"Hoping to have a family with you."

"I…"

A loud buzz from the gate made them both jump, even though they had been expecting it. Gryphon stood and walked to the door. He had two bags of food in his hands when he stepped back into the room.

"Would you prefer I call a cab?" asked the woman.

"There is way too much food for me to eat alone and I cannot stand reheated Chinese," said the man as he passed her a set of chopsticks and began to remove the various containers from the bags.

They spent the next two hours talking about the things that had changed in their lives, getting to know each other again, then they started up the stairs, intent on getting a least a few hours of sleep – in separate bedrooms.

# 33

# Cheating on a Test

Gryphon knocked twice on the office door and waited for the man inside to say, "Enter," before he stepped in.

DJ was sitting at his desk, the end of his pen clasped between his teeth and a medical chart before him that he was flipping through the pages of. He was more skimming than reading. He was hoping to see something he might have missed the first dozen times.

"Interesting reading?" asked Gryphon.

The biochemist looked up, took the pen out of his mouth, held up the stack and said, "One hundred more cases since last night."

Gryphon only harrumphed at that.

DJ set the files aside and smiled at his friend. He said, "So?" excitedly.

"Is there a way to fool a lung efficiency test?"

DJ coughed on his tongue, it was far from what he expected the man's response to his question to be. He took a drink of the coffee beside him to soothe his throat then looked back at his friend and said, "Excuse me?"

"Adrienne went home with me last night," said Gryphon, as if it meant his world was ended.

DJ had hoped she had. He smiled, hoping that meant they were working things out. The look on Gryphon's face told him there was still a long road to hoe before that could happen. He knew the man wasn't one to give personal details either so he didn't ask the next question that came to mind – the man would tell him if he wanted to. He was a little worried that it seemed he wanted to.

"We spent most of night talking… about things I wish I had done before now… all the things I wish we had done… It made me realize… I don't want any woman but her," said the man, sinking into the chair.

"Did you tell her that?" asked DJ, with no joking.

"I tried to… She isn't ready for what I want, and I doubt she ever will be."

"Which is?"

"I want a family."

DJ knew how hard it was for the man before him to admit this. *He* had known this was his best friend's desire for most of the last six months.

316

"Is there a way to fool a lung efficiency test?" Gryphon asked again a little slower.

"Um... Why, might I ask?"

"Adrienne said she wants anyone going over to be tested before she gives them the okay to go – given the levels of oxygen, helium, sulfur and carbon dioxide over there. Which, unless I miss my guess, means a lung efficiency test?" He stood up, walked to the window and looked out over the field that was just starting to green up with spring color.

"Likely," said the chemist.

"Thus my question. Is there a way?"

"What if there were?"

"If I can show pass it she can't deny me going."

"But you aren't okay," said DJ.

"I want the test to say I am though."

"*Gryphon Blake* would cheat on a test?" The very thought of this was foreign to DJ. "I... I am not sure I want to..."

"*Just answer the fucking question,*" said Gryphon, turning to face the man.

This knocked DJ back in his chair but didn't slow him any. "If you go over there in your condition you might do lasting and irreparable damage... You might need more than just an inhaler when you get back... *If* you get back."

"I know," said the man, who had walked to the other window. He turned to face his best friend again. "I have almost everything I ever wanted. I'm rich, beyond my wildest dreams, I have set my parents up to have no worries for the rest of their lives, my brother will want for nothing, if he ever gets out of the hospital, and this company is established well enough that it will continue on well after I am gone – and is left to you, by the way."

"Is this your eulogy?"

"I am being serious, DJ."

"So am I, Man. You said you had *almost* every-thing you ever wanted... Adrienne went home with *you* last night, Gryphon, not the colonel. I think, with a little effort, you and she can start over again."

"Not gonna happen," said Gryphon, as he sank again into the chair before the man's desk.

"Why not?"

"She said she feels safe with the colonel. If she can feel safe with a man like that..." He stood again and walked to the window again.

DJ didn't like how fidgety the usually always calm man seemed to be.

"You know her response when I told her last night that I wanted to have a family with her? Maybe she should call a cab... Meaning, go home to John."

DJ didn't know what to say to that. "So, how does this translate to you being allowed to go on a potentially suicidal mission?"

"I need to be the one that goes over, DJ; I need to know why they know my name." Gryphon turned and looking at the man again.

"I would most certainly *not* want to know this."

"I do."

DJ crossed his arms over his chest and shook his head, not believing he was hearing what he was hearing.

Taking this as a refusal to give him the answer, Gryphon pointed at the door and barked, "If you cannot do this then pack up your shit and get out now."

"Fuck me?!" said DJ incredulously.

"I mean it, DJ, this is no joke."

"I know. I will do this on one condition."

Gryphon was shaking his head.

"I am going with you."

"No."

DJ pushed the intercom button.

Bethany's voice came over it moments later, "Yes, Dr. Wright?"

"I need you to go down to the supply closet and get as many boxes and bubble wrap as there is and come in here to help me pack up my stuff."

"Excuse me, sir?" she asked, sounding unsure if she had heard him correctly.

Gryphon was still shaking his head.

"I've been fired and need to vacate the premises," said the man in a monotone voice.

"Fucking A, DJ!" Gryphon wondered why his friend had to get a backbone now of all times. "Fine, but you get yourself killed don't come whining to me."

"Bethany," said DJ then.

It took a moment for the reply; the woman had taken a couple steps away from her desk. "Yes?"

"Belay that request, My Dear," said the man, smiling as he released the button.

"So, how can it be done?" asked Gryphon.

"She will be looking to measure the force of your breath, to determine how strong your lungs are... If you were to take a hit of your medicine just before the test, to make sure your airways are as open as possible, and put your tongue on the inside of the mouthpiece for a split second before you blew out, build up the pressure, it should give a closer to normal reading. I cannot promise it will work or that she will fall for it though."

"Thank you. I need you to swear to me that you will not tell anyone I am doing this, DJ," said the man, looking his friend directly in the eyes.

"Can I be Batman?" asked the biochemist, getting a playful look in his eyes then.

"Excuse me?"

"The hero? Okay, Superman… though then you would have to be either Lois or Jimmy?"

Gryphon gave him one of his well-practiced annoyed look.

"Do you mind if I change the name of the company to *Wright* Concepts?"

"Alright, DJ, you are having a little too much fun with this now."

# 34

# **The Right Stuff**

"When was the last time you had an asthma attack?" asked Adrienne as she pumped up the band around his arm to check his blood pressure. The reading was one hundred ten over seventy, a little low but nothing unusual. She scribbled the number down and removed the cuff.

"About two days ago," he answered quickly.

"In the warehouse? That one was pretty severe. How often are they that bad?"

"Extenuating circumstances," said Gryphon.

"How often are they that bad?"

"That was the worst attack I've ever had," he said, as his mind was replaying the episode in Callie's shop, when he had actually lost consciousness. Telling her this would've made her admit him to the hospital on the spot,

"It was due to extreme stress, not the condition of my lungs."

Adrienne was looking at him, hoping to be able to tell if he was lying. She was almost certain he was but she couldn't say it in front of so many, she didn't want to embarrass the man. "Take off your shirt." Adrienne felt a flutter in her stomach at being so close to him and at having to touch his bare skin again but she shook it off. She took the end of the stethoscope in her fingers and set it against his chest, just below his right breast then moved it to the space on his back, just below his shoulder blade. She wasn't listening to his heart, she was listening to his lungs, which could be heard better on this side, without the heartbeat around it. "Take a deep breath, hold it then blow it out slowly."

Gryphon did so.

She could hear the noise of his illness inside them without having to try. "When did you take your last dose of medicine?"

"Not since the last attack in the warehouse." He had actually taken a hit of medicine just before entering the office about ten minutes ago and several more earlier in the day as he rode the elevator to his office.

"I want to perform a lung efficiency test on you," she said. She knew the results of that would be definitive enough that the decision to exclude him would be taken out of her hands. She was surprised, and concerned, when he nodded his head.

"When?"

"Right now." She motioned the assistant to bring over the spirometer.

Gryphon wanted to take another hit before the test, just for good measure. "Can I go to the men's room first, you must want a urine sample as well?" he said, hoping he didn't sound pushy or desperate.

"We do but it can wait, the test will only take about a minute."

Gryphon nodded and asked, "Can I put my shirt back on; it's a touch chilly in here." He knew if he could warm up the outside of his lungs it might help to give a better reading as well.

"No, I want to be able to watch your muscles as you perform the test." Adrienne held a nose clip, like a deep sea diver or a long distance swimmer might use, up to him and watched him put it into his nostrils then held her hand up to his face and said, "Try to blow air out of your nose." He did. She felt nothing. She handed him the mouthpiece then, which looked like the breathing apparatus for a scuba tank, except this one had a meter with a small ball bearing on the end of it. Notches along the tube corresponded to the percentage of air pressure in the lungs and it was attached to a tube that went to a tank filled with oxygen. She waited for him to get the uncomfortable bit in his mouth and said, "Practice breathing through it for a moment."

Gryphon was feeling very claustrophobic with his nose pinched off, and his only other airway restricted with the thing in his mouth; he couldn't take in nearly as much air as normal. He forced himself to calm down, counting to ten in his head, and breathing as slowly as he could until he was a little more comfortable. He nodded his head to her that he was ready.

"Take as deep a breath as you can. I don't want you to hold it just push it out as quickly as you can then continue to blow out until your lungs are completely empty."

Gryphon sucked in a raspy sounding lungful of air, set his tongue on the mouthpiece for a split second and blew out.

Adrienne had her eyes on the watch on her wrist so she didn't notice him cheating. "Keep going, keep going," once he had passed six seconds she said, "Good. Now breathe normally for a moment." She had him repeat this two more times before she allowed him to remove the nose and mouthpiece. She handed him a tissue to use when he took out the nose clip.

Gryphon was working the muscles of his face and trying to blow air through his nose as he looked at her. The perturbed look on her face told him he passed.

"I want to schedule a stress test," she said, hoping there was no way he could cheat on that test.

Little did she know, he had never had problems with that sort of physical exertion, it was not the right kind of stress on his system.

# 35

# What the Heart Wants

The governor, his secret service men, the doctors and the scientists were all back in Gryphon's office two days later. In that time another three thousand cases had been reported. Some were still alive, in about the same condition as Sam Blake.

"So, what has been decided?" asked Governor Price as he took a seat across from Gryphon's desk.

Adrienne wanted badly to say she wouldn't let Gryphon go, she knew he had found a way to trick the tests but short of publicly calling him out on it she had no recourse. She knew if she refused to let him go he would refuse to let them use the PSD and that he would likely do it without them monitoring. She knew John would be upset with her for not letting him go and she felt horrible but she would rather send John. "I have run medical tests on several potential subjects."

"Who is going across then?" asked the governor.

Adrienne couldn't find her voice. Her lower lip was quivering and her eyes were welling up with tears as she looked at Gryphon.

Gryphon didn't want to hurt her but he was resigned to this action. "*I* am going across, Governor Price."

John guffawed then pumped up his chest because there was still a chance he too could play hero. He said, "You should not be going over there alone."

DJ shifted then and said, "He won't be. I am going over with him."

"Now wait a minute," barked the colonel.

"There is a better chance of gathering information with only a two man team. We hope to go over and get back without them knowing we were there," said DJ.

"Is this agreeable to you, Dr. Ivekio?" asked Governor Price.

Adrienne still hadn't found her voice and was trying hard not to start crying. She cleared her throat and nodded her head.

"This is bullshit," spat the colonel.

"The doctor is the director of this operation, Colonel Graham, if she says Dr. Blake and Dr. Wright are fit enough to go and doesn't wish to send more than just the two of them at this time then that is to be it," said the man. He looked back at Gryphon then and said, "When do you intend this to occur?"

"As soon as we have found a point that seems the safest to cross through," said DJ.

"Very good. I am on my way to a meeting in Washington the end of this week then on a family vacation. I will check in with you, Dr. Ivekio," said the man as he stood. He put his hand out to Gryphon and shook his, then to DJ and shook his, and said, "Good luck to both of you."

"Thank you, sir," said DJ.

Gryphon nodded. He was watching Adrienne, who was now staring out the window. He could see her reflection clearly from the angle he was in.

The others in the room, other than the colonel, left as well then.

"I want you to be on alert, Colonel Graham. If we find the need you may get your chance to cross over after all," said Gryphon. He really didn't want to subject even the monsters of this other realm to the man but he hoped this would prevent him saying or doing anything foolish.

The colonel only grunted; a little appeased by this. He looked at Adrienne's back and said, "I need to get back to the base."

Adrienne didn't even respond to this.

"I will make sure she has a ride wherever she wishes to go," said DJ, knowing the man would be less upset if it was him that made this offer.

John wanted to demand the woman go with him but knew she would refuse, he had felt her pulling away from him since the day she told him she was going to Gryphon's talk at the college. He stomped most of the way to the elevator.

DJ stood once the colonel was gone and said, "I will be in my office if you need me."

Gryphon nodded and walked him to the door. He turned to Adrienne then slowly walked over to her and stepped up beside her. "Thank you."

"Do not thank me, Gryphon," said the woman, her voice hitching. "Do not thank me for giving you the okay to get yourself killed."

"I am not intending to get killed over there."

"I... I don't want you to do this, Gryphon," said the woman as she turned to him, tears flowing freely down her face now.

"I don't want anyone else taken by these things."

"Why is it you that has to do this?"

"I know it in my heart and what Callie has said."

"I like Miss Summers very much too, but I cannot place you in danger on the word of a woman who claims to be a psychic. I didn't think you believed in that."

"I didn't... before... She showed me one of her premonitions, there was no way she could have faked it and there is no way to deny those things are somehow connected to me."

"What if... what if what they want is your soul?"

"I will do all in my power not to let them have it," he said aloud but he was thinking, *unless it will mean saving all of you.*

"What if I say I am still in love with you...? What if I say I want to have a family with you too, would you stay then?" asked the woman.

"That's not fair, Adrienne."

"But..."

Gryphon pulled her into his arms and held her. "I want you to want that, Adrienne, but not in this way. If you weren't willing to say this two nights ago, when there was no risk to me, then you don't really mean it."

"I do, Gryphon."

"Do you want a ride to your place?"

"I will get a room at a hotel. I don't want to hurt John but I just... I don't want to be near him right now."

"There is no need for a hotel. You will always welcome in my home," said Gryphon. He wanted to offer her a room in his house for as long as she wanted it but he knew that would only cloud the issue. He wanted her to want him back but he wanted her to truly want it not because there was a chance that she may never be able to again.

# 36

# **Arrangements**

Gryphon actually slept better than he expected he would, especially considering what he would be doing in only a few hours. He stepped into the kitchen and smiled, he had thought he smelled pancakes. It still surprised him that his chef always knew just what he was craving. "Good morning, Ms. Hendricks."

"I noticed someone used another room last night. Did your parents stay?" asked Aggie.

"No. Mom and dad went to stay at Sam's. Mom wants to get it cleaned up for when he comes home, and I think they both wanted to feel closer to him."

"More of your family, to see your brother?" asked Aggie as she flipped the pancake she was making then removed it from the pan and poured the last of the batter into the pan.

"No," said Gryphon flatly, the articles he was reading said ten more of the mummy bodies had been discovered and several dozen had been admitted to Biscayne General with symptoms of severe dehydration over the last few hours. This helped steel his resolve for the action he was to be taking that afternoon. "Adrienne stayed last two nights and will likely the next few."

"Dr. Ivekio, Adrienne?" asked Aggie. She was another that had enjoyed them together. She wasn't able to truly feel happy about it given that the woman had slept in a different room than his.

"Yes, Aggie, and no, we have not rekindled the relationship."

She could see how hurt he was as he said those words and didn't want to push him for details but she couldn't help it. "You say she is staying again this evening? I could have a nice dinner prepared? Maybe some candlelight and romantic music, on the patio? It is supposed to be a beautiful night."

"No. We will not likely be arriving at the same times so... Just leave a few takeout menus on the counter for her to pick from, the ones I have accounts with so she can charge it to that."

"Takeout food?" said the woman with obvious distaste. "When you have a world class chef in your employ... Do you know how insulting that is?"

"Let it go, Abigail."

"Yes, sir," she said. She took the last pancake out and set the pan into the sink to cool off then brought a plate with three of them, three strips of bacon and a bottle of syrup over to him. "Should I figure on something for the lady's breakfast?"

"She has already left for the day," said the man, not even looking up as he flipped to the next page of the paper. Gryphon could tell she was very upset by his apparent indifference. He pushed the plate away from him and said, "Aggie, I need you to come here for a moment."

"Is something wrong with the pancakes?"

"No, just my appetite is not so good this morning. Please, sit down."

Aggie didn't like how forlorn he looked all of a sudden. Her first thought was either he had bad news about Sam or he had bad news about himself. She wasn't sure which would tear at her heart more because either would destroy the man sitting before her and in turn her. She sank into the chair beside him and tried to wait patiently as he tried to find the words he wanted.

"I have to go away for a bit… only an afternoon… I hope… but there is a chance it may be longer," he said as he passed her a piece of paper.

The woman took it and saw three numbers on it, 65 – 45 – 25, "What is this?"

"It's the combination to the safe in the den. Right, left twice, then right."

"Why do I need this?"

"There is a substantial amount of cash in there that I wish for you to divide between you, Jerome and Jayne, in whatever manner you see fit, in the event that anything should happen to me. Also documents I need you to give to my attorney, pertaining to patents and precedence's for the business holdings, and my will."

"Why would I need to do that?"

"This is really just a precaution."

"I… don't want anything to happen to you," said the woman, tears starting to come to her eyes.

"Neither do I, Aggie, but I need to be prepared in the event."

The woman only sat still, fighting the tears back. She wanted to know more but she knew it wasn't her place to ask.

Gryphon took her hand in his and squeezed it gently as he said, "I'm just being my overcautious self, Abigail." He pointed a finger at her and squinted one eye as he added, "I know just how much money is in the safe and I will be changing the combination the moment I return." He knew she would never go near the safe until she was certain he was dead but he knew teasing her about it would ease her mind that it was truly only a precaution.

It helped to hear him tease and see the glint return to his somber eyes. "Not if I use it and replace it before you return."

"I told you no more trips to the casino. I will not bail you out again."

"I wasn't the one who started that fight, the woman tried to take my bucket of tokens," said Aggie.

"Yeah, no one ever told me just how much fun it is to employ an ex-con," said the man, smiling wickedly. "Anyway, I plan to be home for dinner so if you wouldn't mind having that fine meal you spoke of prepared... and make enough for extra mouths. I think I may have a few guests join me."

"Yes, sir."

He was happy to see the bounce in her step had returned as she put the piece of paper into her pocket and started for the pantry with the stack of takeout menus he had suggested she have waiting to return to the drawer; no doubt intent on planning the meal, wanting to be sure she had everything there she would need. He hoped he hadn't just lied to her.

He took the plate of breakfast, dumped it into the garbage disposal and flipped the switch quickly then set the plate into the sink and left the room to go to his den and get his briefcase.

\*\*\*\*\*\*\*\*\*\*\*\*\*\*\*\*\*\*\*\*

Gryphon had hoped his brother would be awake when he stepped into his room, and that all the thoughts running rampant in his brain were unnecessary – but he wasn't – meaning they were. A nurse, the same one he had shouted at that had been about to shut the blinds, was setting a new bag of saline solution up.

"I'm sorry I shouted at you the other day, Nurse," he said as he stepped up to the other side of the bed and took his brother's hand in his.

"It's alright, sir, I know you're worried about your brother," said the woman.

He could see she was still nervous about being in the room with him but he didn't say anything. He waited until she left to speak again.

"Hey, Sammy, the Puma's won last night," he said. He wasn't into sports but his brother was deeply and almost obsessively. "Score was 37 to 28 and went into overtime."

Sam shifted a little but didn't awaken.

"I am one that believes they can hear you when they are in this condition," said the voice of Dr. Parsons.

Gryphon looked over his shoulder at the man and said, "Has there been any change at all, Doc?"

"No. His vitals are good and strong though."

"What good does that do if he never wakes up?" asked Gryphon, a touch of anger coming to his voice.

"It's a good sign, Gryphon. Once his body is strong, his mind will be. He still has good brainwave activity. He had lost a lot of weight and his fluid levels were very low. He is gaining day by day. I would be surprised if there isn't a marked improvement within another few days."

Gryphon nodded, hoping the man was right. "The others?"

The hospital was near capacity, extra beds had to be borrowed from area hospitals to contain the other living victims.

"We lost some last night… most are still like your brother was when he first arrived…"

Gryphon was about to step away from the bed and get himself a chair when his parents stepped in. His mother took the few steps between them and pulled him into a hug, one that was much tighter than she had ever given him in the past. He knew she was upset at the condition of Sam's apartment.

"How are you?" asked his father.

"I'm alright," said Gryphon.

"You, DJ and Adrienne have been very busy. Have you had any luck?" asked Bruce.

"Some… progress. DJ and I are attempting something this afternoon that should give us a lot of good information."

"Yeah?"

He knew his father wanted details but he wasn't ready to give them. "Aggie is preparing a fine dinner this evening. I am unsure how many might be there but I was hoping you and mom, and you, Dr. Parsons, might be on the list?"

"A celebratory dinner?" asked Gloria.

"More of a… gathering."

"Alright, count us in," said Bruce.

"I have been called to come to GCI by Dr. Ivekio, to assist in some medical testing there. If that is finished in time, I would certainly be interested."

"I am hoping Adrienne and DJ will be able to join us as well so I am sure they will be."

"Very good. I have to finish my rounds and I will likely see you at your office in a few hours."

"Very good, Dr. Parsons."

"Adrienne will be coming to dinner?" asked Gloria, her eyes lighting up.

"Yes, mom. Don't go getting your hopes up. She and I had a long discussion the other night… We do still have feelings for each other but… we are not at the same place in our lives."

Gloria could see how her son's eyes lit up when he said the young woman's name so she allowed the flames of hope to sputter at least.

Gryphon let his mother have the glimmer of hope, knowing she needed something happy to keep her mind on. He hugged his father then said, "I need to get going, lots to get prepared."

"What time is dinner, Son?" asked Bruce.

"Around six, I would think."

"We will see you then."

# 37

# Playing Hero

"This location seems to be only a few feet off the ground," said Derek. He had been flabbergasted when his boss had brought him into the lab and explained to him what they were doing.

The two had spent most of the evening working on monitors to be implanted into him and Gryphon. They were both excited, the younger had never gotten to see his experiments being used firsthand and the older one had always had a secret, and sick, desire to be tested on – sort of hoping for some freak accident to turn him into Spiderman or something he supposed. The they and Gryphon had spent hours working on miniature versions of the PSD so the men could open a rift back to Earth when time was up.

Gryphon's hand was pressing on his sternum as he nodded to them and shook his head. He was thinking the younger man was following in the elder's footsteps – the implication of this was really quite scary. Adrienne stepped in then with Dr. Parsons behind her. Neither looked happy with him. "I take it Adrienne has told you what we're up to, Dr. Parsons?"

"If she hadn't been the one to tell me I'd have said you were in need of psychiatric treatment. I discourage you from attempting it. Your brother appears to be responding to the latest treatment."

"This is not just for him, Doc, I am doing this for all of them that weren't so lucky, for the others fighting to live and to prevent more from suffering the same fate," said the man, trying hard to keep his voice steady. He could feel his lungs starting to constrict.

"Do your parents know?"

"No. And I must ask you to keep it from them. Dad might be alright with it but I know mom would have a heart attack," said Gryphon, as his sternum pinched again. He was beginning to think he should have taken another hit before he stepped into the room.

"Speaking of which, I am sure you are aware that given your condition there is potential for you to go into respiratory arrest if you go through with this?"

"The tests show I'm just, Doc," said Gryphon, looking pointedly at DJ.

DJ immediately looked at the tops of his shoes.

"I know you found a way to fool the tests," said Adrienne, looking hard at DJ herself now.

DJ tapped Derek on the arm, pointed at the door and said, "Let's go get the nanoprobes?"

"Yes, sir."

"What is it he is after?" asked Gryphon, hoping to stall what the glares from the doctors were about.

"Nanoprobes. We will be injected with them, in our pectorals. They will monitor our vitals and act as a homing device so we can track each other and they can find us if we are… incapacitated and require assistance," said DJ, sounding a touch too happy about it.

As soon as the men were out the door Adrienne said, "I can still call this off, Gryphon."

"We both know you won't, Adrienne," said Gryphon as he checked that the PSD was still aimed at the spot on the refrigerator of the fourth floor cafeteria.

This was the only place they had found that opened to solid ground so they had the employees on this floor evacuated and resituated on the second and third floors, using the excuse that a vial of deadly toxins had accidentally been dropped in the lab next door.

"Why wouldn't I?"

"I know how afraid for me you are, you both are, and believe me I am more than a little for myself and DJ as well, but you won't stop me because in your heart you know it is me that has to do this."

"Arrogant bastard," whispered Adrienne.

DJ and Derek stepped back into the room then, the latter holding a partitioned tray with several vials of a silver liquid and five very large looking syringes. The former had a tray with five each of what looked like large wristwatches and bracelets.

Dr. Kearns stepped into the room seconds later pushing a cart with several monitors and equipment.

Colonel Graham and two other soldiers stepped in right behind him.

"Everything settled?" asked DJ, seeing that all the parties were now present.

Gryphon looked at Adrienne and Dr. Parsons to be certain neither was going to fight him. When they both nodded he looked at DJ and said, "It is."

DJ motioned Gryphon to the single lunch table that had been set up in the back of the room. He told him to sit down and take his shirt off as he removed his own.

Derek set the tray down on the table beside the men, took one of the syringes, removed the needle guard, stuck the end of it into one of the vials and pulled the handle back. The silver fluid was then sucked into the tube. He pressed the plunger a touch, until a small bubble of the fluid was on the tip of the needle and said, "Who wants to go first?"

DJ had a smile on his face as he held up his hand.

Derek handed the needle to Adrienne and said, "Just under the skin, over their heart, Dr. Ivekio."

Adrienne stepped up to DJ, took a small amount of skin between her fingers and inserted the needle.

"Boy does that feel some kind of weird," said the man as the cold fluid entered his system.

"What is it doing?" asked Gryphon.

"Dispersing through my bloodstream. It's made up of thousands of tiny robotic cells that will flow through our blood and enter each of our organs. They will remain in our organs so we can be monitored fully – sounds like wicked sci-fi, doesn't it?"

Gryphon smirked. "How long do they work?"

"We think they will break down in a few months and should pass through our bowels without notice."

"We think?"

"Don't worry; as long as we don't get near any metal detectors, or get an MRI in the next couple days, we're fine." The look on their faces were priceless, "I'm joking. They're undetectable to most devices."

Gryphon was shaking his head as he watched Derek filling another syringe. "Who's the rest for?"

"The colonel and his men, in case they are needed," said Adrienne as she stepped up to Gryphon and said, "Are you ready?"

"I am." He cringed as the large needle pierced his skin and felt the odd cold and warm feel of the fluid being injected. He imagined he could feel the tiny robots moving inside him but knew it was only his imagination – or more hoped it was. His bronchial tubes closing off even more then was not though.

DJ then held one of each of the other devices he had with him up to Gryphon and said, "This is a stopwatch. Dr. Kearns doesn't want us over there for more than five and a half hours. These are set for five hours and are set to give us a ten minute warning. The other is a device that works with the nanoprobes. They will allow us to stay close by responding to them. Mine is set to hone in on the frequency of your nanoprobes and yours to mine." He turned the one for him on and held it away from Gryphon, showing the light on it was flashing red then he moved it toward him and showed him the red light became steadier.

"Alright." Gryphon put both on his left wrist.

"We will close the fissure once you are across. Promise me you will open a return portal as soon as you hear the alarm?" said Adrienne as she held two small PSD units on chains up to them.

"Will do," both said at the same time, putting them around their necks.

The woman held up two other small devices.

Gryphon recognized them as templecams, another piece of technology his company had been working on. A small camera and voice activated two-way radio that attaches to the side of the face by spirit gum. He took the unit from her, peeled off the plastic backing and set it against his face on the right side.

DJ did the same with his.

The two of them and the doctors looked at Dr. Kearns, who was on the other side of the room. He nodded, and said, "Say something."

DJ spoke first, "One fine day in the middle of the night, two dead boys got up to fight. Back to back, they faced each other, drew their swords and shot each other. A deaf policeman heard the noise…"

They all looked at him funny.

"Sorry," he said, smiling a little sickly.

Gryphon grunted and said, "Did you hear him?"

"I am getting you both, loud and clear."

"We ready to do this then?" asked Gryphon as he jumped off the table.

"One more thing," said Derek as he stepped up to them with what looked like two blue wetsuits.

"These will allow you to conserve your body fluids and keep you cooler. I don't need to remind you that it's very warm and dry over there," said Adrienne.

The men nodded and began to take off all their clothes without modesty.

Once they were both suited up, Gryphon asked again, "We ready now?"

Adrienne's heart was screaming for her to say no but she knew Gryphon was right. She nodded to Derek.

He moved to the PSD unit and flipped the switch and jumped when a circular opening appeared about waist high then expanded outward.

Gryphon had intended to go first but DJ stepped in front of him.

He put his hand through the opening then pulled it back. "It is certainly hot over there." He showed them it was already covered in sweat and the inside of the watch face was coated with a sheen of moisture from the temperature change between there and the room.

"Quit joking around, DJ," snapped Gryphon and Adrienne at the same time.

DJ shrugged, nodded then stepped through.

# 38

# Jets of Black

DJ was afraid to open his eyes but he was equally afraid to leave them closed. He could feel an odd heat and a chill at the same time sweeping his skin as hot winds hit his body from various directions and he had the feeling of being way up high. He wasn't sure if he was glad or not when he finally forced his eyes to open.

He saw a purplish-black cloudless sky above him; if he had seen a sky like it on Earth he would have been looking for the tornadoes next. Streaks of silver and black were zipping across it at uneven intervals. He didn't know if this was some alien form of lightening or not, and didn't want to find out the hard way. All around him was huge jets of black, red and purplish rocks, as far as he could see. The monoliths were of varying heights and sizes; some were only spikes others looked several feet across. He looked behind him then and realized he was on one of the same, only his was mere feet across. He was standing on a thin ledge barely as wide as his boots, near the top of it. He wondered how they could have thought this was solid enough ground to have them cross over to.

He rubbed at his nose as the sulfur odor hit it; he hated even how fresh eggs smelled. He wished he had brought something to rub under his nostrils to mask the odor. He knew it wasn't harmful, just unpleasant. That and everything smelled just plain hot – like burning plastic or hot electronics. He reached out and touched the rock behind him. It was slick and cold – it reminded him of slate or shale – more the latter with how easily it flaked in his hand as he touched it. He hoped the small ledge under his feet wouldn't give way so easily. He looked down, hoping to see the ground, or a wider ledge, only a few inches or even a few feet, few enough to be able to jump to with little and or no injury, below but he saw neither – only down a great distance then coalescing grayish clouds swirling around violently. He had no way to know if there even was ground below him. With his luck it would be one of the methane lakes.

"So, Gryphon, what do you think we should do now?" he asked. He got no answer. He looked around his tiny ledge and saw, with heart-gripping realization, he was alone. "Gryphon?" GRYPHON!" He still got no answer.

*Oh, God,* he thought. What if the unit had accidentally been moved after he went through so it had opened to an entirely different place for Gryphon? Just a micrometer in either direction could be enough to send him hundreds of miles away. How would they find each other then? What if he hadn't landed on one of these ledges? What if he had come through in midair and had fallen to his doom? He looked at his right wrist then, the magnetized band was still there but the LED light on it was blue, either Gryphon hadn't made it through the rift or he had but he wasn't anywhere near him. He had to hope the man was nearby and that if he didn't find him before that they would see each other again when they opened portals back to the lab.

"Well, DJ," he asked himself, "You wanted to play hero... what are you going to do now?" He tried to go over his options but he came up empty. He looked at the watch on his left wrist and saw he had four hours and forty five minutes before he had to jump back. He needed to find firmer ground to do that from. He hoped he could do this within that window of time.

He began to shift his position on the small ledge, hoping maybe the view on the other side of the rock tower would give him an answer to his dilemma. It did, but not in the form he would have chosen. He felt the ledge beneath his boots giving way.

"Oh, shit!" It fell away entirely knocking him into the jagged rocks of the wall behind him. He felt those sharp rocks cutting into the tender skin of his back and felt it shredding the skin of his palms as he tried desperately to get a hold of something. There was nothing solid to hold onto – he felt himself falling.

**\*\*\*\*\*\*\*\*\*\*\*\*\*\*\*\*\*\*\*\***

Gryphon was actually still on Earth, in the corner of the cafeteria, bent over with his left hand on his left thigh and his right clutching his throat; trying to catch his breath and make the tightness in his chest go away. He was ghostly white and was gasping and wheezing loudly.

They all looked at Dr. Kearns when DJ's voice came through the speakers, asking where Gryphon was.

"Fuck!" croaked the man. He jumped when he felt a hand on his shoulder and looked up to see Adrienne holding his inhaler before him. He grabbed it, shook it, stuck it in his mouth and pressed the bottle to get the medicine out. He sucked in and held his breath for a few seconds then took another hit. He could feel her hand still on his arm "Back off, Adrienne," he said sternly.

"You need to lie down, Gryphon."

"You lost the privilege of telling me what to do when you walked out on us!" He instantly felt sorry, knowing she was only trying to help, but not enough to apologize to her.

Adrienne realized, for all their friendliness over the last few days, he was still upset with her.

"GRYPHON?" came DJ's desperate voice again. It was starting to be tinged with fear now.

Gryphon stood up on hearing this. There was no way he was going to leave his friend over there all alone, wondering what had happened to him. He used his forearm to wipe the sweat from his forehead, took another hit of the medicine, just for good measure, then stormed past them and started toward the opening.

"I cannot let you go," said Adrienne.

"You cannot stop me," said Gryphon.

"If I say you are not fit then you are not going," she said. She had crossed her arms under her shapely breasts now.

"Adrienne." She had the look on her face that said she meant business; the one he had always thought was sexy. This almost made him smile as it brought back memories of how they would say they were sorry after having fought, much like the other night in the doctor's lounge.

She looked over at John and said, "Get out of your gear so I can inject you with the probes, John."

The soldier immediately began to remove the Kevlar vest he was wearing.

Getting his mind back on task, Gryphon said, "I'm alright, it was a stress induced attack."

"All the more reason why you shouldn't go," said Dr. Parsons, to which the others quickly nodded.

They all froze when DJ's voice came through again, "Well, DJ. You wanted to pay hero, what are you going to do now?"

"My friend is over there in God knows what kind of danger. *I am going*!"

"I am trained in martial arts, and I have a really big gun, Dr. Blake, I can handle a few spooks," said the colonel.

"These *spooks,* as you call them, suck the fucking life out of you, Colonel Graham. It doesn't matter how much training you have and your bullets went right through them, if I recall," said Gryphon, grabbing his throat again. He wasn't having another attack, this time it was because his throat was dry from the medicine.

"Still, this is only a test run anyways, we aren't planning to confront them," said Graham.

"They aren't likely to back off just because we are only there as a test, Graham. You think you need to go play hero, and I'm guessing you're thinking the way to do this is with a pile of explosives?"

"It would damn sure keep them from returning here, wouldn't it?"

"Or piss them off enough to come over in droves and take all of us at once instead of only one at a time." Gryphon was inches from the opening now.

Adrienne was shaking her head violently as she watched him step his foot through the opening and test the ground beneath it. "Gryphon, get out of there."

He didn't move.

"Gryphon, stop," said Dr. Parsons.

The colonel brought his rifle up then, which prompted the other two soldiers, to do the same.

"If I find anything that suggests we need to take them out I will *damn sure* let you know Colonel," said Gryphon. He saw the guns hadn't been lowered yet. "Go ahead and shoot me."

"If you have an attack over there, Gryphon..." said Adrienne.

"I have my inhaler."

"Doctor?" asked Colonel Graham.

"Alright," said Adrienne as she stepped closer.

Gryphon tensed up, thinking she was trying to stick him with a tranquilizer or stop him by force.

Adrienne only gently touched his arm then leaned forward and kissed him. "I know you have to do this. Just, please, be careful," she whispered.

Gryphon set his forehead against hers and said, "I will, I promise." He had to fight the urge to touch her cheek and kiss her again, watching her lower lip quivering. He looked at the others then and saw the soldiers still had their rifles aimed at him.

"He can go," said Adrienne.

The colonel looked like it bothered him to but he finally told his men to stand down.

"Thank you," said Gryphon, this time he did caress her cheek. "Sorry I barked at you."

Adrienne quickly nodded.

He gave her a quick hug then stepped through the opening before she could change her mind.

Just as he stepped through they heard DJ shout, "Oh, shit!" This sounded stretched out as if the man that expelled it was falling.

# 39

# The Fog

Gryphon was on a landscape only slightly less treacherous than the one DJ had found himself on. He, at least, was on solid ground but the gray fog around him was so thick he couldn't see his hand in front of his face. It was far warmer where he was as well because there was no wind blowing across his skin to help cool him down. He knew the suit he was wearing was supposed to keep him cool but it was constricting so much it was making it hard to breathe. Adrienne and Dr. Parsons wouldn't like it but if he didn't he would have another attack – he pulled the zipper on the front of the suit down to his stomach and pulled it open, exposing his bare chest.

"Can you hear me, Adrienne?" he called out.

"Yes, Gryphon," came through the earpiece but he could barely hear it, "but just barely."

"Must be the distance," he said sarcastically, sounding more like DJ.

"Are you alright?"

He knew she wouldn't believe him if he said he was fine. "The air is a little thick and I'm in the middle of a dense fog, which isn't helping my claustrophobia, but I am alright."

"That explains why we can't see anything around you," said Dr. Kearns.

"We cannot seem to get DJ anymore; we have lost both his voice and his camera signal. Is he there with you?" asked Adrienne, sounding panicked.

"No," said Gryphon, feeling his chest tighten up again. "Where is that son of a bitch?"

All the people in the cafeteria heard were the last four words. "Are you alright?" screamed Adrienne, coming through loud and clear that time.

"Yes, Sweets, just worried about DJ." He realized after he said this that her current lover was there with her and likely would be quite upset with the term of affection. He said, "That was bright, you idiot," under his breath.

He didn't want to walk into a hole or slip on the loose stones he felt beneath his feet but he couldn't just stand there either. He wished now he had thought to bring a walking stick. He slowly moved his feet before him, wondering why he had been so certain he was the one to do this. He called out, "DJ? You near me? DJ?" He looked at the device on his wrist and saw the red light was blinking, telling him he was but he had no idea in what direction. "Adrienne, my wristband says DJ is near me now. DJ, are you here?" He cocked his head around then, thinking he had heard something.

"We still have no signal from him."

"Hang on a minute," he said. It almost sounded like someone shouting but he couldn't say what or from where. He guessed the fog was distorting the sound. He stopped in place and looked at his wristband again, hoping it was not giving him a false signal. The red light was now solid telling him his friend should be close. "DJ?" Gryphon said hopefully.

"AAAHHHHH!!!"

Gryphon didn't have time to react as something hit him and knocked him to the shifting surface. It took him a moment to figure out which direction the thing that hit him had come from and what it was. Gryphon rolled his friend off him and said, "DJ, you alright?"

"Ah...owe... am I still alive?"

"I believe you are. Can you move?" Gryphon was pleased to see his friend seemed in one piece, though a scraped up and dusty piece.

DJ started to sit up then groaned and lay back down.

"Do you need to go back?"

"No, just give me a minute… I think I just fell the equivalent of about forty stories."

Gryphon looked at him sternly, thinking he was joking, the look on the man's face told him he wasn't.

"Thanks for breaking my fall. Are you hurt?"

"Nothing I won't survive," said Gryphon, offering him his hand. "Sorry, I was a little late getting here."

"It's alright. As it turned out your timing was about perfect, otherwise I would be a rock flavored pancake right now." DJ checked his suit for holes. The back of it was nothing but stringy threads and his back underneath looked like hamburger but otherwise he was intact. He looked at his friend and said, "What happened here?" pointing to the wide open front of his suit.

Gryphon pointed to the camera attached to the side of his head and mouthed, 'Is there any way to mute this?'

DJ shook his head.

"Gryphon, is that DJ we are hearing?" asked Adrienne's voice.

'Nothing about this,' the man mouthed to his friend, indicating the open front of his suit, which would negate its affect. "Yes, Adrienne. He quite literally fell upon me."

"Is he alright?"

"Both of us are a little battered but fine," said DJ into the speaker of Gryphon's unit.

"Stay close to Gryphon."

"Got that figured already, Doc." He looked at Gryphon and said, "So, where to?"

"I don't know; I can't see a fucking thing."

DJ looked at his watch, "We have three more hours, pick a direction and I'll follow."

Gryphon pointed ahead of them, or what he thought was ahead of them, and said, "We are going to see if we can get out of this fog, Adrienne."

DJ was looking around them as Gryphon said this. He tapped him on the arm and held a finger to his lips.

"Hang on, Adrienne. What is it, DJ?"

"Shush," spit the man.

Gryphon could hear noises now too, the sound of something being dragged across the ground.

They began to turn around, their backs to each other, trying to look in every direction, unsure where the sound was coming from. Four faceless things separated themselves from the fog around them. They were a white-ish gray and were wearing white robes, which is what they had heard scraping against the loose rocks on the ground. They were surrounded by them.

"Son of a bitch," screamed Gryphon, DJ, Dr. Kearns and Adrienne at the same time. The latter two had seen the things through the camera on Gryphon's head.

"*Which of you is Gryphon,*" asked the voice.

This didn't make the hairs on Gryphon's neck twitch as the ones they had heard before had. He spun around and brought his fists up, he had no idea if he could physically fight these things but he was intent on trying to.

One of the four stepped closer to them, the one that was across from DJ.

"Get the fuck away from him," Said Gryphon, jumping in front of his friend.

The thing turned its body toward him. "*Are you the one called Gryphon?*"

They had no mouth so neither knew for certain whether the thing had spoken this or if it was only in their mind.

Gryphon ripped the camera from the side of his head and handed it to DJ, not wanting the woman back on Earth to see him getting his soul sucked out. "Yes, I'm Gryphon. I will let you have me as long as this man can leave here."

"Gryphon, No," said DJ, and Adrienne's voice through the small speaker on the camera.

"It is *my* fault we are here," said the man, not paying his best friend and the woman on Earth any attention. "I will let you have me but let him leave here."

"*We do not wish either of you any harm*," said the thing. "*If you wish to return to your world we will open you a portal.*"

"Wha… what?" asked the man.

"*We do not wish you or any of the people on your world harm.*"

"You don't think that sucking the life out of the people of our world is causing us harm?" screamed Gryphon then he was gasping. He suddenly couldn't pull air into his lungs and they felt like they were on fire. He had never felt so much pain – hot, searing pain. He would have cried out if his throat would have let him. Tears were streaming down him face, which was painful as well because the tears were hot and was burning his skin. The closeness of the thick fog was making him feel like he was being squeezed. He thought he was going to pass out. He went down to his knees and almost prayed they would take the life from him them.

The closest being stepped up to Gryphon and placed one of its three fingered hands on the center of his bare chest.

DJ screamed, "Leave him alone," and launched himself at the thing.

It swung its other tiny hand out without turning or removing the one on Gryphon's chest. DJ froze in place, half off the ground half in the air.

"What is going on?" came Adrienne's panicked voice. "John, get ready to cross over."

"Stop. Wai… wait!" screamed Gryphon. He was breathing again, though it was raspy.

The people in the cafeteria heard Gryphon shout 'wait' then everything went dead.

"We lost them," said Dr. Kearns. Both monitors were nothing but snow now.

"Get them back," said Adrienne, with more than a little fear in her voice.

"I can't. Their signals are gone," said the man.

Adrienne didn't know what to do. Did she dare send more men over, at risk of losing them too?

"My men and I are ready," said the colonel.

She jumped and turned away from him. She cleared her throat and said, "No, I cannot risk it. We will have to wait and see if they return on their own…"

The colonel didn't look happy with this decision but really couldn't do anything about it.

# 40

# Pholanhdies

When Gryphon opened his eyes he found himself in a huge domed chamber. It looked to be cut out of the reddish rock, as they had seen with the ASP. He had to squint his eyes because everything was so bright. He couldn't see anything that would be putting out so much light – unless it was the rocks themselves. He had no idea how he had gotten there or why he was lying on the cold floor of this chamber. DJ was beside him, but he wasn't moving. He sat up to check if his friend was alive and saw the four white beings were standing in a circle around them. He knew he should be frightened but he wasn't – in fact he felt amazingly comfortable and his lungs weren't burning at all anymore.

*"Do you fare well?"*

He couldn't tell which had spoken, or thought, this; the words didn't echo as he expected them to in a rock chamber like this. One of them floated a little forward then so he guessed it was that one that had asked this. "Where are we?" His words did echo.

"*Our world is known as Pholanhd.*"

"And why are we still alive?"

"*We do not wish to harm you.*"

"You said that before but I know of about five hundred people who would disagree."

"*It is closer to several thousand.*"

"Excuse me?"

"*I believe we need to explain.*"

"I think maybe," said Gryphon with a pointed guffaw, "Starting with what is wrong with my friend?"

"*He is unharmed. He is only asleep.*"

As if to prove this, a slight snore came from the other man's throat.

The thing leaned over Gryphon and held its small hand out to him, as if in offer to help him stand. The scientist in him wanted very much to take it, wanting to learn all he could of these things – like why they were doing what they were doing and how they were doing it. The man in him was screaming that they were only trying a new tactic. "Why should I trust you?"

"*We did not harm you when we first learned of you, we do not wish to now.*"

"Excuse me?" The thing still had its three fingered hand held out to him. He took it then got his feet under himself and stood up.

"*You were much smaller then... but a child.*"

"You mean in the closet?" The things surrounding him seemed very tall at that moment and the walls around him felt very solid. His throat and chest started to compress again. The thing waved its hand over him. His breathing became steady and the pain was gone. "What do you keep doing to me?"

"*Your lungs are injured. We are trying to ease your discomfort. As we did so long ago.*"

"What? How?" asked Gryphon, almost afraid of the answer.

"*You could not breathe in your atmosphere so we made you better.*"

"What?"

An image of a dark closet with a small boy sitting with his knees to his chest in the corner – him – fighting for breath because he felt like the walls were closing in on him came to him. "I wasn't having trouble breathing my atmosphere, I was frightened."

"*Explain,*" said the thing.

"I wasn't having trouble breathing my world's air, I was afraid," said Gryphon, getting a little angry. These things, that claimed they didn't want to harm him, had made the last thirty-three years of his life living hell.

"*Explain frightened,*" said another of the things, stepping forward. "*Explain afraid.*"

"It was you that offered an explanation," barked Gryphon. He had decided if he was going to die he wanted to know why. "What is this proviso of yours?"

"*It is not ours,*" said all four of the voices.

"Then why are your… people… coming to my world and taking my peoples' souls saying it is to complete your proviso? Is this a mind game?"

"*Explain mind game.*"

Gryphon couldn't swear to it but he thought this was the same one that asked him to explain frightened and afraid. The one he thought was the leader put its tiny hand up as if to quiet the others.

"*It is the Pholanhs that are doing this to your world. We are Pholanhdies.*"

"Are you two different races?"

"*Once we were all the same… Many cycles ago a rift opened to your world. Some of us crossed over and lived in your world, in your dreams. We fed off your energies as you slept, not enough to cause harm just enough to sustain us. You had so many minds that we could visit a different one every night and leave little effect behind. To you they were only bad dreams*"

Another stepped forward then and continued the first one's thought. "*One of us took it too far. We did not know a person could be killed in their sleep, we were always so careful. We do not think the one meant to do the person harm, we think it only didn't know what to do with the essence that escaped the body."*

*"It took it, hoping to give it back, but the body had withered up so there was nothing to instill the force back into,"* said the first.

Another spoke then, *"It brought this essence back here and showed it to the others. They fought over it until it became separated. The first one sucked it inside itself, thinking again to keep it safe. It became different then, turning blackish gray and more solid."*

The fourth one spoke, *"Some of the others wanted this too. They began to go over and make your people die in their sleep so they could take their essence and become more solid."*

The leader spoke again then, *"Throughout your history there have been dried carcasses discovered – they were left by the Pholanhs."* This one waved its hand and various time periods of Earth began to play in midair before Gryphon like a slideshow.

He saw the stone ages, throughout the middle ages, Rome, Greece, Crete, Egypt, China, Japan, Mayan and Inca cities, various Indian tribes, the bog people found in Great Britain and dozens of other cultures finding bodies; some only days old, some hundreds of years old before they were discovered. Some had believed it was a punishment of the gods, some saw it as a reward – that the body had been so preserved, like it was only being kept for the soul to be returned to, others – in more modern times – knew it was anything but natural. He saw cave drawings and written texts from all these points in time and heard stories told to children throughout the ages of creatures coming to take your soul away. He heard the famous childhood prayer even his parents had made him and Sam repeat as children, '*If I should die before I awake, I pray the lord my soul to take...*'

"That was all you?"

"*That was all the Pholanhs,*" said the second one.

"Alright, say I believe you and they are different, what does all this have to do with me? Why do you... they know my name?"

"*Fewer and fewer of your people are being born each generation with the construct of the mind we need to gain access to your world. Yours is one of them.*"

"Great!" He wasn't sure how else to respond; it did explain why Callie felt there was a connection between him and these creatures. It wasn't exactly the explanation he was hoping for but at least that was one less mystery – his scientific mind was pleased to have it even if his rational one was not. "Alright, why aren't you doing this as well?"

"*We do not wish to harm your people,*" the four said in unison.

"Where does that leave me and my world? The people of my time know what these… these Pholanhs are doing and will not stand for it. We are not so bent on everything being an act of God or some mythical beast. We know about the rift and can access your world. We came through intent on stopping any more of your… of them crossing over. We are a resourceful people. I am not sure how we will do it but we will find a way to stop them." Gryphon didn't know if they could read his mind but he hoped they couldn't, or weren't right then, or they would know how feeble the threat he had just made was.

*"We must ask you to send no one else across. The Pholanhs are already alerted to your presence and are angered."*

"Which means?"

*"We found you before they did. We made you safe from them,"* said the four in unison.

"Why?"

*"We do not wish them to harm any more of your people,"* said the four in unison.

"Is there a way to stop them?"

*"Destroy the proviso."*

"What is this proviso?"

*"They use it to hold the essences they gather,"* said the second.

"The proviso is a sort of storage unit?"

*"Of sorts."*

"So what? You need me to act as a distraction, keep them busy, so you can go in and destroy it?"

*"We cannot do it,"* said the third one. *"We are worried if we enter their domain we will be turned. We four are the last of our kind."*

"So how can it be done, how can they be stopped?

*"Destroy the proviso,"* said all four in unison.

"Yeah, been over that already. If you can't do it then how do we destroy it? Do I need to bring an army and explosives over?"

*"No foreign object can be used. Only one who is of this world can destroy the proviso,"* said the first.

"But I thought you said none of you can?" He was confused now.

*"One of us would have to become solid form. To do this we would have to take in an essence, meaning we would have to harm one of you... We have sworn never to do this,"* said the first one.

*"We cannot guarantee that we would still want to stop them then,"* said another.

"So if one of you can't do it, but whoever does must be of this world... and solid, but to become solid you would have to take an essence and then might not want to stop them? Not making this easy are you? I was never good at riddles. Is there a weapon or tool that is of this world that can be used?"

*"You are the tool."*

"Excuse me? You expect me to be your savior?"

*"You must save us,"* all four said at once.

*"By saving us, you will save your world, too."*

"I am getting very confused now."

*"Explain confused?"*

"You *are of this world*," said the first.

"I'm what?"

*"The air in your lungs makes you like us,"* said the second.

"The fuck?"

*"Explain fuck?"* asked the second one. *"Explain frightened."*

"Fuck is an expletive some of the people of my world utter when we're angry, confused or frightened. Frightened is what your people, sorry, the Pholanhs, make us just before they take our... what is it you called it? Our essence?"

*"That is frightened? Is that also afraid?"* asked the second one.

"Yes. Frightened... terrified... horrified... *scared fucking shitless*."

*"That is what you felt as a child?"* asked the first.

"Yes. When a human is frightened they sometimes have a hard time breathing. This makes our hearts race and makes some of us hyperventilate or breathe faster."

"*So you were not having trouble breathing in your atmosphere?*" asked the second one.

"Yes and no. Once I had calmed down I would have been fine."

"*Then we harmed you?*" asked the second one.

All four backed away a little.

Gryphon didn't want to say yes but they had.

"*We apologize for harming you,*" said all four.

"*We can change you back,*" said the second one.

"Would I still be able to destroy the proviso?"

"*No.*" all four said in unison.

"Shit!"

"*Explain shit?*"

"What will it mean for you all if I destroy this proviso? Will the Pholanhs revert back?"

"*We do not know but we are growing old and tired. We should have already turned to stone,*" said the first one.

"*It is our time to turn to stone,*" said all four.

"So, you want me to destroy the proviso in hopes that it will allow your race to die?" asked Gryphon. He was having a hard time grasping that they'd be willing to sacrifice themselves.

"*It is our time,*" they all four said in unison.

Gryphon wanted to say thanks for placing all that added pressure on him. He guessed he had already sealed his fate the moment he crossed into their world in any case. "I will destroy the proviso on one condition. My friend leaves this world unharmed."

One of the four waved his hand and a portal opened to a room Gryphon recognized. About a month ago he had carried his friend into this room after picking him up and taking him home when he had gotten drunk after a bad date – it was DJ's bedroom.

*"We cannot go through the portal,"* said the one that had opened it.

Gryphon nodded. He reached down, lifted DJ off the floor of the cavern and carried him through the opening. He laid his friend down on his bed then turned and went back through the portal. As soon as he was back in the cavern, the thing waved its hand again and the doorway closed. "Alright, how do I do this?" The four beings surrounded him and clasped hands then his head was flooded with images.

# 41

# Time's up

Five hours went by slowly for the people at Griffin Concepts, Inc. They had lost the radio and camera feed three hours ago so they had no idea what was happening to the two men or if they were even still alive.

Adrienne had paced almost all three hundred minutes of them, refusing John's attempts to get her to leave with him. She couldn't go until Gryphon was back, and safe. She had to be there when he came through so she could slap him as soon as he stepped out, to tell him how angry she was that he had frightened her like this, then kiss him when she saw that he was alright. She knew that John was very upset with her that she was so upset but at this moment she really didn't care.

Dr. Parsons wanted to stay but he had to get back to the hospital and Derek left because his ride was leaving and he hadn't been given the okay to stay for overtime. So it was only her, Dr. Kearns and John left in the room – which made it very tense.

"Is it time yet?" asked the woman, as she looked at her watch then the clock on the wall. She had been asking this every few minutes since about a half hour before.

Dr. Kearns nodded to her this time, "Their alarms should be going off right now."

Adrienne moved to just before the refrigerator, wanting to be the first thing Gryphon saw and wanting to see him very badly. Ten minutes clicked down and there was no sign of a doorway opening. "Where are they?"

"I don't know," said Dr. Kearns.

"Are you picking up any of the nanoprobes?"

"I haven't gotten any readings from them since just after the signal stopped."

"I don't understand; they worked fine on the test dummy..."

"There are only two reasons I can think of; either something is blocking them or they are ..." He didn't finish what he was about to say because he knew how the woman would react. He could see, by the look on her face, she already feared this second possibility.

Adrienne walked to the PSD unit and flipped it on; hoping the signal from it wouldn't cancel out theirs. She stepped before the opening and saw only the same thick fog. She strained her eyes but saw nothing moving in it. "Are you getting anything now?" she asked, hoping it was only the distance from the portal and the aperture being closed that was blocking the signal.

Dr. Kearns turned the dials, trying to find any kind of signal. "I am sorry, Adrienne."

"Should we get ready to go in?" asked John.

Adrienne desperately wanted to know where the men were, but she couldn't let her heart make the decision. "No, I can't risk it."

"You're going to leave them over there?" asked Dr. Kearns.

"No. I want more than just three to go."

"I will request a full troop deployment and make plans to mount a rescue mission in the morning," said John. He knew the chances the men were alive was slim and none, and would be greatly diminished by morning, as did Dr. Kearns and he guessed Adrienne also. He knew there was no way she would ever forgive herself if it wasn't attempted though and that there was no way she would ever return to him if he didn't at least pretend to make an effort to find the men.

"Did you want me to close the rift now?" asked Dr. Kearns, pointing out that two of the grayish black things were coming toward it.

Every ounce of the woman was screaming no, imagining the two men were running for the opening and would be reaching it just before it closed but she couldn't let the things enter their world and take her and the men behind her either. She turned and shut off the unit.

Dr. Kearns shut off the monitoring equipment as well. He wished them as good a night as they could have and left the room.

John told his men to head back to the base.

Adrienne jumped when she felt a hand touch her shoulder.

"Let me take you home, Adrienne," said John, he started to reach around her, intent on kissing her.

The woman pulled away from him.

"What is the matter?"

Adrienne wiped the tears from her eyes and fell into the chair Dr. Kearns had been sitting in.

"Enough of this foolishness, it is time for you to come home, Adrienne."

"I'm sorry, John, I never considered your place home."

"What?" asked John, getting very upset now.

"I am sorry, I just… I never had feelings for you." She knew she should never have moved in with him but, as she told Gryphon, it was convenient.

"You said you loved me," said the man angrily.

"I'm sorry."

"You fucked him, didn't you?"

"It wasn't planned, it just happened. He was upset about his brother… I was only trying to offer him some comfort… some support."

"After all the shit I put up with, all your fucking ego trips? This is what I get? Dumped for a dead man?"

Adrienne wanted to shout that Gryphon wasn't dead but why else wouldn't he have returned? Either way, she could no longer live the lie that John was the right man for her; if for no other reason that in honor of Gryphon. "I will be by the apartment in a few days to get my stuff and I would appreciate it if you can not be there when I do."

"Knew I never shouldn't have gotten involved with you," spat John.

"I ask you take your leave now, John," said the woman, not entirely comfortable being alone with him right then. He had never lifted a hand to her before but the memory and the point tenderness of the bruise on her thigh from him shoving her away during the fight between him and Gryphon lingered. "I am going to ask a different officer to be assigned to this duty in the morning."

"I hope Gryphon Blake is not but a fucking shell when you find him. See if he is as warm as you think he is then." He spun around, stomped through the door and slammed it closed behind him.

The force of this cracked the glass in the window and made her jump.

# 42

# Head and Heart Aches

Callie couldn't believe how much her life had changed in the last few weeks. She truly liked Gryphon Blake and was seriously considering taking DJ Wright up on his offer to take her to dinner and a movie. She was no fool, she knew he wasn't completely finished with his wild lifestyle but she could see he did truly like her – as more than just a sex object.

She thanked and paid the taxi driver as he pulled up in front of her building. She grabbed the bag of groceries she had picked up and climbed out. She was yawning as she opened the door to her loft apartment. She was more than ready for a hot bath and a good night sleep. She had been at the hospital with Gloria most of the day, hoping to keep her occupied so she wouldn't wonder where her other son was and why he hadn't been to visit his brother all day. She had forced herself not to reach out to them, not wanting to know what they were doing because she knew it was dangerous. She hoped whatever they were doing stopped these attacks.

She saw the light was blinking on the answering machine on the stand just inside the door. She pushed it as she walked by. Gryphon's voice came through it asking her if she wanted to come to his house around six that evening for dinner with him, his parents, DJ, Adrienne and Dr. Parsons. She smiled. She started to set the bag of groceries on the counter then she suddenly felt very lightheaded.

The bag slid from her hands, hit the edge of the counter and smashed to the floor; spilling the contents of the cereal, bottle of orange juice and all but two of the eggs in the carton of them. She had to grab hold of the countertop to keep from falling into the mess herself. She knew what was happening instantly, she was having a premonition, but that didn't mean she was ready for it, or for what it showed her...

Gryphon was sitting at a large desk, in his office, she guessed. This didn't bother her but what she saw he was doing did. He was reading over a legal document, his pen in his hand, about to sign it. Again, this wouldn't have bothered her, except this document was his last will and she saw he had two life insurance policies before him as well.

The fact that he was completely calm as he looked the documents over, that a stack of letters, one addressed to each of the people he cared most about, and a glass with about a double shot of something alcoholic were beside him, which she watched him down in all but a single gulp, did bother her.

The image flashed to another scene then. This one was of Gryphon looking down at Adrienne, who was sleeping before him, as if he wanted to memorize her face, as if it would be the last time he would ever see it. She heard him sigh deeply and whisper, *"Take care of yourself, Love."* He then turned, stepped through a swirling wall of light and disappeared.

Callie jolted again as the scene changed again. The place she was seeing was out of a nightmare. The sky was blood red with black clouds. It smelled hot and there was an underlying scent of rotten eggs, rancid meat and melting plastic. Strange and eerie noises were echoing all around her. She was seeing this through someone else's eyes, which wasn't entirely surprising to her. She often saw these in the point of view of the person involved. She looked down and realized it was Gryphon's.

The scene changed again then. Callie was still seeing through Gryphon's eyes and DJ was with him this time, standing beside him. They were staring at what looked like a shaft of light that was shooting out of a hole in the floor, going up to another in the ceiling of a large arched chamber. That shaft was blindingly bright and had lines of even brighter light swirling inside it. Both men were squinting and DJ had a hand across his eyes as they tried to look at it.

*"They said we have to disrupt the shaft?"* DJ asked then. She saw him looking around as if he were looking for something to use to do this.

Callie was not only seeing through Gryphon's eyes but seeing into his mind, reading his thoughts. Her heart clenched. He was wondering how many of the souls trapped inside the shaft before them were of people he had known. She felt as much as heard him thinking there was no way he was going to let them have Sam's, or anyone else's, as long as there was something he could do to stop them. She saw what he was planning to use to disrupt it. She wanted to scream for him not to even think about it but she couldn't make her voice come from her throat.

Both men, and Callie, jumped as the device on DJ's wrist, the one Gryphon's mind was telling her was meant to warn them it was nearing their time to leave, beeped loudly.

*"We only have ten minutes left, Gryphon, we will have to come back,"* said DJ, starting out of the room.

She saw twelve of the ugly blackish gray things coming at them then, surrounding them, and heard DJ calling desperately to Gryphon.

"They won't let us back in here, DJ," her lips mouthed as in her head Gryphon spoke. He said this as if their being there and the things getting closer to them were no big deal. Callie saw the man's eyes turn to his best friend's face and, in a voice far calmer than it should be with the thoughts he was having, heard him say, "*Get back to our world.*"

"*Good idea, let's go,*" Callie heard DJ say then.

She saw him starting to turn through Gryphon's eyes but Gryphon wasn't moving. The reason for this was clear in his mind. She was trying to scream for him to stop as his eyes went back to the shaft. He did start to move then but not toward DJ.

"*Gryphon?*" Callie heard DJ ask; the sound of fear in his voice got deeper. "*Gryphon, NO!*"

The shaft of light, the chamber and the man were all gone.

Callie jolted violently and opened her eyes. She saw only her apartment before her again. At that moment it did not especially comfort her. She looked at the clock on the wall and saw almost three hours had passed. She must have passed out. She was lying on the floor, covered with sweat. She could tell she had been crying.

She did more of the latter, hysterically, for several minutes again; her knees clutched tightly to her chest, praying what she had seen had truly been only a premonition and was not after the fact as it had been when she had watched the Stubbs dying.

She wiped her face, crawled to her phone and quickly dialed Gryphon's home number. Her heart was beating harder with each ring, praying the man would answer and she would hear the voices of his dinner guests behind him, waiting for her arrival. She jumped when she heard the click of the receiver being picked up then a moan left her lips when she heard a female voice answer.

"Hello?"

"Is… This is Callie… is Gryphon there?"

"Hello, Callie," said the woman.

She recognized the voice as his mother then. "Hi, Mrs. Blake."

"How many times do I need to tell you to call me Gloria, Dear?" asked the woman kindly.

"I'm sorry, Gloria… Gryphon left a message inviting me to dinner…"

"Yes, we're here waiting for him, Dr. Parsons, DJ, Adrienne and you."

"Oh… Has he called or anything… to let you know he is on his way?"

"No, he hasn't, but I should think he will be along any minute. Did you need a ride? I can send Bruce over to get you."

"No… no, thank you," said Callie. "Actually, I was calling to beg off. I have a headache. I wanted to ask if I can join you all another night."

"I am sorry to hear that, Sweets. Take a nice hot bath, drink a warm glass of milk and go to bed early."

"Thanks. I'll stop by the hospital tomorrow."

"I will enjoy seeing you. Maybe we can finish the game of rummy we started."

"I would like that. See you then. Tell Gryphon I will see him tomorrow as well."

"I will, Dear. Sleep well and don't hesitate to call if you need anything."

"Thanks. Good night," said Callie as she hung up then. She was a little less worried then, surely if something bad had happened to her older son Gloria would have known it, right?

She crawled over to the counter and used the stool to help pull herself up. She picked up the mess she had made then went to the bathroom and started to fill the tub with hot water and a healthy squeeze of bubble bath.

\*\*\*\*\*\*\*\*\*\*\*\*\*\*\*\*\*\*\*\*

Adrienne walked to the parking garage in a daze and climbed into Gryphon's Magnum. She took a deep breath of the air inside it, it still smelled of new car but there was also his smell in it. This made her smile and made her heart clench painfully. She started it, backed it out of the spot and put it in gear without really even paying attention. She wasn't sure how she was made it to Gryphon's house without wrecking the car on the way; she didn't remember much of the trip.

She heard voices as soon as she stepped inside. She listened, hoping more than anything that two of them were Gryphon and DJ. She recognized Aggie's voice, and Gryphon's parent's, but heard no others. *Crap*, she thought, how could she explain why she was here without Gryphon and where he was? She had planned to just slip up the stairs and pretend she wasn't there, not ready to face them. She froze when she saw Gloria step into the hallway.

"Adrienne, is Gryphon and DJ with you?"

"Hello, Gloria. No, They... They're both still at the lab... think they're planning an all-nighter."

"Oh, that's a real shame. I swear that boy of mine is going to work himself to death one of these days. Aggie has worked her butt off to make a huge meal for us all too. Gryphon had asked us over and said he was planning on you, Dr. Parsons, DJ and Miss Summers to be here as well... some sort of celebratory dinner."

This actually made Adrienne feel a little bit better. This told her the man had intended to come back... It was a short lived joy. She had another thought then... "You said Miss Summers is here?" She hoped the woman could tell her if Gryphon was alright.

"No, Dear. She called about a half an hour ago and said she had a headache. She said she'd be around to the hospital in the morning though."

"Oh." Adrienne fought to not start crying, she was sure the other woman's headache was actually heartache because she knew the men's fate. "I'm not feeling overly hungry just now myself... Would you mind if I just to go upstairs, take a bath and lie down? I promise I will stop by the hospital tomorrow. Maybe we can all get together for lunch."

"Certainly, Dear. You do look pale. Do you want me to ask Aggie to fix you some soup?"

"No, I'm fine, just a little lightheaded."

Adrienne just stared at Gryphon's bed for several seconds. It had been their bed once. She wished more than anything to see his form under the sheets. It was perfectly made up; she wondered if the maid had changed them since he had last slept in it. She climbed onto it, pulled one of the pillows to her and took a deep breath.

His smell flooded her nose and made her smile sadly as tears came to her eyes. She hugged the pillow tight to her, lay down on the bed, curled herself up and began to sob quite hysterically.

She was crying so hard and loud that she didn't hear the rush of air or feel the heat of a portal opening or the man who stepped out of it, nor did she feel the man sit on the bed and set his hand on her shoulder until he had done so.

It took Gryphon a minute to recognize where he was, his head was so foggy, another to realize why there was someone before him crying, and another to realize who it was. His heart began to beat faster, with pleasure, pain and fear – the reason for the first was obvious enough, the second was because the woman was most likely crying because she though he was lost or dead, the third reason was he might not really be there, and the last, and worst, reason was worry that she would be frightened to death. He was comforted, and a little of the third dissipated, when he sat on the bed and felt it give with his weight, and more when he reached out and touched the woman's shoulder.

Adrienne expected to see one of Gryphon's parents or Aggie, come to check on her. She couldn't believe she was seeing whom she was actually seeing, for all she wanted to be. She closed her eyes, set her head back down and began to cry even harder; thinking it was only her imagination. She felt herself being lifted up and the man's strong arms going around her. She wrapped hers around him and said, "You bastard!"

"I'm sorry, Baby," said Gryphon as he took her face in his hands, wiped away the tears and kissed her eagerly. "I am so sorry. I didn't mean to scare you."

"What happened? I thought you... I thought I would never see you again," said Adrienne as she leaned forward to kiss him again, still not believing he was really there.

"I will tell you it all about it tomorrow, Baby," said Gryphon.

"I love you, Gryphon," said the woman. "I never want to be away from you again."

"I love you too, Adrienne."

# 43

# Reality Check

Callie's night hadn't ended nearly as well as Adrienne's. Premonitions of people being taken haunted her all night, coupled with the fact that she had called DJ's place five times and got his answering machine all five times. She wasn't getting anything but the annoying "out of the service area" alert from both his and Gryphon's cell phones. She had tried to reach out to both men's minds several times and couldn't get a feeling of where they were, which was odd since DJ's mind had all but flooded hers almost every second of every day since she first was introduced to him.

As soon as the numbers on her alarm clock changed over to seven o'clock she grabbed the phone and dialed Gryphon's office. She found she was holding her breath, hoping someone would answer it.

"Good morning, Griffin Concepts, Dr. Blake's office," said his secretary in a very pleasant voice.

"Is Dr. Blake in?"

"Who should I say is calling and what this is in regards to?"

"I'm Callie Summers, a friend of his and Dr. Wright's. They asked me to call them to see about getting together for lunch today. Is he there yet?"

"Oh, hello, Miss Summers," said Sandra. He had told her it was alright to put her calls through to him as soon as he arrived.

Callie sighed heavily and put her hand over her heart. "Um, he hasn't happened to ask you for any… any legal documents recently, has he?"

"No," said the woman quizzically.

"Good… okay," said Callie.

"Did you want me to transfer you to him?"

"No, I'm on my way in to see him now." Callie's heart was in her throat as she threw a sweater over her tank top, pulled on a pair of jeans and slipped her feet into her flip flops. She didn't take the time to put on make-up or brush her hair even, she only grabbed her purse and ran to the elevator.

\*\*\*\*\*\*\*\*\*\*\*\*\*\*\*\*\*\*\*\*\*

"Enter," said Gryphon. He expected it to be his secretary or DJ. He smiled when he saw it was Callie, then frowned at the state of dishevel she was in. "Good morning, Callie…" he said a little tentatively, praying she hadn't just come from the hospital.

"What are you doing?" she barked.

Callie had been telling herself the whole taxi ride over it was all just a misunderstanding, that she hadn't been seeing a premonition, what she saw him doing when she stepped into his office was a slap back to reality. The only difference she saw was he had a cup of coffee before him instead of a whiskey but she could smell whiskey in the coffee from where she was standing.

Gryphon was a little shocked by the question and the anger behind it. "Uh, I am wishing you a good morning, I think." He had been trying to be cute but the look she gave him, which was almost exactly one Adrienne had given him more than once; more than once only the day before in fact, told him she didn't find him that way. It was a look that said she knew what he was up to. "What is it you think I am doing?" asked Gryphon; feeling a bit like he was being called to the carpet by a teacher.

"You often update your will and life insurance policies over a cup of spiked coffee before eight in the morning?" asked the woman.

"Forgot, you're clairvoyant."

"Have you written the letters to them all yet?"

"Yes," he said, holding them up. "Suppose I can rip up yours since you already know what it says."

"You act so cavalier," she said sarcastically.

"I am anything but, Callie, but I have no choice. I'm guessing you had a premonition?"

"Yes," croaked the woman, finding her throat suddenly tight.

"Am I to assume it isn't good?"

"I... The premonition ended before I saw."

"Well then, you don't know for certain that I am doomed then, do you?"

"How *can* it end well though?"

"If I am able to stop those things from harming anyone else it will have ended well," said Gryphon.

"At risk of your life?"

"Even at risk of my life."

The conviction in his voice stopped the woman from saying anything more to try to talk him out of the course he had set, for all she wanted to; she knew he had to do this.

"I understand the connection to me now. The Pholandie said there is a certain type of brain chemistry needed for their kind to gain access to our world. Mine is one of the only ones left to them."

"That is… not exactly reassuring."

"Understatement," said the scientist. "It also lends itself to why it can only be me that does this."

"What about DJ?"

"He is asleep in his apartment," said Gryphon as he made a neat pile with the legal documents.

"But he was in my premonition."

"See, your premonition has already served us well. We have changed the future. Which means the chances that it will turn out for the best is increased."

Callie wasn't sure what to say. She hoped for all she was worth it were that simple but DJ not being with him wasn't going to change what he was going over there to do it only meant he'd be doing it alone.

Gryphon stepped around his desk, pulled the woman into a hug and held her as she cried.

\*\*\*\*\*\*\*\*\*\*\*\*\*\*\*\*\*\*\*\*

Gryphon hung round his office for about another half hour then decided he had stalled long enough. He locked his office door, told his secretary he was heading out for the day, went to the door to the stairs and walked down them to the fourth floor quickly.

The floor was still closed down so he didn't have to worry about anyone finding him. He looked around the cafeteria to see if there was anything he should bring with him. He shook his head, deciding there was nothing he wanted to take with him. He had thought about taking one of the templecams, thinking briefly it would be good for science, and history, to know what he had done, but he wasn't sure he wanted anyone to see what might be going to happen to him.

He had rigged a timer on the PSD so it would shut off just after he went through so none of the things, the Pholanhs, as he now knew they were called, could come through. He set the stack of letters, one for Adrienne, Sam, DJ and his parents on the stand beside it and flipped the switch on. He watched the aperture open and stretch to full size. He took a deep breath, walked to it and stepped through it without a second thought.

\*\*\*\*\*\*\*\*\*\*\*\*\*\*\*\*\*\*\*\*

DJ awakened with a start. He looked around, he wasn't certain if he was glad to see he was in his own bedroom or not. He was having a hard time getting his mind to work and was trying to figure out if he had been dreaming. The sulfur smell still in the hairs of his nostrils, the very tight suit the doctors made him and Gryphon wear in the other world to keep them cool, still being on his body and his back feeling like it had been put through a grinder told him it had all happened.

The last thing he remembered was the four white things coming at him and Gryphon and seeing one of them touch his friend then all went blank. How was it he was back in his condo, in his bed, without remembering how he got there? Had those things sent them back?

He looked at the clock on the table beside the bed and saw it was eight fifteen, meaning he was forty-five minutes late for work. He picked up his phone and checked the messages; there were several from Callie, all from last night, but none from Gryphon, either from last night or this morning. Why hadn't he called to see if he was coming in? He had a sinking feeling in his gut.

He got up quickly, got out of the constricting suit and put on normal clothes then ran out the door to the garage. He made it to the front doors of GCI in record time and amazingly didn't get a ticket doing so. He was surprised, and not so, to find Gryphon's bike there. He was glad to find it was still warm or not. Maybe he had just not had time to call him and ask if he intended to come to work today. He knew there was no chance of that. He started fast for the elevator, he was all but running by the time he reached it, something in his heart was telling him he needed to hurry.

The sawhorses telling anyone that happened to stop on the floor by accident the place was quarantined were still in place but the tape partitioning off the cafeteria was gone. DJ had no doubt it would have been put back by Adrienne before she left last night, not wanting anyone to happen upon the equipment. He was only a few feet from the doors of the room when he saw a flash of bright light he had come to recognize. "Shit!" He pushed the door open just as Gryphon's back went through the opening to the other world.

He didn't see Dr. Kearns or Adrienne anywhere and all the monitoring equipment was off so he guessed the man was attempting to play hero all by himself. His eyes fell on a stack of envelopes; the top one had Adrienne written on it in Gryphon's handwriting, he guessed he would find one with his name as well if he were to look at them. He saw the timer on the PSD was counting down fast and knew he had to do something quick if he was going to.

He grabbed a watch timer and one of the chains with the miniature PSD's they had constructed then leapt through the fast closing doorway.

# 44

# The Proviso

Gryphon stood still and waited for his body to adjust to the intense heat, his eyes to the ugly reddish sky and his nose to get over the initial blast of the strong odors of this world. His lungs were on fire but not because he was having trouble breathing, they actually felt better in this place, which, if the Pholanhdie were being honest, was because he had part of this world in him.

He was standing outside the vaulted chamber the four creatures had brought him and DJ to, and explained the situation to him. He was listening to see if there was any danger. He was about to step inside when he was shoved by something from behind. He turned around quickly. He half expected to see a Pholanh behind him – knowing what he was there for and wanting to stop him.

He was glad it wasn't but he wasn't glad to see who it was.

"What are you doing here?"

"I could ask the same of you. Think I am going to let you have all the fun?"

"This is not a joyride, DJ." There was no teasing annoyance in Gryphon's voice as he said this.

"I am beginning to think you don't want me here, Gryphon," countered DJ with none of his usual teasing.

"I don't."

"Why not?

"Because it's dangerous."

"For you as well," said DJ he quickly added, "I am not going back so forget even asking."

Gryphon knew he had very little time before the Pholanhs detected his presence so he nodded and said, "Alright."

He walked into the chamber.

DJ followed him in. He was awed be the enormity of it and how bright it was inside. He started to point out the glowing rocks as he watched his friend walk over to three stone stalagmites near the center of the chamber as if not expecting them to be there. He thought it was a little strange there were no stalactites on the ceiling over them, Gryphon, however, didn't seem to be too worried about this. Something told him his friend had been in the chamber before.

"*Shit!*"

"What's the matter?" asked DJ, Gryphon didn't answer. DJ watched him look around as if he was trying to find something. "I am guessing something happened the last time we were here, that I wasn't involved in, since I don't remember anything after those white things found us and I awakened in my bed in my condo, and you seem to be on a mission."

"The things that found us are called Pholanhdie, they are... I suppose you'd call them the good guys. The ones that have been stealing souls are called Pholanhs. They were the same race once. The Pholanhdie leader said it was their time to turn to stone," said Gryphon pointing back at the three man-sized pillars.

"Okay. Where was I during this conversation?"

"Asleep"

DJ nodded then asked, "There was four of them, wasn't there?"

"Yes."

"So, where is the fourth?"

"I don't know."

"What are you looking for?"

"He... it... one of them said there was a tool I would need when I returned."

"When *you* returned? A tool for what?"

"The Pholanhs have been taking human souls for centuries. They are storing them up in a thing they call their proviso, trying to hold off the natural order of their realm. The Pholanhdie want it to end. They say they have already survived beyond what they were supposed to."

"How does this translate to you having needed to return here alone?"

"The proviso needs to be destroyed." Gryphon. He was about to turn to face DJ when his eyes stopped on the thing he was looking for. He went to it and picked it up.

DJ saw a crystal pyramid in Gryphon's hand. He was about to ask what it was and what he planned to do with it when he saw his wrist clearly – his bare wrist. The wrist of his other arm was bare also. "Why aren't you wearing one of the bands, Gryphon?"

Gryphon didn't answer him. "You need to go back, DJ."

DJ stepped up to his best friend and pulled the collar of his t-shirt down. He wasn't sure if he was surprised to see no PSD unit hanging from a chain there or not. "Without a PSD unit you… If I hadn't come through you wouldn't have had a way to get back," said DJ. His mind replayed the discussion they had in his office when the man asked how to cheat on the test to get himself okayed for crossing over to this world. Starting to see what was happening now, he said, "You didn't plan to ever go back."

"You need to go back now, DJ."

"I will not leave here without you."

"DJ."

"No, Gryphon, I am not going to let you commit suicide."

Gryphon, painfully aware of how little time he had now before they would be discovered, nodded and said, "Fine," then he grabbed his friend's arm.

DJ felt a strange pulling sensation and like he was falling at the same time, very similar to how he had felt when he first arrived and fell the forty something feet from the top of the rock tower. Luckily then the air, being so much thicker here, had slowed his rate of descent and he had the padded landing in the form of his friend so he had survived it.

"What happened?" he asked as he felt solid ground beneath his feet again. He opened his eyes to find them in another chamber. It looked identical to the one they had just been in but this one didn't have the stone pillars, instead it had a blindingly bright column of pulsating light in the center of it.

"We shifted," said Gryphon as if this was an everyday occurrence.

"We what-ed?"

"It's how the things of this world move around it," said Gryphon offhandedly.

"How is it you know this and how is it you can do this?"

"The Pholanhdie showed me how before they sent us home," said Gryphon. He prayed the man didn't dig for how he could be able to move on an alien world so easily with only a brief explanation of it – that would require far too much information and time.

"What the fuck is that?" DJ asked as he stepped up to the bright shaft.

"That is the proviso."

"You said that's where they're storing our… the essences?" DJ stopped beside Gryphon and looked from the shaft to his friend and back.

Both men were squinting and DJ had a hand across his face as they tried to look at the shaft of bright light. It was shooting out of a hole in the floor and went up to another in the ceiling of the chamber some twenty feet above them. It was blindingly intense and had lines of even brighter light swirling inside it. Every little while one of those lights would slow down and press itself against the side of the shaft in a humanoid body-like shape. The stone rings on the floor and ceiling, that seemed to contain the bright shaft, had odd hieroglyphic like writings around them.

DJ walked around the thing, looking at each for a few seconds, trying to commit them to memory. He wished he had a camera with him.

Gryphon had done the same the night before when the Pholanhdie brought him to the chamber.

DJ stopped after a third trip around and looked at his friend. "So, we need to destroy this?"

"Yup," said Gryphon sedately.

"And what do we need to do?"

"The Pholanhdie say the shaft has to be disrupted," said Gryphon. He left out that it had to be done by someone of their world.

"And, how are we supposed to do this?" asked DJ looking around for something to use. His eyes stopped on the crystal clutched in Gryphon's hand, wondering if it was what they would be using. The device on DJ's wrist beeped loudly then, startling both men. "The fuck? This thing must be broken." He shook his wrist like it might change the readings, "It says we only have ten minutes left."

"It is likely fine, time moves differently here."

"You seem to know an awful lot about this place, Gryphon. What aren't you telling me?"

"Nothing, DJ."

DJ noticed Gryphon hadn't taken his eyes off the proviso since they arrived. He wasn't sure he liked the reasons his mind was coming up with for his friend's intense concentration. "Whatever the case, we will have to come back and complete this mission you seem to be on another time; any longer here will begin to adversely affect our bodies." He started to turn around to open a doorway back to their world when he saw that they were surrounded by several of the blackish gray things. "Uh, Gryphon?"

Gryphon already knew they were surrounded, he had felt the things approaching from the moment they arrived.

DJ saw his friend hadn't moved but the things had. In a strained voice he said, "They are getting closer."

Gryphon wasn't listening to his friend anymore. He was staring at the shaft, wondering how many of the souls trapped inside it were people he had known and how many might be added if he didn't complete his task. There was no way he was going to let them have Sam's, or anyone else's, to add to it as long as there was something he could do to stop them.

He turned to his best friend then and, in a voice that was far calmer than it should have been with the thoughts he was having, said, "Get back to our world, DJ."

"Good idea, let's go." DJ saw Gryphon moving but not toward him, toward the shaft, with a look of resignation on his face. "We will find a way to get back here another time, Gryphon."

"They won't let me, us, back in here, DJ," said Gryphon in a monotone voice.

"I will not leave without you." DJ stopped halfway between the bright shaft and the opening of the chamber and crossed his arms to make his point.

Gryphon knew the man was being serious. He couldn't put his friend's life at stake so he nodded and said, "Alright, DJ," then turned and looked around them.

DJ looked around as well and remembered again how much trouble they were now in. There were more than ten of the things Gryphon said were called Pholanhs coming at them fast. "Shit, what do we do now?"

Gryphon held the crystal the Pholanhdie had left for him before him. He closed his eyes and recalled the words, or thoughts, of the thing that had explained how to use the weapon-of-sorts, '*There are thirteen of the Pholanh; you must wait until they are all in the room before you break this.*' It hadn't said what would happen just that it would give him time to do what needed to be done.

He counted quickly; he could only see twelve.

The band on DJ's wrist had gone off almost nine minutes ago, if the calculations in his head were right, meaning they had no time to wait. He prayed the device would work in the same manner with what was there as he slammed it to the floor.

The thing shattered and threw sharp shards across the room then a strange non-light came from where it landed. This concentrated darkness grew larger and larger then began to coalesce like thick black smoke. Tendrils of this smoke moved outward. It shot at the twelve Pholanhs.

They all began to grab at their throats, gasping as if unable to breathe.

Gryphon felt a brief flash of guilt for causing them pain but it was very brief as he remembered what they had done to his people. He turned to DJ then and shouted, "Open the doorway."

DJ watched the thing just before him fall to the ground as if the pocket of air it had been riding had gone away and was mildly amused that it was actually quite a bit shorter than him when its robes touched the ground.

"DJ!"

The man jumped when he heard his name said more sternly. "Oh, right, yeah." He turned from the thing and pushed the mini PSD unit around his neck. The doorway opened with a flash and swirl of color. DJ whooped excitedly as he saw into the cafeteria of GCI. He could see there were several people waiting in the room as well. "Come on, Gryphon," he said as he turned to his friend. He saw he was standing still, back to looking at the strange shaft of swirling bright light. "You coming?"

Gryphon hadn't moved.

"Gryphon?"

The older man shook his head and swore under his breath. He knew DJ would refuse to go if he didn't as well. The smoke was already starting to dissipate meaning the things would be able to move again soon, he didn't have much time. He turned to his friend and said, "Let's go."

DJ breathed an audible sigh of relief. He had thought sure Gryphon was going to order him to leave without him. He really didn't want to refuse him anything but he would have, for all he knew it would have meant them both being trapped in this hideous and terrifying realm and likely being added to the shaft of light. He wasn't ready to be a hero, for all he had joked he had wanted to be one. He still had a lot more wild, crazy and dangerous things he had yet to do in his life.

He watched Gryphon take the steps between them slowly, like he was fighting with the idea, then he turned and saw the doorway was shrinking. "Hurry, Man."

"Go, DJ, I am right behind you," said Gryphon as he sped his steps up.

\*\*\*\*\*\*\*\*\*\*\*\*\*\*\*\*\*\*\*\*

Adrienne had expected to find the men working on the equipment for their next attempt when she arrived at GCI. What she found instead was an empty room and the letters from Gryphon, explaining what he had done and why he was doing it – he actually made it sound like this was the right thing to do.

She started to reach for the button to turn on the PSD when a portal opened beside her. A whoosh of heated sulfuric air hit her in the face. She began to cough and her eyes watered. She looked into the opening and screamed in excitement. DJ was just on the other side, Gryphon was a few feet for him, a strange bright swirling thing was behind them and nearly a dozen of the ugly things were around them. The things seemed to be fighting with a blackish wispy smoke but the men seemed fine. She could see their mouths moving but couldn't hear what they were saying. She could read Gryphon's lips as he told DJ to go and that he was right behind him. She saw him turn and start toward the opening and felt her heart begin to beat faster. It stopped when she saw the doorway was getting smaller. DJ was jumping through the opening then and falling forward. She fell back a few steps but caught him before he hit the PSD unit. "Are you alright, DJ?"

The man was covered with sweat and was shaking violently. "Ye… yeah… I th… ink so," he said through teeth that were chattering. Going from 110 degrees to about 70 degrees was a shock to his system.

She helped him sit down and threw her lab jacket over him then looked back at the opening, ready to catch Gryphon. The doorway had shrunk further, if he didn't come through now he wouldn't be able to. Her breath caught in her throat when she saw he didn't have a chain around his neck with a unit to open another. She shouted at him and waved for him to come through then saw his lips moving, mouthing the words, 'I love you' in slow motion. The opening had shrunk further. It was now too small for him to get through. "Gryphon? Gryphon?!"

DJ stood up as he heard the woman's desperate plea and said, "That fucking asshole."

They both shouted, "Gryphon, NO!" as the portal closed off completely, sealing the man on the other side.

DJ gently shoved Adrienne out of the way and turned on PSD. The beam of light hit the front of the fridge but no doorway opened. He shut it off and checked to be sure it was still set to the right frequency. He counted ten seconds off in his head then turned it on again. Again, no doorway opened.

At that same time, in the room at Biscayne General. Sam Blake suddenly took a deep breath and opened his eyes, and Callie, having just watched the whole scene play again in her mind, knowing this time it was while it was happening, had her face was in her hands. She was in tears and she was rocking herself back and forth. She had heard each and every anguished plea from Adrienne's mouth as if she had been right beside her and clearly heard Gryphon say his last words. They both tossed their heads back and screamed, "Gryphon, No!" at the same time as the others, at the top of their lungs.

# 45

# Eyes Wide Open

Gryphon waited to make sure DJ was through the opening before he moved. He saw him fall into Adrienne's arms and her help him to sit down. He couldn't hear them but he could see her lips saying his name so he knew she could see him as well. He saw her waving for him to come through and slowly shook his head. He said, "I love you," then closed his eyes as the doorway closed. There was no turning back now, even if he wanted to.

The smoke was gone now and the Pholanh were beginning to rise around him. He heard his name called out by all of them. The combined volume was pounding his eardrums painfully. He wanted to cover his ears but he knew it would do no good. He knew he had only seconds now to do what he needed to do. He turned back to the shining column, their proviso. He prayed the Pholanhdie was right that he had enough of their realm inside him to make this work. He started to run toward it.

The Pholanhs all began to scream as they realized what he was doing and began to converge on the man, intent on stopping him. Gryphon threw his hands out. They all bounced back as if they had hit an invisible shield several feet away from him. They continued to try to reach him but each time one would get near him he would point at it and it would be tossed backward. He could feel them changing their strategy and knew at least three of them were coming at him from behind, thinking he wouldn't know they were there so he wouldn't stop them before they reached him. It was too late; he was already before the shaft.

He took a deep breath and said, "Thank you, God, for all you have given me. Watch over those I am leaving behind. Please take my soul as a final offering and let the rest of my people be free of this plague." He knew this sounded clichéd and silly but it felt right at that moment to say. He closed his eyes and mouth tight, spread his arms out from his side and fell forward into the shaft of light.

The Pholanhs all stopped in place. If it were possible their blank faces would have been stretched in surprise and fear. A collective "NO!" sounded from all of them.

Gryphon couldn't fully describe what he felt inside the shaft of light. He could see all the souls swirling around him. He felt gentle touches and soft caresses, as if they were welcoming him. They didn't have any bodies or faces but he did see a representation of them. He wanted to cry but couldn't. Unlike the wisps of light, he was still solid and could still feel all his extremities. He felt his heart clench and his lungs spasm then his mouth flew open. The hot and viscous fluid in the shaft filled his mouth then and he started to gag. It tasted foul. He told himself not to swallow but he did. He felt the stuff filling his lungs and stomach. It felt hot and cold and wet and dry, it was extremely painful and yet pleasurable at the same time. He could feel his organs filling with the gelatinous stuff. His body began to convulse and he could feel himself twisting up.

He opened his mouth again, to scream, but nothing came out. Something told him this was because he no longer had a mouth or tongue or vocal cords to do it. He wondered why his mind was still so sharp but only for a moment then he no longer remembered who he was. The face of a beautiful woman formed before him, one he knew. He fought to put a name to the face. He tried to smile as the name came to him but he couldn't do this either for the same reason that he couldn't scream. A strange heat began to burn where his heart had been then he saw himself becoming a bright swirling light like all the others around him. His final thought was wishing he could have seen the woman with that face just one last time.

The shaft bulged outward the moment the foreign body entered it, then it shrank back and twisted to barely a few feet in width. It blinked a couple times as the corporeal body that had entered it began to be consumed by it. At the moment the body became nothing but light like all the others inside it, it exploded outward. The cacophonic blast would have burst the eardrums and internal organs of any human that was standing before it and the wave of energy that flew outward from it next would have consumed those torn and wreaked bodies. It swept past the wraithlike beings in the chamber and, other than a few robes billowing a bit, left them un-moved. A sonic-like boom spread out from the chamber and swept the planet, making a loud bang on the other side of it.

The brighter swirls of light, which were the thousands of souls the thing's had collected over the centuries, burst forth and began to move around the room. They looked like tiny stars. They came together and formed a large sphere. It pulsed once then grew in size until it had consumed all of the Pholanhs. Each being was left as a pillar of stone as it passed over them. When it was done, it shrank back to about the size of a large beach ball then it blinked twice and disappeared. The ceiling of the chamber began to crack and collapse, chunks of it began to rain down, hitting the now stone beings. They broke apart and crumbled to dust. Within minutes the entire thing was one flat pile of rubble.

\*\*\*\*\*\*\*\*\*\*\*\*\*\*\*\*\*\*\*\*

The last being on the dying planet, the fourth Pholanhdie, was standing on the edge of a thin cliff. It was watching its world beginning to break down into the elements that made it. It had no mouth but it was smiling. The human, Gryphon Blake, had done what he had been drawn to their world to do.

It felt bad for having to use the human. Their race truly hadn't liked doing this, but it was the only way for them to receive redemption. It knew the man was not sorry for having done it. It waved one of its hands over the other and a small shaft of light, much like the proviso, formed in its hand. This one didn't have the brighter lines of souls moving around it, it had only a small body of a man floating inside it. It spoke in its language and brought its hands together. It squeezed the shaft of light until its palms came together and it disappeared. With it, so too did the planet, shrinking in on itself then blinking out as if it had never been there in the first place.

# 46

# Awakening

The man opened his eyes wide. He sucked in a painful lungful of air through a throat that was dry and on fire. It felt like it was being blocked by something. He started to panic as he tried to clear it by coughing. He couldn't make the muscles of his stomach, lungs and throat respond. He wanted to scream that he wasn't supposed to feel pain when he was dead. Did this mean he had gone to hell? He heard a shrill beeping noise in his left ear then; loud enough to make him squint his eyes. He then heard, "Dr. Yakamoto to OR3, stat, Dr. Yakamoto to OR3."

*That is an odd thing to hear in hell,* he thought.

He started to raise his left arm, to scratch an itch on the end of his nose. He heard other voices then. They were saying a name too but he wasn't sure whose. It sounded familiar to him. He remembered hearing others speak this same name, in raspy, dark voices that made his skin crawl. These voices didn't make the hairs stand up on the back of his neck though; they made his heart leap in his chest. Was it his name? Yes, it was his name, he remembered now.

He felt something take the hand he had been moving to his nose and something take the other that had been at his side then felt something wet against them. He tried to see what this was but he couldn't turn his head. His heart began to beat faster as fear began to take hold of him. He noticed the beeping in his ear got faster then and wondered why.

He jumped when something appeared before him. A face he thought. It was gray looking and seemed to be featureless. He was about to scream for the thing to get away from him when his vision began to clear. It was a face and it did have features – male features. He thought he should know who the man was; he strained to remember his name. Out of nowhere it came to him. It was Dr. Douglas Parsons' face he was looking at.

How could that be, unless the man's soul was in this hell with him. *God, no, I failed,* he thought. Tears started to pour down his face then. He jumped when he felt something soft touch his face and brush those tears away. He realized the doctor's mouth was moving. He tried hard to make out what he was saying.

"You have a tube down your throat, don't try to talk, you could injure your vocal cords."

*That is a strange thing for a soul to say. Can a soul speak?* He wondered.

\*\*\*\*\*\*\*\*\*\*\*\*\*\*\*\*\*\*\*\*

Adrienne started to leave the room, needing some fresh air. She stopped when she thought she saw the hand of the man in the bed move. She stepped up to his side and saw his eyes were open. She breathed in a shocked breath.

Dr. Parsons heard this and turned to look at the man in the bed as well and saw his eyes were open. He looked at the hopeful faces around him shook his head. "It's normal for someone in a coma to open and close their eyes; it's more a reflex of the nerves." He said as he started to reach for the lids to close them, "If I leave them open they will dry out. I will have a nurse bring in some drops. Can one of you give him a couple in each eye and close them whenever you catch him like this?"

Adrienne swallowed down the lump that had suddenly formed in her throat and started again to turn away to do what she had been about to do before. She stopped again because this time the man's arm had moved. It had come off the bed and was kind of hovering – like it wasn't sure what it wanted to do.

"Is that normal?" asked DJ.

Dr. Parsons turned back and watched this. He saw the man was blinking his eyes as well. "No, it isn't." He leaned over the man and looked at him. He watched his pupils dilate and grow and dilate again as they tried to focus on him. "He is waking up."

Everyone in the room began to laugh and cry then.

Adrienne stepped back to the side of the bed. She saw his eyes focus on her then look at the others in the room. Tears started to flow down his cheeks. She wiped them away then took the hand he had been lifting.

Gloria grabbed the other.

Both woman brought those hands to their faces and kissed them, getting their tears all over them.

"You have a tube down your throat, don't try to talk. You could injure your vocal cords," said Dr. Parsons. He motioned for the women to step back. He grabbed a tissue from the stand beside him and took a hold of the end of the tube that was connected to the oxygen tank. He slowly began to withdraw it from the man's throat.

The man in the bed felt a scratching pain as the tube moved up his esophagus. It was excruciating. He wanted to tell him to stop but he couldn't. He squinted his eyes and grunted then began to gag as it moved past his tonsils.

"Easy, just relax your throat muscles," said Dr. Parsons. Once the tube was out the doctor grabbed a bottle of throat spray and sprayed three pumps into it.

The anesthetic instantly began to numb the sore edges but it was still burning and very dry. He jumped when he felt something touch his lower lip then.

"It's a straw. Try to drink some of this water. It will help."

The man wasn't sure how he was able to make his lips close on the thin plastic tube or command his facial muscles to suck in the liquid but he did. The cold stuff felt like heaven as it flooded his mouth and entered his throat. He didn't want to stop. He heard the doctor telling him to take it slow and forced himself to.

The doctor set the cup down and said, "I am going to bring the head of the bed up just a touch. Let me know if I bring you up too far."

The man managed to nod his head, which felt odd on his shoulders. He felt his upper half moving then and saw the rest of the room come into view. He saw several people standing around him then. It took his slow mind a moment to put names to the faces. "I'm so sorry," he managed to croak out of his dry throat.

"Oh, Gryphon" said his mother.

"You fucking well oughta be, Asshole!" spat DJ. Hearing shocked breathes around him made add. "Pardon my French but he should be."

"What should he be sorry for, DJ?" asked Gloria. She was the only one in the room that didn't know what the man had done.

"I'm sorry I didn't save you all," said Gryphon. He felt tears build in his eyes and start to flow down his cheeks again.

Adrienne wiped them away then leaned over and kissed him, "You did, you idiot."

"Wha? How?"

"We were about to leave the cafeteria when a bright light flashed in the center of the room and you appeared. Completely naked, I might add," said DJ. "You quit working out, didn't you?"

"I am not dead then?"

"No, Sweetie, you are not dead," said Adrienne as she leaned over and kissed him again.

"Sammy?" he asked.

"Here," said a voice that made Gryphon's heart beat fast, with hope and fear. He turned his head in the direction he thought it had come from to see his brother sitting in a wheelchair at the end of the bed. He looked thin and pale and his eyes were red but he was smiling.

"He awakened the day you came back." said Dr. Parsons.

"He is alright then?"

"I am," said Sam. "Still weak, but yeah."

"He has a ways to go and is undergoing physical therapy. The others are beginning to gain in strides now as well. About a third of them have awakened as well."

"Am I alright?"

"As a matter of fact," said Dr. Parsons. He put his hand up to Adrienne, to tell him the good news.

"Your lungs are perfect, Gryphon. Your asthma is completely gone."

Gryphon took a deep breath and realized he didn't feel or hear the gurgling he'd felt and heard every time he took a breath for the last thirty-three years. "How?"

"We aren't sure..." said Dr. Parson. "But, if you will give me the okay, I would like to run some tests to see if I can determine how."

Gryphon only halfheartedly nodded. He had spent as much time in the hospital over the last few weeks as he ever wanted to. He would not be happier if he never step foot in a hospital again. The scientist in him wanted to know how his lungs were now perfect though. The Pholanhdie had said he had a piece of the other realm in him, he wondered if when the place was destroyed that piece was as well. "How long have I been here?"

"You were in a coma for two weeks."

"How much longer do I have to stay?"

"Already rearing to go back to work," said DJ.

"No, to life."

"As soon as we can schedule you a visit, we will have a physical therapist check your motor functions. I should think you will be released by the end of the week," said Dr. Parson.

Gryphon closed his eyes and tears began to flow again. "I'm sorry I scared you all so much."

"Stop it, Gryphon, you have nothing to be sorry for," said Adrienne as she brought his hand to her face again and kissed it again. "Just promise me you won't leave me like that again."

"I promise I won't. I love you, Adrienne," he said, forgetting all the other people in the room for a moment.

"I love you too, Gryphon," said the woman, her hand going to his cheek and holding his face.

He heard his mother and Callie both giggling then and smiled. "Adrienne…" he asked. His voice trailed off as his throat constricted a little. He looked at the Dr. Parsons and said. "Can I have some more water, Doc?"

Dr. Parsons nodded and held the glass with the straw back up to him.

Gryphon took several pulls then nodded and looked back at Adrienne. "Will you marry me?"

This took the woman a little by surprise but she quickly recovered and said, "Yes, Gryphon Blake, I will marry you."

# 47

# Back Of Beyond

Gryphon was released from Biscayne General Hospital three weeks after his trip to the beyond. He had spent two and a half of those deep in a coma, during which he had relived his time inside the proviso over and over again.

There hadn't been any more reports of mummy bodies being found and all the tests to try to open the rift to the world he said was called Pholanh failed but he felt something still wasn't right. He still felt a tugging in the back of his mind. He knew of only one way to prove his suspicions right and or finally to put them to bed.

He pulled his motorbike into the last spot open on Fifth Street, dropped four quarters into the parking meter and walked up the alley to Callie's shop.

He remembered how cynical he had been when he had come here for the first time all those weeks ago. Back then he had wanted to find out what the strange woman knew of his brother's situation, now he wanted to know if the woman could tell him if his speculations were right. Just as with the first visit, he was feeling apprehensive. This time it was nothing to do with thinking she was only an obsessed crazy lady.

He pushed the door open and was pleased to see the shop had several customers in it. She had told him how business had slumped recently and had thought she might have to close and get a real job. At the same time this made him anxious because it meant he would have to wait for them to leave to have the woman's full attention.

It was almost an hour later, and half of a book on the theory that the pyramids all over the world were built under the supervision of aliens and were actually landing pads for their space crafts, before the last person finally left the shop.

He watched Callie lock the door then turn to him slowly. He wasn't sure if the look on her face was good or bad. "Do you believe this?" he asked as he held the fancical book up to her.

"Who is to say? Those that do are said to be brilliant scientists no different than those that do not," said the woman frankly.

Gryphon wanted to argue with her on the subject but he didn't. He reminded himself that he hadn't believed in psychics, monsters or parallel dimensions just a few weeks before either but he had been proven wrong on that account. He had no more physical evidence of his trip than those scientists had had and he was called a brilliant scientist by some as well.

Callie felt odd as she looked at the man before her. He was alive and well now but for a few days he had ceased to exist. She'd had a strong connection to him since the dream that had started the rollercoaster ride they had lived the last few weeks. The connection had shattered the instant he had jumped into the Pholanh's proviso... She knew he had died, then suddenly he was there again. DJ told her later that he had appeared in the middle of the room in a flash of light – at the same instance as he was open to her again.

He seemed to be the same Gryphon physically, he had no visible scars to show he'd been through any kind of trauma, but she knew he would never be the same mentally or emotionally. She had gone to see him only one time while he was recovering in the hospital. Her avoidance of him wasn't because she didn't care; it was because it hurt too much to look at him. It hurt to see how much he had changed on the inside. She had relived what he had endured each time he did. She had known he was a man of integrity but she was struck hard by what this man had done, at how much he had been willing to give up, not only for the people he knew and cared about but for everyone – friend and stranger alike.

She had known he would be coming to her shop again, she had seen that too. And, she knew why. "Hi, Gryphon." She was trying to sound happy to see him, as she opened her arms to him.

"Sorry I haven't been around before now."

She didn't need the apology; she knew what he had been through. She technically was to be open another hour but he was more important than any money that might be made so she quickly closed the door on the back of the last patron – who had been in for a love potion – and turned the lock without hesitation.

She directed the man into the booth. She heard and felt him sigh when he sat down. She knew he was hoping she would tell him his suspicions were wrong. She couldn't. She tried not to rush him; wanting him to be sure he was ready to hear what she had seen.

"You know why I am here," said Gryphon. This wasn't said as a question, he had no doubt she did. Since she hadn't told him yet that he was wrong, he guessed he wasn't – which was twisting his insides up. "Why didn't you say anything?" he barked.

"I'm sorry, I didn't think you were ready to handle it, I guess," said the woman then she sat up straighter and said, "No, I'm not sorry. I don't want you to be hurt, again, anymore, Gryphon. You've been through enough. For God's sake, you *died*," she added sharply.

This didn't deter him, if anything it made him more certain he had to know. "I have to end it, Callie."

The woman nodded, she already knew her plea was going to fall on deaf ears.

"Do you know what needs to be done?"

"Put the piece you brought back on the table."

He hadn't told anyone, including her, that he had brought a piece of the other realm back with him the first time he returned. He knew Adrienne and DJ would have immediately wanted it quarantined to be certain it wasn't a health risk. He didn't know what had possessed him to take it. Yeah, he did. It was to prove to himself it hadn't been just a dream. He took the thing from his briefcase and set in before him.

Both of them shivered as they looked at it.

It was a six inch by six inch square block of rock that had an impression of the things' three fingered hands. He guessed it had been part of some sort of security feature – like the palm reading devices his techies had been working on for years.

Callie swallowed hard and said, "Place your hand on it."

Gryphon wiped the palm of his right hand on his jeans then placed it on it; his thumb in its thumb, his index and middle finger in the first of the two fingers and his ring finger and pinky in the second.

"Clear your mind," said the woman as she placed both of her hands on top of his.

Both of them jumped and drew in deep breaths but neither removed their hands.

They couldn't say where they were but they knew it wasn't the booth in her shop. The room was dark and smelled of baby powder and a slight hint of dirty diapers. They could hear a soft lullaby playing telling them it was a child's room.

They weren't alone.

Gryphon tried to speak but couldn't make his mouth move. He jumped when he felt something touch his hand then settled down when he realized it was Callie's hand.

"*It's here.*"

Gryphon didn't hear this as words, more as a thought. He wasn't sure how he did it but he realized he had responded to her when he saw her nod her head. "*I feel it to.*"

They jumped when the headlights of a passing car shined into the window. At first all they saw was body shaped shadow in the corner then the Pholanh stepped out of that shadow and floated over to the crib. The baby asleep in it made a slight cooing sound but didn't wake up. They watched the thing stretch its arms over the baby and saw it had one of the urn-like vessels in its hand.

"*Must rebuild the proviso,*" it said.

"*I can't let you do that. Leave that child alone,*" said, or thought, Gryphon.

The thing turned to them.

If Gryphon didn't know better he would have said it jumped.

"*The destroyer,*" said the thing. It turned from the crib and started toward them. "*You will be added to the proviso.*"

"*Gryphon!*" Callie watched him step forward, as if intent on meeting the thing in the center of the room.

"*Stay back, Callie,*" said Gryphon. He spanned the distance between him and the thing in two giant steps then reached out for it. He cringed as his hands closed over its shoulders. They felt slimy and cold. "*Your proviso has been destroyed.*"

"*You will be the first in the new proviso,*" it placed its tiny hand on his chest and a bright glow began to come from it.

Gryphon jumped and grunted in pain. His face contorted, his eyes rolled back in his head and his legs bent a little. The only thing keeping him up was the connection the thing had with his chest.

"*Gryphon!*" shouted Callie.

*"Stay back, Callie!"* Gryphon yelled in his. His chest was burning and constricting, worse than it ever had during the any of the many asthma attacks he had suffered through the years. His skin itched, from the inside, and it felt like it was being ripped from his bones. He opened his mouth, or thought to, to scream again but nothing came out. He started to release the thing's shoulders; he knew if he did it would be over for him. He had no idea where he got the strength to do it but he straightened his legs and stood back up. *"Your proviso has been destroyed,"* he repeated. He brought his right hand down from its shoulder, took hold of the vessel in its other hand and squeezed his hand together. The thing shattered as if it had been made of powder.

A painfully shrill screech sounded in their heads then. Callie brought her hands to her ears, trying to block it out but there was no way to. The baby in the crib woke up suddenly and began to scream at the top of its lungs. Gryphon fought back the pain of all three sounds ramming into his ear drums and moved his hands to the side of the thing's head. He pulled it toward him, leaned forward and kissed its forehead.

The screech diminished to not much more though a low wail then the thing began to shiver. It sank to the ground, its form began to waiver a little and a sound like crying came from it.

Callie put her hands to her mouth, this sound ripped through her heart.

The baby in the crib was now screaming even louder, if that was possible.

The door of the room burst open and the light overhead came on in a flash. The baby's mother stepped into the room. "What's the matter, Daniel?" she asked.

The thing in Gryphon's arms flickered once then dissolved into dust and disappeared in a quick flash of light.

Gryphon and Callie's minds were still in the room. They watched the woman take her son from his bed, hold him close to her chest and begin to coo at him, oblivious to them. The baby turned its head to them and reached out for them. The woman's eyes scanned the room, looking for what her baby was seeing. "What is it, Honey?"

Gryphon and Callie's minds left the room then.

Their physical bodies jumped as their minds re-entered them.

Callie pulled her hands from the top of Gryphon's, slapped her right one against her chest over her heart and fell back.

Gryphon lifted his hand slower. His fingers had fallen asleep and were cramped from the position they'd had been in to stay on the mold. He rubbed and flexed his fingers, grimacing, as the pain turned to the pins and needles feeling of the blood beginning to flow back through them.

They both jumped when the slab of alien rock on the table between them jumped and then began to vibrate. They watched a bright light came from the three-fingered impression then the thing cracked and fell to the table as powdery dust.

"Is it done?" asked Gryphon.

"It is done," said Callie.

"Only one problem," said the man.

Callie looked at him funny.

"We're in the wrong bodies."

Callie smirked at him and said, "And I thought DJ had a sick mind."

**The End?**